Spies
WITH BENEFITS

OTHER BOOKS BY DOCTOR JAC

Rough Waters

Undaunted Lovers

Spies with Benefits

London's Secrets (2018 Release)

Spies WITH BENEFITS

A MIKE AND GRACE NOVEL

DOCTOR JAC

Printed in the United States of America

ISBN Paperback: 978-0-9962921-3-9

Book Cover and Interior Design: Ghislain Viau

*To book readers who keep an important
part of our culture alive and thriving*

CONTENTS

ACKNOWLEDGEMENTS

Writing books is a collaborative affair. These people helped bring this book into being.

My beautiful wife Laura was, as always, the story consultant reviewing and advising throughout the process. Editor David Colin Carr helped me become a better writer. Book designer Ghislain Viau patiently did a great job with the cover and interior layout. Frank Langben did a superb job editing the final text. Beta readers Mary Manning and Tony Illich helped polish the original copy. Col. David Fitzenz, USA (Ret.) assisted on military issues. My long time mate, Neil Peters, provided the Aussie toast at the wedding. Dr. Linda Lu taught me how to pronounce Cixi's name in Mandarin. Jeanette Campa and my 94 year young mother-in-law, Laura Sanchez Dubois, checked my Spanish. Sara Palmer, Paul and Pierce Jamieson have picked up the marketing chores again.

Thank you all very much.

PROLOGUE
FROM UNDAUNTED LOVERS

Michael Holmes grew up next to a Sioux reservation in North Dakota. He's one-quarter Sioux, an attribute that's very handy at times. He escaped those frigid plains by winning a Rhodes scholarship to Oxford. He studied Asian Political Economics and Mandarin Chinese. He spouts a bit of Edwardian English at times, just for fun.

A naval intelligence officer stationed in Hawaii five years ago, Mike met Grace Donaldson, nee Liu Chan-juan, at a squadron party. Grace, the daughter of General Liu, former chief of staff to Chiang Kai-Shek, had immigrated with her parents to Hawaii fifteen years earlier. Mike and Grace fell in love immediately, but there was one problem, she was married.

Her traditionally minded Chinese mother pressured her not to divorce her playboy husband. Over the intervening years Mike and Grace struggled to keep in contact, exchanging short letters and sharing two brief visits as Mike traveled the US and Asia Pacific on clandestine missions. While Mike was on a year-long absence for a deep cover mission in China, Grace's navy pilot husband was killed in a plane crash. When Mike returned, Grace had disappeared and their future seemed to have vanished.

In the final chapter of *Undaunted Lovers* they met unexpectedly at the United Nations where he was newly assigned. Given her China experience, Grace had been hired several months earlier by the State Department to work in the US delegation.

That meeting links the last chapter of Undaunted Lovers with the opening chapter of *Spies with Benefits*.

Chapter 1

FRESH WIND

September 1972
United Nations General Assembly Hall

Mike relaxes his arms and Grace steps back a few inches. She looks up at him and starts laughing convulsively. When she comes up for air she looks again and once more doubles up. He grabs her shoulders and pulls her upright, "I say, Madam, please control yourself. This chamber demands decorum."

"Oh Sherlock, it's wonderful to hear you're still spouting that British mumbo jumbo."

"One learns that, even in the most severe circumstances, respect is always appropriate."

Now she's on full giggle, trying to get control.

"Just what is so amusing, may I enquire?"

"You. You have a mascara streak running from your ear to the corner of your mouth. Also, you have a little pink smudge on your collar. It's a priceless picture."

"Well, you're not exactly a Vogue model yourself. Your eyes look like two exploded ink wells."

She moves back into him. They hold each other and snicker like teenagers. "I left my purse in my office. I'll use the wall phone to call Laurie in Mexico's office upstairs. I'll meet her in the ladies room across the hall and clean up. You better repair the damage also."

Mike tears his handkerchief in half and gives one side to Grace for emergency repairs while he tries to wipe incriminating evidence off his face.

"We need to go back to the office and stay away from each other until we can figure out how we're going to play this. There's a little bar on Lexington near 43rd Street. It's called Lexor's. Laurie knows the maître d' and can get us a booth in the back corner. Don't worry. She can keep a secret. Can you meet us there tonight after work? But bring a friend so it doesn't look obvious."

"How about my mother?"

"No, silly, bring someone who likes you."

"What time?"

"About a quarter to six."

"I'll . . . we'll be there."

He tries thinking, but there aren't any synapses firing. *After five years and lost hope this comes out of nowhere. Am I truly awake or wishfully hallucinating?*

Chapter 2

THE DATE

September 1972
New York City

1745, Mike arrives at Lexor's with his Aussie mate, Ned. He met this husky, brash, red-faced fellow during Mike's tour at Barber's Point seven years ago. Ned's a pilot and flight lieutenant in the Royal Australian Navy. When the Australian aircraft carrier HMAS Melbourne called at Pearl Harbor, Ned was aboard. During that visit the Aussies participated in joint maneuvers with US Navy and Marine air units. There were several receptions and parties involving officers from these groups. The Aussies developed a reputation as great partiers. Ned excelled in upholding their reputation.

When Mike arrived at his UN post he found a note saying Ned was in the Aussie delegation. They met for a couple drinks and reveled in old times. Tonight they fight their way upstream through the rush hour sidewalk brutes and find Lexor's. On opening the door, the odor of alcohol, perspiration and raging hormones nearly bowls them over. The bar is crowded, somewhat dim and as noisy as these Friday night meat markets become. They plow their way through the smoke and gloom toward the back until Mike sees Grace sitting with Laurie, a pretty, dark complexioned girl in a corner booth.

"Well, Commander, you certainly look better than the last time I saw you."

Introductions. Grace – Ned, Ned – Laurie, Laurie – Mike. Grace says to Ned, "Why don't you sit next to me, handsome?"

Ned drops into the booth, a little too close to Grace. Ned and Mike face each other, the girls in between. A large bouncy waitress lands at the table and introduces herself as Renee. The women order white wine. Mike asks for a vodka tonic and Ned orders a Fosters. Renee boogies off toward the bar shaking her ample booty to the music.

The conversation is labored. "Laurie, that's a beautiful name. Where are you from? What brings you to the UN? What's your job? How long have you working at the UN?" until they all start laughing. Mike's aching to touch Grace. From the way her fingers play on the table top, it looks like the feeling is mutual. In time the conversation reaches that awkward point where no one has anything to say. Ned is smitten by the big Latina smile and uninhibited laugh. Mike thinks, *If I wasn't already crazy about Grace . . .*

After an hour of banter and a second round for all but Grace, Ned breaks in, "Is anyone hungry? Would you ladies like to find some grub close by?'

Laurie checks with Grace for a signal. Grace nods and volunteers, "That sounds like a good idea. There's a nice Italian place just a block down 43rd Street."

By now the bar has turned into a tightly packed, deafening, hot house of bodies engaged in various mating dances. They fight their way to the door and pop through to the coolness of the street with an audible sigh. What a relief to be out of that coop. It's only a short walk on 43rd to Geno's. Mike tries to finesse himself to be next to Grace, but Ned and Laurie are dancing along, getting in the way. Mike feels like kicking Ned, but keeps his testosterone level in check.

Geno's is a typical neighborhood Italian bistro half a flight down. Not too crowded. Most of the patrons look like locals, greeted warmly with hugs and kisses as they arrive.

The group is seated in a quiet corner. Grace places Ned and Laurie on either side of her.

The waiter asks if they would like drinks. Laurie looks around the table, "Maybe a bottle of wine for the table since we've already had drinks?" Mike orders the house red. Ned adds another Fosters. Grace and Mike try to be nonchalant and not make too much eye contact. The other two are concentrating on their little mating ritual.

Ned is in love already, and Laurie really likes his playful brashness. If Laurie knew that Ned's wife, Vivian, is visiting relatives in England and will be back in a fortnight, she might be more restrained. Laurie and Ned devour their dinners between giggles, Grace just nibbles at her Italian salad.

Mike feels like his chair is teetering on the edge of a cliff. One wrong move and he'll disappear.

Laurie knows the score and is having a ball watching sparks ricocheting across the table, at the same time teasing Ned. The HMAS Melbourne could cruise through Geno's and Ned won't have noticed.

Dinner, dessert, coffee and liqueur are stretched to the limit. It's time to call it a night. Back in the street the September evening is warm and it's relatively quiet—as quiet as Manhattan ever gets.

At the corner Grace stops. "Boys, it's been delightful. Thank you so much. We live just two blocks away so we'll say good night and walk home."

Ned and Mike live in the same building a couple blocks closer to the UN. As they walk, Ned babbles on about Laurie. Mike's in a haze.

Chapter 3

PLAYING HOUSE

September 1972
New York City

Saturday afternoon, Mike calls the number Grace gave him. There's no answer. After an unsettled weekend, inevitably the sun comes up Monday morning. Mike skips breakfast and is on his way to the UN by 0800. Grace isn't in yet. By nine she's still not in and he wonders if their tete-a-tete upset her. On an unnecessary trek across the office, Mike sees her at her desk.

1138, his phone rings. She teases him, "Have a good time Friday night, Commander? I hear that you and some friends nearly closed Geno's. You have to be more discreet. There are eyes everywhere in this place."

"I don't know what you're talking about. I was in bed by nine."

"With who, you bastard?"

He almost falls off his chair. "OK, I give. How are we going to play this game?"

"Unfortunately, there will be a slight game delay. I've been assigned to shepherd a group of visiting Taiwanese to a meeting in D.C."

"Do we get a few minutes before you leave? When will you be back?"

"Slow down, sailor. I'm leaving this afternoon and be back next Thursday. Do you think you can survive?"

"I'll survive all right, but I didn't know that inside your gorgeous body lies the heart of a torturer. You know I've been tortured before and I'm not interested in a repeat performance."

"What do you mean tortured? You're just trying to throw me off, aren't you?

"Don't you remember my Hong Kong episode? You saw me at Letterman and again at Tripler? Don't tell me you don't remember that."

"Oh yes, please forgive me. Of course. It was so painful to see you like that I've tried to put it out of my memory."

"I have too, but it won't go leave."

"I'm really sorry. I'll be gone about ten days. I'm aching to be with you too. While I'm away I'll figure out how we can manage this. Til then, sweetheart."

For the next several days Mike sits looking out over the East River to Long Island, wondering what Grace is doing. He fanaticizes about her in a dozen ways, some X-rated. After work he goes for lengthy runs along the river to work off the tension and invite sleep. Eventually he exhales and relaxes. *I say, old bean, it appears you're feeling a bit of angst in this area, wouldn't you say? Get a grip, my lad.*

Monday, Ned pops into his office. His smile almost cracks his skin. "Thanks for introducing me to Laurie, mate. She's fair dinkum."

"You do remember mate that you have a very strong-minded wife who will be home in a week or so? Don't go off the deep end."

"No worries, mate. Just a harmless flirtation."

"Harmless for whom? Does Laurie know?"

"Yes, and she knows it isn't going anywhere. "We're just having a bit of fun."

"Caution. A lot of people in this place make it their business to know your business."

"No problem, mate. How're you doing with Grace? She's a right spunky sheila, I'd say,"

"She's on a trip for a few days. Haven't seen her since she and your Mexican jumping bean left us on the corner. Did you know I only spent a couple hours talking to her at a party five years ago and a few days during rehab at Tripler? I went off on a mission for a year and when I got back she'd disappeared. I thought I'd never see her again. Suddenly, bingo she's here. I'm in a bit of shock."

"Well mate, if it's any comfort to you, I got the vibes she's as truly mashed about you as you are about her. Be cool until you can find a time and place where you can talk, or do whatever fits the mood. Till then, go home tonight and have a deep conversation with your Scottish friend. I don't know if it will help, but at least it'll relax you. No worries, mate. It'll all work out. If you want to double again, let me know. "It's got to be before the 15th you know."

"I'll circle the date on my calendar."

*   *   *

Midweek, the Deputy Director for Political Affairs calls Mike in. Phil Hunt is standard Ivy League. Fortyish with a budding pot belly and receding hair line. Brooks Brothers all the way. He's in the right place for who he is, and looking forward to forty years of public service. He stands up and shakes Mike's hand briskly. "Hello, Michael. Are you finding your way around this place okay? It can be a little daunting at times, people from all over the world packed into one building."

"So far, so good. But I'm wondering what my job is. Nice place for a vacation, but it won't do my career any good if I don't accomplish something."

"Don't worry, my friend. You're going to have a chance to do something significant. ONI (Office of Naval Intelligence) didn't send you here for a holiday. Your first get-acquainted assignment is to sit in on a subcommittee of the Social and Economic Council on Monday. You'll get a flavor of how things work or don't work here. When you return, come see me and give me your impression. Then we'll talk about your job. Good luck."

Monday, Mike heads for the meeting. When he arrives there are a couple dozen people milling about a central table. A bank of chairs lines the wall. Gradually the group finds seats and settles into some sort of order. Mike shakes a few hands and picks a spot on the periphery where he can see the chairperson. At twenty minutes past the hour the leader shows up. She's a tall black woman with a serious demeanor, dressed in a central African costume Mike can't identify. She doesn't look like she believes in participative management.

The meeting starts with a roll call and quickly degenerates into a round robin chinwag. Madam Chair turns out to be more a mother hen than leader. Arguments on obtuse points last minutes without a focus. The published agenda is lost in persiflage. After an hour of this, both the room and Mike's temperature rise. Boredom is replaced with nausea. After two hours he contemplates slashing his wrists. He's thinking. *If we ran meetings like this in the navy we'd never get a ship out of port." But, this is my first test so I'll ride it out.*

That afternoon Mike, books a return visit to Phil's office. Normally he'd write a report of the meeting. But he hasn't determined what the meeting was actually about and if any conclusions were reached, beyond scheduling another meeting.

"Honestly, Phil, I've never seen such a chaotic mess."

Phil laughs. "Let me tell you how things actually work here. The meetings are just for show and to let delegates feel like they're doing something worthwhile. The fact is that many of the people here have been sent by their countries to get them out of the way or perhaps to reward them with a two year paid vacation in New York City. There are, of course, many sincere, honest, talented people here. But in practice, a few people meet on a back channel to determine what can be done on their issue. Once they agree, they let the others in on the plan, off line, one or two at a time. Everyone feels they've played a useful insider's role. In the end the plan is executed with some degree of success, or not, by the small leadership group. If nothing happens, few people get excited. The deadline here is eternity."

"I understand. But I've been involved with kidnapping, suicides, torture, murder and face to face killing. Don't tell me I'm here to attend meetings like this."

"No. I just wanted you to get a feel for the game."

"Okay, so what's my job?"

"Mike, your mission is to turn a couple delegates our way. Recruit them. You know, to spy for us. You have experience in espionage. You've shown a talent for working with difficult people, and you speak Mandarin. We believe you can apply all that to this challenge. We're especially interested in the commercial attaché from the Chinese delegation and the technology delegate from the Russian delegation."

"Isn't that what the CIA is for?"

"Yes, that's one of its major goals. However, despite a lot of expense and effort, they've not been successful. We don't know why, but the fact remains they've not been able to recruit them. We have a couple advantages. One is your record in Asia. In addition, you aren't CIA. You should be able to strike up a relationship without raising suspicions. Also, we have a woman on our staff who grew up in China, daughter of a former Kuomintang army general. He repudiated Chiang Kai-shek and immigrated to Hawaii about twenty years ago. You have to meet her. You'll like her. She's very sharp. Her name is Grace Liu."

Mike holds his composure, an act worthy of an academy award. "I met her briefly the other day. I'll make it a point to talk to her immediately. I presume you've alerted her?"

"Yes, she's expecting to talk to you and work out an approach. The Chinese fellow is Jiang Gao. He's early thirties, young for such a high level job in China's system. When his UN tour is over he'll return to a position in the hierarchy. Jiang's family emigrated many years ago from Henan Province to Taiwan, where they prospered as traders and bankers. When Chiang was defeated by the communists and fled to Taiwan, he oppressed the locals. Jiang's family escaped to the mainland and found their way back to Henan. We believe he's been angry about Taiwan's success, angry that the PRC didn't take it back when Chiang first went there. This may be where he's vulnerable.

"The other person is a Russian woman, Ivanova Petrov. She's a widow about thirty-five years old, grew up during the postwar starvation. She's short, frail and sallow, with a drab aura of sadness. Her husband was well connected across Russia. He died during Brezhnev's reign. We believe she harbors a grudge against the leadership because her husband might have been saved with better medical treatment. She has broad knowledge of the petroleum and telecommunications industries. Additionally, Ivanova is known to have contacts with successful business leaders and bankers, due to her husband's connections. In Russia's system there are a small number of very wealthy people. She's not wealthy, but she seems to be on the edge of that circle. Brezhnev might have sent her here to get her negative attitude out of the country."

Phil can't guess the depth of Mike's gratitude. He walks back to his office with a new spring in his step and risqué thoughts in his head. It's as though the rain has stopped and the sun is shining. That night he pays a lengthy visit to Macallan farm's Elchies Scotch while enjoying the company of a Montecristo cigar. In a moment of clear-headedness he realizes the joke is on him. *That woman knew about this all along and never told me. She thinks she's so clever. I'll make her pay somehow.*

The following Thursday Gace is busy in her office writing the report of her trip to D.C. Mike decides to wait for her to come to him, though he can hardly stand it. She'll know that he's been briefed, but he's going to play hard to get, despite aching to burst into her office and sweep her into his arms. In a couple hours she starts circulating and dropping off copies of her report for all who have a need to know. Mike isn't on that list. To his surprise, towards the end of her rounds she strolls into his office and hands him a copy of the report. With an enigmatic smile she asks, "How are you, Commander? Here's a copy of my trip report. You might find it interesting. Phil tells me we're going to work together on a new project. That should be fun. On a different topic, I'm having a little buffet dinner for some of the newcomers on Saturday night. You qualify. Here's your invitation." She hands it to him. Below the greeting she has written a personal note:

You are invited to a buffet dinner Saturday evening, October 14th to welcome new staff to the Delegation

Cocktails at 7 — Dinner at 8

Grace Liu
328 West 45th Street
Apartment 4A

M.

Don't be the first to arrive, or the last to leave.

G.

This girl is a barrel of laughs. "Thank you for the invitation, madam. I shall scrutinize my schedule to determine if it is possible to cancel another engagement."

That stops her for a second. She rebounds with an, *I'll-get-you-for-that* scowl. "I do hope you can make it, Commander Holmes." She turns on her heel and walks seductively out of the office.

My god, I love this girl more every day. Nothing makes me happier than a bit of jousting.

* * *

Mike spends a fretful hour Saturday trying to decide what to wear. He's new to New York's rules of attire. He tries jackets, shirts, ties and slacks in every combination. The only item he's certain about is dress loafers. At 1830, he throws on the ubiquitous blue blazer with a gold silk pocket handkerchief over a blue, button-down oxford shirt and a gold and navy rep stripe tie. Charcoal gray slacks make the ensemble boring, predictable, yet suitable. He approaches her building at 1855. She was clear: not too early. From the corner he watches a number of people in party dress entering the building. Finally he leaps five steps into the building, is passed by the doorman, and takes the elevator to her floor, ringing her doorbell at 1910.

"Commander Holmes, I'm so happy to see that you could join us. I know a handsome young man like you is in high demand. You've noticed the women at the office ogling you, yes?" she teases. Introducing him to the dozen or so guests, she warns, "Look out girls this one looks like a real charmer."

The apartment is a bit larger than expected. She must be augmenting her housing allowance with personal funds. Pale cream walls and soft lighting complement her red silk cheongsam. Two exquisite small Chinese sculptures and a few antique brush paintings are not something she picked up at a souvenir shop. In three corners of the room exquisitely carved dark mahogany tables hold orchids in full bloom. His Asian experience helps him identify a delicate white cymbidium with yellow centers, a large dendrobium with distinctively speckled lavender petals and a psychopsis, red and yellow petals and three rose antenna-like leaves. The flowers set an intimate and exotic tone. There's a subtle hint of elegant incense in the air. All Grace's trademarks.

1915, the last of the guests have arrived. Grace has laid out a beautiful buffet. No sweet and sour pork here. Chinese delicacies include Xinjiang barbecue, three types of Baozi, Tibetan Shab Tra and Mongolian hot pot. Fried mantou for dessert along with a bowl of green, black and red grapes and aromatic teas complete the tasteful feast. Guests continually return to the table for "just one more bite." Her evening is a gracious, warm affair.

He mingles, purposely avoiding Grace except for a perfunctory comment here or there. Mike notices that she isn't eating. Yet, she's watching him, testing his social graces no doubt.

2130, the first person leaves. When Mike sees another preparing to go, he does the same. At the door he takes Grace's hand and thanks her for a lovely evening, "I'll probably see you around the office."

She smiles. "I look forward to it," she says with an acceptable formal tone. She's keeping him and everyone else off balance.

Monday, Laurie comes over from the Mexican delegation and stops by his office. "Grace has three girl friends from Hawaii visiting this week. They arrived on Sunday and will be here until Thursday. She will probably be in that afternoon or on Friday. I hope you can stand it," she mocks him with a wicked wink. "She gave me this note for you. Good luck."

"Dear Sherlock,

I'm sorry I didn't have an opportunity to tell you about my visitors. I'll be out just a few days. I'm longing to be with you. We've only had a few days together in five years and most of those were when you were rehabbing your wounds at Tripler.

It won't be long now, I promise you.

Love,

C.J.

Thursday afternoon, Grace sails into the office and shares pictures and details of her trip with the ladies. A half hour of chatter and giggles ensue. Mike waits until 1630 before sticking his head in her door. "Thanks for the lovely party. You were so gracious making us newcomers welcome and comfortable. I was delighted that I could clear my calendar for it."

"I'm also happy that you enjoyed the party." She hands him a document. When he reaches for the paper she holds onto it. There's a small piece of folded paper attached with his name on it. She lets go with a sly smile and sits back, arms folded as though she just did something clever. Mike pockets the scrap and walks nonchalantly to his office.

He turns his chair so no one can see he's looking at the scrap.

Seven p.m. Friday. Be there. Very casual.

Are they going to be together at last or is this another tease?

* * *

1900, Grace greets him wrapped in a white terrycloth bathrobe. It's not what he expected. She doesn't say a word as she closes and bolts the door. He tries to hand her the bouquet of stargazer lilies and jasmine vines. She jumps into his arms, wrapping her legs around his waist and smothering him with kisses. She lets go and drops to her feet on top of his. "If you're not in bed with me in sixty seconds I'm going to kill you. Then I'm going to kill myself!" Taking his hand she pulls him toward the bedroom, a trail of his clothes scattering behind. From ice to fire.

Two hours later they're lying in each other's arms. "That almost made up for five years apart, didn't it my love?"

"Almost."

"Are you hungry?"

"Food hasn't crossed my mind. What would you suggest?"

"How about a root beer float?"

"I'd never have thought of that, but I am thirsty and my blood sugar is depleted."

She gives him a little kiss. "I have a robe for you. I thought you might misplace your clothes."

Root beer floats in brandy snifters at the kitchen table. "I have no idea what kind of food you like. In fact I don't know much about you at all. What did you say your name is?"

"We can get to names later. My favorite dinner is poached salmon, angel hair pasta with Danish butter, cilantro parsley with a dash of parmesan cheese accompanied by a glass of Dry Creek pinot grigio. What about you? I've noticed you don't eat much."

"Good observation, Sherlock. I'm not a big eater. To me eating is more a necessity than entertainment. When I was a young girl my mother and I studied food with a woman who viewed eating that way. We took a rather Spartan approach, natural foods with enough liquids to stay in balance. When we arrived in Hawaii with fresh fruits and vegetables so abundant, we felt at home. I love all kinds of grapes. They're sweet, wet, and nutritious. So many people in New York are very overweight and not very healthy. I don't know how they function. This root beer float is pure indulgence for me. But it tastes great and complements our mood."

"What else can you share about yourself? A Chinese woman living in a foreign land? There must be something interesting there."

"Interesting is an understatement. Are you ready for this?"

"Of course. I need to understand everything about the woman I love."

"Okay, sit back, but pay attention. The story starts with our arrival in Hawaii when I was a young teenager. Although there is a large Chinese population on the Islands, it wasn't that easy to assimilate. We were welcomed with caution. Our people didn't know if we were truly nationalists or actually communists. It took a few years to get past that. Then I went to Stanford. Again people didn't know how to relate to me. Among the liberal students I found my way. I finished my BA in three years and started on a Master's, but my dad got sick and I had to come home and help mom care for him.

"When I came back to Hawaii, I met Jerry and he swept me off my feet. Being married to a white man added another dimension. By nature I'm Chinese. By circumstances I'm American. I felt that I didn't fit well into either culture. That's partly why I married so young. I felt the need for protection. Big mistake with Jerry-the-party-master. For several years I was rather lost. When dad died I was even more alone. You showed up and that really messed with me. Along with all the other issues, I was married and falling in love with another man, another haole.

"It all came to a moment of discovery in the spring of 1970. In the space of two months you left on your secret mission, mom died, and Jerry was killed in the plane crash. Suddenly, I was totally alone. I had to grow up fast. After selling mom's house and moving into an apartment in Manoa, I went back to UH to finish my masters. Coincidently, I was asked to shepherd Taiwanese visitors from the UN. When a fellow from the State Department heard about my background he asked me if I would like to join the UN delegation. It was a great opportunity to test myself. It was sink or swim. When I looked in the mirror I saw a grown woman with all the tools for a successful life. I decided to become an expert swimmer. No more waiting for something good to happen. So here I am, a big girl who can take care of herself and deal with anyone or anything that comes along. My reward was that the gods brought you back to me."

* * *

The conversation of discovery goes back and forth for nearly an hour. Finally Mike says, "I'm getting cold. I need to go back to bed or get dressed."

"I'll show you where the bedroom is. You may not remember the way, you were so eager to get there last time."

0810, he rolls over and sits up, "I say, I'm a bit peckish. I could stand a bit of something to fill the void, don't you know."

"Good morning John Bull, or whatever your name is."

After a continental breakfast accompanied by the ubiquitous bowl of green and purple grapes, they go for a walk. The sky is overcast and the air is quite brisk. A stiff breeze whistles around the buildings, just what they need to clear the cobwebs. Late morning they stop at a neighborhood bakery for a warm bagel, cream cheese and strawberry jam. Tea and espresso clear the clouds inside and out. Across the street a rectangular neighborhood park is vibrating with kids and dogs chasing each other, kicking leaves and throwing sticks.

"Honey? That word feels as good in my mouth as a spoonful of honey. How are we going to play this? You didn't tell me you knew we were assigned to work together. That's a fact for which you'll have to be spanked."

Grace laughs and leans into him. "We'll just have to try to act normal. When we're together, no winks, no smiles—especially no touches. Just be professional, but friendly, like you are. Make believe I'm Laurie. We'll just let things develop. At the end of the day, we can come home and play house."

"There's an offer I can't refuse."

Chapter 4

ON DUTY

October 1972
New York City

Monday, Mike and Grace begin gathering background on Ivanova Petrov and Jiang Gao. Their delegation rosters provide basic information neither especially helpful, nor necessarily truthful. They don't list delegates as spies. CIA and FBI dossiers are slightly more useful. When asked why they want them, they make up a story that they're pulling together a study of banking practices in China and Russia. Feds are suspicious, but agree to share information. One of the great problems about intelligence, or espionage if you want to call it that, is that no one ever tells the whole truth, even the ones on your side. Secrecy underlies and demands caution, but it also inhibits operations.

First target is Jiang Gao, Commercial Attaché of the Chinese delegation. CIA reports there's a nervousness about him. He's very bright but socially immature. This inhibits his interactions with some of the older delegates.

CIA hasn't found his soft spot, but Grace claims she has a couple probes they can try. When Jiang's family returned from Taiwan they settled in Zhengzhou. The city of over seven million is the capital and largest city of Henan province. It's the political, economic, technological, and educational center of the province and the major transportation hub for Central China. The city lies on the southern bank of the Yellow River.

Jiang excelled in the best schools, attracting attention from the aging politicos. Upon graduation he was given a position in the banking system where he performed brilliantly. The central party's aging leadership recognized that a new generation needed to be trained. Accordingly, they targeted him for advancement.

Commercial Attaché Jiang is concerned with trade policies, import and export duties, trade financing and the establishment of Free Trade Zones. He spends much of his time with foreigners, though he's not at ease dealing with them.

Mike and Grace are invited to a Chinese delegation reception to honor a visiting dignitary. Mike's still living most of the time in his own place, so he cabs to Grace's apartment. She's dressed in a dark blue cheongsam richly embroidered with flowers. On the front a red bird with a very long neck flying upward draws attention to her gorgeous figure.

"It isn't fair that a woman so beautiful should be allowed to wear a cheongsam. You should have to dress in a gunny sack to keep men from going insane."

"Not my problem," she replies coquettishly.

Reception is at the Roosevelt Hotel. "The Grande Dame of Madison Avenue" is the epitome of grandeur, from its thirty foot lobby ceiling to its golden ballroom with massive chandeliers, arched windows, and the famous suspended clock. Long tables are loaded with a sumptuous array of Chinese delicacies. Three bars provide an endless supply of potables. Grace accepts a champagne cocktail, though she barely sips it.

Touring the huge ballroom slowly but deliberately, they locate Jiang and work their way around to him. He's tall and slim, with round glasses partially hiding intense eyes and an uneasy smile.

Halfway through the maneuver Grace turns and bumps into him. She introduces herself in Chinese. When Mike also greets Jiang in Mandarin, he's surprised. Jiang is enchanted by Grace, of course. The conversation is light and short. Later in the event they pass him again and Grace remarks on how nicely the evening has gone.

"Thank you. I hope to see you again," nodding pointedly at Grace. Little does he know how much he'll see of them.

Middle of November they meet at the Committee on Trade and Tariffs, and Jiang comes over. Mike observes that he has the same last name as Jiang Qing, Mao's third wife and a prominent member of the Central Cultural Revolution Group. "Are you related?" Jiang twitches slightly. Bingo, a key to his psyche. Grace asks if he knows her. Jiang warms to the topic. He met her briefly one time and was struck by her beauty and intelligence. Grace lets the conversation drift, but Jiang keeps bringing it back to her. It's enough to realize the CIA agents missed the boat thinking he was concerned about the Taiwan situation. His feelings for Jiang Qing are the opening.

Over the next months they cross paths with Jiang several times, slowly probing the Jiang Qing connection. You only have one chance to turn a person into an asset. Better to go slow and win, rather than fast and blow it.

Simultaneously they're studying Invanova Petrov. She's an entirely different story. Ivanova's a second level delegate to the UN, working on energy issues. This puts her at the heart of the petroleum and banking systems. In Russia they're tied together under control of central party mechanisms.

Banks provide financial assistance to Soviet enterprises with cash flow shortages or expansion plans. Credit usually depends less on the credit-worthiness of the borrower than the priorities of the central planning policy makers. Ivanova has ample opportunity to work with central planning people as well as emerging business leaders. Although the Chinese are somewhat cautious with foreigners,

Russians are inherently close-mouthed and suspicious. It's part of their national paranoia.

Tracking Ivanova they discover she meets frequently with communist delegates from several other countries, including Jiang, about trade financing. Mike and Grace find their way into a subcommittee meeting on this topic where Ivanova and Jiang will be present. Jiang sees them before the meeting opens and waves. The meeting itself is intriguing, like a medieval ballroom dance. Everyone circles and touches lightly, but there is no intimacy. After the meeting they approach Jiang. He introduces Ivanova and a delegate from East Germany. They focus on the proceedings just witnessed. Ivanova seems to be relaxed, no doubt because of Grace's presence. The woman is covered in a drab, boxy number that is hard-pressed to call a dress. She compliments Grace on her suit and they fall into a discussion about spring fashions, which enthralls Ivanova. "Russian women have never been known as chic dressers," Grace comments to Mike in their debriefing later.

Grace dazzles Ivanova with information about sales from Saks and down through Bloomingdales, Macy's and Loehmann's. Ivanova admits that she doesn't know how to navigate the retail jungle. Perfect. Grace offers to give her a tour two weeks from now. The Soviets probably need that much time to check out Grace. Strike two, the CIA should have used fashion as an entry point, rather than politics.

In the next month they move slowly but steadily, finding opportunities to meet Jiang casually. By March they have a steady flow of contacts with both targets. Jiang continually expands on his admiration for Jiang Qing. It's clear that he has deep feelings and is very upset with how she's being treated. He considers her to be the true and best successor to Mao. Periodically Grace or Mike make a date with him for tea or a drink after work. Mostly, they listen to him go off on Jiang Qing's problem at length. To keep things moving, they agree with him that she's logically the proper one to succeed Mao. He seems to be remarkably outspoken on the topic, seemingly without fear of surveillance unlike the Russians.

In the meantime, Grace is enlightening Ivanova on the undercurrents of New York fashion. She's making as good a friend of the middle aged woman as the scrutiny of the KGB allows. Every couple of weeks they have lunch or high tea at Tea and Sympathy in the West Village or the Russian Tea Room on 57th Street. Slowly Ivanova opens up to Grace about her anger over her husband's treatment and subsequent death. Grace empathizes with Ivanova by sharing her anguish over her father's and husband's deaths. A true bond is growing between them.

*   *   *

While their work life bonds Mike and Grace in mystery, New York offers opportunities for recreation and intimacy through great restaurants, the Staten Island Ferry, Rockefeller Center, Sunday brunch at the Palace, and carriage rides in Central Park. Eventually they make it to Ellis Island to find a record of Mike's grandfather. He emigrated through Rotterdam on the SS *Champagne*, landing in the new world in 1900. From there, somehow he managed to make it to North Dakota where a relative lived. It's very satisfying for Mike to learn more about his family history.

As spring opens them to the outdoors, they rent a car and tour the upstate and Connecticut countryside. One warm May day they pass a golf driving range. Grace says, "Let's go hit some balls."

"When we met in Hawaii I vaguely remember you mentioned golf. Did you say that you played golf in Hawaii?"

"Of course. I played a lot. If you can play in the wind there, you can play anywhere."

"Then let's stop and you can show me your form."

"You said you had a single handicap. Is it still true?"

"It's been a couple years since I've picked up a club. I'm very rusty. Did you have a handicap when you were playing in Hawaii?"

"Of course. If you're serious, you have a handicap. If you don't have one, you're just a wannabe hacker."

They pull into the range, get balls out of the machine, and pick up a couple well-worn clubs. Mike stretches and takes a few swings to warm up. The only question is, if his knees will hold up. When Mike turns around Grace is addressing her first shot. She makes a nice swing and hits a straight shot about 80 yards. As she loosens, up her shots go higher and farther. "You have a nice trajectory, Dragon Lady." He's delighted to see she's probably a pretty good player.

"I'm guessing your handicap was somewhere around 15."

"The lowest round I ever shot was an 81. My best handicap was 14. Someday if I ever have a home on a fairway and get the chance to play consistently, I think I might break 80. How about you?"

"I got as low as a 4 at one point when I was at FAD. My lowest round was a 71."

"Wow. You never told me you were that good. I'm impressed."

"I'm afraid it's a thing of the past. Haven't played much since my knees were broken. I don't know if I can ever get back under even 6 of 7."

"What do you mean your knees were broken?"

"I mentioned it the first night we were together, but I guess you were so focused on my magnificent body and brilliant repartee that you forgot about it. I told you about being kidnapped in Hong Kong. The bad guys broke both my patellas trying to get me to talk."

"What else haven't you told me?

"When we get home I'll make a full disclosure."

Robed over tea, a few rice cookies and grapes, Mike spins the tale of his early life.

"I grew up next to a Sioux reservation in eastern North Dakota. Tough environment. Parents never got through high school because they had to work. I have a younger brother, Bob. We all worked as soon as we were able. Mom's idea was by the time you're twenty you should be married, working and making babies. Romance wasn't part of their dream. I think my dad never felt much loved. I disappointed mom and sided with dad's notion of getting educated and escaping North Dakota. I stood out in high school and got a college scholarship and then a Rhodes. Spent two years at Oxford studying Asian politics and economics. I learned Chinese with a British accent from an Edwardian era Foreign Service retiree. When I came back I joined the navy, went to OCS for a commission, and met you a couple years later. Now that we're baring our deepest truths, fess up. How did those blue eyes sneak into your regal lineage?"

"I admit it's a bit unusual for a Chinese lady to be blue-eyed, but use your imagination. There are Europeans in my ancestry. From what I've been told, the first was a Catalonian. During the Napoleonic Wars, around 1800, much of Catalonia was occupied by the French. You know what occupying soldiers and sailors do, don't you? They make liaisons with the local ladies. That's where the blue eyes came in. Some unknown blue eyed Frenchman must have connected with an ancestor of mine."

"Okay. But that doesn't explain how they got to China."

"Simple. My great-great-grandfather was a Catalonian officer on a Spanish trading ship that landed in Shanghai about 1865. The date was never verified. The marriage license didn't show it either. Anyway, he met and fell in love with my great great grandmother and jumped ship. From what little we know of her, she was an independent, brilliant young woman, characteristics not highly valued in women at that time. Despite many objections they married and ran off to Henan Province. Somehow he obtained a position in a local university, perhaps because he was a master navigator and mathematician. She established centers for widows and orphans that led to her being recognized by the Guangxu Emperor. I was born in Henan of this notable family. The blue eyes skipped through the generations and I was the lucky one in my generation. Satisfied?"

"That was a long way to go to get blue eyes, but in your case it was worth it."

"Thank you. Any other questions Agent Liu?"

Chapter 5

MAKING IT LEGAL

July 1973
Manhattan

Summer's swelter drives them out to the Adirondacks and the Jersey shore for weekends. The City is not a great place to develop your golf game. At work they're discreet, yet it's beginning to show. Smiling too much when they're together. Mike's never been so happy. He's doing what he loves at work, and he's living with the love of his life. Still, is this real? Can it last?

Grace feels none of the apprehension she felt with Jerry. Mike is clear and straight forward, no quirks or hidden agendas, and very affectionate. They both realize that sooner or later they're going to have to go public. Until then their mission is to recruit Ivanova and Gao. It fills their days and even impinges on their nights.

Over tea amidst a Saturday ramble Grace comments to Ivanova that she seems distracted.

"Soviet Union disregards its people," she says. "They call everyone *comrade*, but treat them like slaves. Communism is ugly. It's a lie. People at the top only want power for themselves. Infighting and treachery are unrelenting. If I were a man I'd be afraid to turn my back. It's disgusting."

Ivanova's level of trust is clearly growing. Here's the opening, but Grace lets the comment rest. When you rush people in this business, they question your motives and you have to back off and start over.

Meanwhile, Gao is tuned into what's happening with Jiang Qing. Mao seems to be softening, inviting people he had disavowed back into party positions. There are rumors that he's quite ill. Just rumors but as Jiang Qing edges into power positions, opposition to her grows. Gao is nervous about her fate. When he seems comfortable with them, Grace invites him to dinner at her apartment. Once they tell him they both studied politics and economics in college, he relaxes. He goes on all night about how Qing has been persecuted within China's changing political scene. They sympathize until he's on the edge. A small shove and he should come over.

At the personal level Laurie confirms to Grace that all the women in the section know about their year-long relationship. So do even some of the obtuse guys, she adds. One evening at her apartment, Mike brings up moving to the next level. Although it seems to be a tacit agreement, he wants to make it official. He's brought a bottle of Dom Perignon in anticipation.

After pouring her a flute of the bubbly he says, "You may have noticed that I'm hopelessly in love with you. You seem at least moderately receptive to me. Do you suppose you could consider being my wife, if I were to ask you?"

"Why don't you give it a try, handsome? If you don't ask, you don't get."

"Grace, I've been insanely mad about you since the first night in Hawaii. Despite both our adventures and intrigues since then, we've come back to that magical night to replay it. The idea of losing you is incomprehensible. I don't know what I would do if we could not be together. This is the best way I can tell you how much I love you. Mike kneels down and takes her hand. He half sings, half recites parts from his favorite song.

"I know that there are men who would give you the world to enjoy. All I have is my heart for your toy, and a promise to be here whene'er you call. If you wonder what I'm asking in return, my demands are really quite small. Just say you'll love me and me alone. That's all."

"Michael that is so beautiful, very sweet. But don't try for a career in music. Thank you, my love. It was a fateful night in Hawaii. The gods must have meant for us to meet. Chinese believe in fate and I believe our fates are intertwined forever. I do want to be your wife."

A weight pours off Mike. The light in Grace's crystal blue eyes burns more brightly and a dazzling smile lights her face.

* * *

This calls for an engagement party. They'll invite the staff, as well as friends from other delegations because Ivanova and Jiang are on the list and should not stand out. Nights and Saturdays they shop for a ring that they will keep under wraps until the party. They choose a date, September 10, two weeks before the annual UN week. In late August they send out the simple invitation.

Please join us in celebrating
our engagement

Delegates' Dining Room
September 10, 1973
Cocktails and Hors d'oeuvres
6 to 7:30 p.m.

Michael Holmes and Liu Chan-juan

R.S.V.P. US Political Affairs Office

They will have red and white floral arrangements on small tables, an open bar, conventional delicacies, of course small bowls of green and red grapes, and a few Chinese specialties. No soggy dim sum.

September 10 there isn't a lot of work being done. The ladies are totally wrapped up in the event—as if a war had ended or someone gave birth to septuplets. As they take the elevator to the Delegates Dining Room at five, Mike comments, "It's nice to see everyone just having fun and not worrying about the state of the world." They check with the chef and the maître d', and then try to relax with a glass of wine looking out over the East River.

Mike's beyond joyful. "I never anticipated that a day filled with so much love would come in my lifetime."

Grace looks at him and wonders, *how could a man with such a tender heart be a spy?* Are you okay Sherlock?

He nods. "It's like my life is passing in front of me from Dakota through Oxford, Vietnam, China, meeting you, losing you and now…."

She sits on his lap hands him a cold champagne flute. "Here, big boy. It will make you feel better."

"What a life! And now it's beginning all over again. No more alone. I've found my home at last."

1800, the guests start arriving, Mike's grinning like a carnival monkey and Grace is taking it all in stride. Ivanova and Gao arrive separately. Both are effusive in their congratulations as if they've been lifelong friends. The party is going quite well, the noise level deafening. At 1845 Mike calls everyone's attention. Gradually, after much rapping on glasses, the group quiets down. Mike clears his throat with a large gulp of cold champagne.

"Ladies and gentlemen, Grace and I are most grateful that you have come to join us for this joyful occasion. We cannot adequately express our profound appreciation for your friendship and support. Now I would like to share with you the reason why we're here." He takes Grace's hand and kneels down, gently. The crowd is silent. Mike palms her ring in his left hand and holds her left hand with his right. He asks her in Chinese,

"If I can have only one wish come true in my life, I wish it to be next to you forever. Liu Chan-juan, please marry me!"

Many people have no idea what that means. After a long moment, Grace nods and answers "*Hao, wo hui de.*"(Yes, I will.)

He puts the ring on her ring finger. Standing up slowly and shakily, he kisses her hand as he did in Hawaii many years ago. She chokes up. He takes her in his arms gently and kisses her. She waves her ringed hand for all to see. The room explodes with applause. The maître d' hands them champagne flutes. Mike holds his high before draining it in one big gulp. Grace sips two milligrams.

To their surprise, without asking, the maître d' plays a recording of Mendelssohn's Wedding March, though it's barely audible above the laughter and clapping. Grace and Mike waltz, the guests backing away to give them room to fly.

Everyone is having such a grand time there are no signs of them leaving at 1930. Ivanova and Gao are laughing together and mingling with other guests. Grace is happy that the party was so pleasurable. About 2000 the last stragglers wander out. Grace and Mike sit down and take a deep breath in unison. They share a final glass of champagne.

Chapter 6

UNEXPECTED STORM

January 1974
United Nations Headquarters
New York City

Phil Hunt calls Mike and Grace into his office on Monday morning. Without a word he hands Grace one sheet of paper, a note.

Grace's face turns red. "What in the world is this? Where did you get this, Phil?"

"It was in my mail this morning in an envelope marked Personal and Confidential."

"What is it?" Mike asks. Grace hands him the paper.

Mike scans it and rocks back like he's been kicked. He reads it very slowly again, then looks from her to Phil.

Grace reads the note aloud, as if she's trying to digest the words.

Mr. Hunt:
You should know that you have engaged a communist agent on your staff. Her name is Liu Chan-juan. She calls herself Grace to take away doubt regarding her background and political sympathies. Ms. Liu was born in China and lived there for many years before immigrating to America. Her father was deeply absorbed in Chinese military and politics. He came to America as a secret agent for his old communist friends in

*China. She still has relatives in China who are prominent
communists. Have you noticed that she spends much of her
time with the Chinese MSS and Russian KGB agents in their
delegations? You need to weed out this seditous woman before
she does more harm.*

"There's no signature," Grace notes. "And, she misspelled seditious. Michael, these are all lies. You know my father fought the
communists in China. He wasn't a communist agent when we came
to Hawaii. I don't have any contact with family in China. I was only
twelve when we came to America. It's all terrible lies." She looks at
Phil then at Mike, clenches her fists, grits her teeth and hisses, "I'm
going to find out who did this and crush them, annihilate them."

Mike puts a hand on her shoulder, "I don't know what's behind
this, but we'll find out who did it, I promise you."

"Grace, I don't believe a word of this malicious note," Phil says. "I
don't have any idea who or why. Unfortunately, I have to take this to
the Director. I can't ignore it. If I do, and and there is another letter
to me or to him, I'll be in trouble. You understand. He'll probably
report it to the FBI and they'll be in here like a swarm of locusts. It's
their job, even if it's a crank letter. We'll keep it as quiet as possible."

"I understand, Phil. No hard feelings toward you. But I'm going
to destroy the person who wrote this note. FBI, CIA or anybody else
can get involved, but I'm going to kill this snake."

"Grace, this is a terrible act," Mike exclaims. "I'm mad as hell that
someone would do this to you. Phil, I have an idea how to get on
with this. You have a couple of CIA agents on your staff pretending
to be attachés Between them and us we'll flush out this coward and
keep control of the investigation."

"How do you intend to do that?"

"We set about doing an organizational analysis. You announce
that to improve your operation, you are asking staff to respond to a

short questionnaire regarding their responsibilities, work and suggestions for improvements. Personnel can provide the forms. Now we have an excuse to go through the section asking questions. The CIAs and I will take the point and do the questioning. Grace will be covert, talking to people informally about their reaction to the project. The combination of the overt and covert approaches should uncover who wrote the letter. Grace, what do you think?"

"It sounds workable to me. I can talk with the people casually, around the water cooler so to speak. Someone will show reactions that point us toward the culprit."

Phil sits back with his hands behind his head staring at the ceiling for a long minute. "I like it. It's a way to keep control of the investigation without having outsiders running amok in here and upsetting everyone. My bet is the guilty person will give off clues inadvertently." "Good. Phil, if you can have Personnel prepare a questionnaire, we'll map out a plan of attack. I appreciate your support. We'll be back to you in a couple days."

* * *

When they reach Grace's office, she's still boiling. "Michael, we're going to find this rat and make her pay. I'm sure it's a woman. A man would go about it in a different way. You made a great suggestion. Let's lay out our plan and then go back to Phil to involve the local CIA.

A week later the interviews begin. The routine goes smoothly. Mike and the agents meet the staff one at a time in a conference room. The script starts with,

"The purpose of this project is to find ways to make our work easier and more productive. Job descriptions are seldom an accurate account of what we really do. In your own words please describe your basic tasks and responsibilities."

They ask for clarification or expansion. Then they probe about process relationships with other staff. "Who do you work most with in terms of exchanging information?" This gives information about relationships and frustrations. The person is usually relaxed enough to pour out feelings that are both job related and personal.

Next phase: "What are the basic knowledge, skills and aptitudes needed for this job?" This is the point where they hear about any inefficiencies or injustices that exist in the present method for selection, assignment and promotion. They'll hear, "She really isn't qualified for that job. I could do it better. I should have gotten it because…" Those themes paint a picture of who is angry with Grace because she got the job without formal State Department experience. Within a month the interviews have been completed and a wealth of information compiled.

Grace has been talking off-line with the staff about their reactions to the project. There are many opinions as well as feelings. There is hope management will actually do something positive with the data this time.

Most people are reasonably happy with their work, seeing the larger goals of the UN, feeling committed to them, and acknowledging nothing is perfect. A couple people seemed to want to be more candid, but wouldn't speak up. They didn't trust the questioner or maybe felt that he was part of the problem. They send in three perceptive staffers to follow up. From those conversations they've homed in on two women whom they think might be the target.

The primary one is Eleanor Lodge. Miss Lodge, as she prefers to be addressed, is from a family that arrived in America in the early 1700s. She's active in the DAR (Daughters of the American Revolution) and is the latest in a long line of public servants. One ancestor had been an ambassador somewhere, and others have held positions of high responsibility and esteem within the political establishment. A very proper Boston Brahman, she wants everyone to value her pedigree. Her bespoke suits are obviously expensive. There's never a speck of lint on her or in her office. According to several staff, she has complained about not being appreciated or recognized despite her distinguished lineage. And after a couple martinis, she has been known to let down her façade and mention Grace's name, among others, who have gotten unwarranted preferential treatment not earned by their experience or background.

The second suspect is Cathy Bruno, dark-complexioned, hard-working dynamo who doesn't hold back on how things should be run. She's the opposite of Eleanor, grew up in the slums, first generation Italian. Unsophisticated, worked her way to a bachelor's degree. Many of her peers have at least a master's, so she's not extraordinarily qualified. Although she's vocal, she's not too upset with Grace. In fact she spends time around Grace asking questions about China.

When all the data are organized, Mike and Grace meet with Phil.

"Our first impression is that although you should interview both women, Eleanor is most likely the author of my poison pen letter. Did you get the same impression from our report?"

"Yes, although I'm not totally sold on her just yet. What do you suggest as the next step?"

"You set up bogus interviews for promotion to a new Special Agent position. You've narrowed it down to Cathy, Eleanor, and me. Call Cathy in for a talk. If she opens up a bit, ask her, confidentailly of course, what she thinks about me and Eleanor. Do the same with Eleanor."

*　*　*

"Good morning, Cathy. Have a seat. There's coffee on the credenza if you'd like some. You received my memo so you know why we're here and what we're looking for. I'm hoping to fill this new position, if we get it funded, from within. But I might have to go with an outside candidate who looks highly qualified."

"Phil, I don't think you should go outside. There are a couple people here who are capable of filling the requirements on the Requisition."

"You're probably correct. The competition is keen though."

"Well, you know I've been on the job for five years and have a degree in Asian Studies. I'll have completed the course work for my master's next semester. No one works harder or is more dedicated or loyal than me. I learn quickly and would be good in that job."

The conversation goes on for a half hour until Phil says something about seditious actions.

"What did you call them, *seditious* was it? What do you mean? That's not a term I hear very often."

"I meant treasonous."

"Oh yes, I understand."

"Cathy, who do you think might be ready for this job—besides you—of course?"

Suddenly she sits erect and says, "Well Eleanor has been here a long time and has a deep background in this type of work. She's kind of stuffy, walks around as though she has a stick up her you know what. But she doesn't have the social skills that are needed in this position. Grace is very smart, but other than being Chinese, I don't think she has the depth of experience for the job. If I may speak openly, I was very surprised when she was hired at this level with no prior agency experience. I didn't think it was fair to the rest of the staff who've worked their way up like I have."

"I see. Is there anything specific that makes you say that?"

"We don't really know that much about her background or her feelings toward China and its leadership, do we?"

"You have a good point there. She was vetted, of course, but we might need to go into that a bit more. Well, I've got to interview others, so thank you very much for your input, Cathy. I promise to give you every consideration."

Eleanor is up next. "Come in. Good to see you. You're always working so hard I don't spot you walking around the office as much as some others."

"Mr. Hunt, my job is not to chat up the staff. I have major responsibilities, and I focus on them assiduously."

"Yes, I know you do, and I appreciate it. You know why we're here. Let's get into it, so I don't take you away from your job too long."

When Phil mentions the nature of their work and seditious acts as outlined in the Alien and Sedition Act, she responds, "I'm very familiar with that. In fact, an ancestor of mine from Massachusetts supported President Adams when he signed that into effect in 1798."

"Wow. That's great. You know I have trouble with that word seditious. It's hard to pronounce and I sometimes misspell it."

"It's really not a problem. It's s-e-d-i-t-i-o-u-s. Perhaps you should use treasonous instead. It's easier to spell, and everyone knows what it means."

"You're right. I'll remember that. The last question I want to ask is who else on the staff might be qualified for this job. You're clearly the leading candidate, but I'd appreciate your views since you've been here longer than most people."

"That in itself speaks volumes regarding my qualifications. But if you want my opinion, I'll be frank. Cathy is a bright, hard-working young girl, but I don't think she has the background, if you know what I mean, to represent this office before the public. I won't go as far as to say she's somewhat crude at times, but she doesn't present herself as professionally as she might. Her wardrobe looks like something from a Filene's fire sale. There *is* something to be said about breeding."

"Yes, I see what you mean."

"As for Grace, I have misgivings. I won't say I'm suspicious, but I do see her spending an inordinate amount of time with the Chinese delegation. Obviously she is well-received there and has many friends among that communist rabble. Excuse me, I shouldn't call them that, but when you come from a family with the public service background of mine …"

* * *

Phil suggests that Grace and Mike meet with him off-site, so there is no suspicion. "Now I'm more confused than when we started. Cathy didn't know what seditious meant, so she probably didn't write the letter. But when I asked about Grace, she was not as negative as Eleanor. On the other hand, Eleanor not only spelled seditious for me, but gave me a mini-lecture on its history and use. Yet she was much more critical of you, Grace, for being Chinese and spending a lot of time with the Chinese delegates."

"Cathy is much friendlier toward me, though Eleanor isn't very friendly with anyone on the staff, given her exalted view of family history. I would say she is more concerned about me than Cathy is. The misspelling could be a typo."

Mike jumps in. "Though we're leaning toward Eleanor, we really don't have a case yet. Let's get someone to examine the type element of her Selectric. Phil, you can have the IBM technician check both women's typewriters at night for unique characteristics."

"Excellent idea."

Three days later Phil reports. The type ball in neither Selectric matched the fonts on the letter. It could have been typed by one of them at home.

Mike volunteers, "I'll ask the tech if anything was changed on their typewriters since the date of the letter."

The tech looks at his log, "Yes, both of them have been serviced. Cathy's needed an adjustment and Miss Lodge's needed a new type element ball."

"Why did she ask you to change it?"

"She said it was sticking."

"So you changed the ball for her?"

"Yes."

"What do you do with the old elements?"

"It depends. If the problem is obvious, I write a short note and send it back to quality control. If it isn't, I examine the element closely for flaws."

"What did you do with Eleanor's?"

"I still have it. I haven't had time to check it."

"Do me a favor, please. Put it on your typewriter and type several lines from this letter. This is a very sensitive matter. Don't talk to anyone about it."

"No problem. I'll check it after I finish my calls today."

Next morning Mike hands him the element and the paper with a couple of sentences typed on it. "There wasn't a problem with the element. It just had something sticky spilled on it. That happens surprisingly often. Staff drinking coffee with one hand and typing with the other."

Grace joins them to compare the letter to the tech's paper. "No, nothing unusual but," the tech says, "you have to use a magnifying glass to see any irregularities. Still, a magnifier doesn't reveal anything.

Grace suggests "You're the pro here, why don't you have a look?"

"Okay. You have to look at each letter slowly and meticulously. The type face on this element is the typical elite with serifs—that little extra stroke. Obvious flaws in the main strokes are relatively easy to spot. But serifs are very thin, almost invisible even with a magnifier. Imperfections in the paper can affect whether the serifs print crisply.

"I always start by looking at the vowels because they occur more often than most consonants. The "a"s and "e"s show nothing unusual in either paper. But in the "i"s I see a flaw. It's almost invisible to the naked eye. But the left side of the bottom serif line is cut off on the test sentence. Same in the letter."

Mike and Grace take the glass to see what he's pointed to throughout the letter.

"It's not a paper irregularity problem, cause it's always there," the tech clarifies. Grace's letter was written using the old element from Eleanor's machine. However, when I compare it with what I typed, I found another anomaly. My typewriter doesn't have any problems. The letter was written on another machine. Periodically, it shows an irregularity in the spacing between sentences. It's not there every time, just sometimes. I can go to Eleanor and tell her I want to check her machine to make sure everything is okay."

Next afternoon he reports, "Her machine is perfect. The space problem isn't on hers."

"Now what?" Mike asks.

"We have to find the machine that also has the spacing problem on which this element was used." he replies.

"But there are hundreds of machines on this floor alone. And the letter could have been written on a typewriter somewhere else," Grace suggests.

"What was the problem with Cathy's machine?" Mike asks.

"I think it was the space bar hanging up."

"Tonight, put this element in Cathy's typewriter and type the first few lines of the letter."

"No problem."

1800, everyone except for Grace, Mike and the tech have left the floor. The tech reports back in thirty minutes with a smile.

"That's it. This element was put on Cathy's machine. I readjusted the space bar to the hang up I corrected earlier. I can see the spacing problem in what I typed. This element was put on Cathy's machine and the letter was typed there."

"That's great," Mike exclaims. "We've got her."

"Slow down, sailor. We don't know who did the switch. It could have been either woman."

"You're right. We'll take the evidence to each woman separately and see who cracks under questioning."

"Phil, I recommend we show the letter to Eleanor first since she is the prime suspect. If she confesses, we don't have to go to Cathy and the incident remains a secret among just us."

"Okay. She'll think I'm following up to the job interview."

Eleanor is surprised to see Mike and Grace there at her interview. Phil offers coffee and explains, "Eleanor, we have a problem. I received this letter a couple weeks ago. Our investigation concludes it was written on your typewriter."

Eleanor straightens up and pulls her head back. She scans the letter. "I don't know where this letter was written, but I didn't write it. Why would I?"

Looking down she reads it slowly. "I'm insulted that you would implicate me. Look at the writing. The syntax is egregious. I would never say things like 'have engaged a communist agent on your staff.' One doesn't engage someone on staff. Who would say, 'absorbed in Chinese politics'? And seditious is misspelled. Is that why you brought it up in our interview, Mr. Hunt?"

"Yes, Eleanor. We're trying to determine who wrote it, and misspelling is a good clue."

"Well, find someone with a fifth grade education on your staff and you'll have your culprit. Would you really believe me to be capable such a slanderous act?" She stands up, tugs her suit jacket down, and stomps out of the office with her nose at forty-five degrees above the horizon.

"I guess she told us."

Mike laughs, but Grace is resolute. "That self-righteous bitch! I'd like to shove that stick so far up that she'd choke on it."

Phil lets his laughter clear the atmosphere. "I'll see if Cathy is here. People will have seen the smoke coming out of Eleanor's ears, so we need to finish this before the whole place goes up."

Cathy saunters into the office. "What's happening? Eleanor just stormed through the office like a locomotive. Didn't she get the job?"

Phil repeats his opening with Eleanor and shows her the letter. "It was typed on your typewriter using the type element from Eleanor's machine. How do you explain that?"

"I don't know what you're talking about? I have nothing to do with this letter."

"Cathy, we've spent the last month investigating. All clues point to you. Why did you do this?"

Her light olive complexion turns beet red. She's breathing hard and her hands are twitching in her lap. After a couple of deep breaths she almost yells, "You're a terrible manager, Phil. You hire and promote people who aren't qualified and ignore the competent, hard-working people on your staff. How long do you expect you can keep this up? I suppose you're going to tell me I didn't get this new position, after I've given five years of loyalty and great performance. Eleanor isn't getting it either, is she? Is that why she left so angry a few minutes ago? You're giving it to this Chinese bitch who has no public service experience whatsoever.

Mike steps in. His face is deep crimson red and hard as stone. His dark eyes bore directly into her. "Cathy, there is no position. We used it as a ruse to uncover who is behind this slanderous letter. Give it up. You wrote this letter."

She pauses, takes a deep breath, "You bastards. You'll pay for this. I'll see to it personally. Yes, I wrote it and I'm glad I did. I have a copy I've been saving to send to the Director. If you don't do what's right by me, I'll send the complete story to the newspapers. The yellow horde is trying to take over our country—and *you* are aiding and abetting them. Pretty soon hard workers like me will have no opportunity at all. The American dream is being hijacked by the yellow peril." She lunges toward Grace, swinging her fists.

Grace dodges and flips her hip to knock Cathy off balance. The momentum carries Cathy toward the coffee table. Her shins hit it with an audible crack, scattering coffee cups and magazines across the floor. She lies there sobbing. When Mike moves to help her, she screeches, "You too. You're part of it, too. You and your Chinese bitch."

"Brilliant Aikido move, Grace," Phil says. "Cathy, clearly there is no place for you here any longer. I'm not going to press charges for slander, and I advise you not to go to the press where slander will become libel. Please take your personal things. Leave quickly and quietly. I don't want to have Security escort you out in front of everyone. Date a letter of resignation today. You've been a good employee for several years. You'll be paid through the end of next month. "

In Mike's office Grace asks, "Where did that come from? I've never seen you so intense or menacing. It was a positively scary mask you put on."

"My Sioux cousins taught me how to channel all my energy. Cathy was about to go off track. I needed to bring her back to the facts, quickly."

Chapter 7

FIRST CATCH

February 1974
New York City

With the incident cleared, Grace and Mike focus back on their assignment. Grace reports, "Phil, we believe the assets are on the cusp. We need to know just what you or the Director have in mind, before our final pitch. What can you tell us?"

"The key is, for the prospects to have an itch that you can scratch. Is there something they're unhappy about? Do they need money? Would they like to take revenge on something or someone? Are they feeling undervalued? Have they lost faith in their system or ideology? The other side is: can we take advantage of it? What do we have for scratching their itch? Money is the most reliable bait, but it's not always the key. Sometimes it might be defection or asylum.

"Finally, we have to evaluate if they have something we want. Anyone can be upset or needy, but if they don't have anything of value for us, we're wasting our time. Grace, do you think you can answer those questions about Ivanova or Gao?"

"I know what Ivanova is upset that party leadership didn't take proper care of her husband after all his years of service. Poor medical treatment eventually led to his death. She's questioning leadership, as well as the viability of the Soviet communist system. We don't know yet exactly what she has to offer that we would want. Now that I understand the game better, I can go back and work on her. As for Gao, we know he is angry about the fate of Jiang Qing. But again, we don't know what he might have that we want. I think we have to work with them some more before we try to recruit them."

"I agree," Mike adds. "Phil, thanks for the tutorial. We'll get back to you when we find their scratching posts."

In Grace's office they assess their position. "Our focus has been on developing the relationships. We've done that well, I believe. Now what?"

"But we don't know the details of their responsibilities," Grace points out. "Let's make a list of starter questions:

- What is their mission?
- What do they do every day?
- What skills, knowledge or information do they have?
- Who do they report to—and why?
- Are they having any problems, personally or professionally?"

* * *

The second week in February Ivanova invites Grace to lunch to thank her for being included in the engagement party. Too good to be true. It confirms that Ivanova sees Grace as a close friend. She probably hasn't struck up relationships with other Americans, or even other delegates, given the Russians' suspicious personalities. Could it be that Ivanova is trying to recruit Grace?

"Wouldn't that be a stunner," Mike laughs.

Tea and Sympathy on Greenwich Avenue is a couple blocks west of Washington Square, the heart of Greenwich Village. Hidden behind a modest façade is a soft place, an intimate dining room with delicate pink walls. Besides being a lovely setting, Tea and Sympathy advertises itself as a comfortable environment for a cup of tea with a trusted friend. The whole atmosphere is designed for intimate conversation. To sustain the true British manner, they offer etiquette tips:

- Spread your scone with cream first, then jam on top
- Avoid talking with your mouth full and take dainty bites
- Swallow your food before you sip your tea
- Look into your teacup when sipping, not over it. Eye contact is creepy!

Keeping these and other admonitions in mind, Grace and Ivanova call the college age waitress over and order a combination plate of the specialties of the house: Scotch Egg, Welsh Rarebit, Lancashire Hotpot, Lemon Drizzle Cake and, of course, Typhoo Tea. Grace is happy to hear that they have grapes. Their opening conversation is light and follows Ivanova's lead. Grace senses that Ivanova wants to unburden herself, so she lets her set the pace. When they finish, Grace suggests a walk around the Square. "On the weekend there is always something fun going on there."

Although the weather is unseasonably warm, the trees are still barren and black. In a couple months they will begin to show the first tiny buds of spring. Vendors walk among the people offering fun trinkets for the kids. While they stroll about the Square, Grace asks, "Ivanova, I have no idea what you actually do. What are you responsible for?"

"It's funny that we haven't talked about work. Actually, it's refreshing. I really appreciate just having a girlfriend, Grace. When I go out alone and New Yorkers hear my accent, either they want to practice the five words of Russian they know, or they turn their back and mutter 'Damn Russky.'"

"New York is hard, even for me," Grace adds "and I've been a citizen since college."

"Basically, I'm an electronic technician. I'm the Russian consultant on the database of the International Petroleum Institute, which is a consortium of petroleum producing countries. It's a clearing house for industry information. We issue periodic reports of experiments, occasional technological breakthroughs, and a monthly report on industry trends. Each member country submits their monthly production data. IPI summarizes it. It only circulates within the membership, they can see only the mean figures, the averages, as well as the highest and lowest costs and production volumes. It captures the trends by country, region and type of oil: Brent, Texas Sweet Light, OPEC and Dubai, as well as natural gas. Countries are not identified, but knowledgeable industry people can read the origin by country, sometimes by producer. I monitor worldwide production for the Russian banks. Several databases help me determine trends in costs and production, as well as any anomalies."

"Couldn't you do that in Moscow?"

"No. The US maintains the best public database in the petroleum industry, plus they have the most advanced and reliable computer technology. Besides, IPI is here in New York, so I have to be here to work on development of the software and reporting system. If you know what and how to do it, you can open doors that allow for deeper dives."

"What do you mean?"

Ivanova looks around and whispers close to Grace's ear, "Laugh when I tell you this, in case I'm being followed. IPI produces top level benchmark data. But since I know the system, I can get raw data by country, things that are not publicly disclosed, including emerging directions in production. This affects futures price speculation. Sometimes I can even get behind firewalls and see communications between executives and producers. In the right hands, it's very powerful information."

Grace throws her head back laughing. "Ivanova, you're a hacker. How cool is that?"

The little Russian is beaming. "Yes, in school in the Ukraine I was top of my class in computer technology, such as it was in those days. That came to the attention of people in the central bank, so

I was called to Moscow. They put me though intensive intelligence training. Because so much of the industry is centered in the Arabian Gulf, I had to study Arabic. Now I know how to get the raw data and pry into communication channels to hear what they're talking about—behind the curtain, if you will.

Grace giggles loudly. Then she lowers her voice. "That's amazing. Why are you telling me?"

"It could be that the KGB is watching me. Besides that, I would like to know how I can take advantage of this secret information. I need to tell someone. You are the only person here that I trust. Maybe you can help me make something from this information. People you know might be interested in this data. It's hard to live in New York on a Moscow technician's salary."

"How do you think I can help you?"

"Your fiancé is an intelligence officer and you are so well-connected, perhaps you can guide me?

"I'm flattered that you trust me so deeply. I'll talk to Michael about it. Don't worry. It won't go beyond us. Call me in about a week. By then we should know if there is something we can do for you."

They meander among the people in the park until it becomes uncomfortably cold. They share a cab to midtown. Grace pays the fare.

Back at her apartment Grace makes a cup of hot strong tea and savors a handful of grapes. What a break, Ivanova is coming to them.

Although Mike maintains his apartment as a safe house, he now lives with Grace. She pours him a Macallans in anticipation of telling him the good news. Grace is at the door before his key is out of the lock. Mike envelops her and steps her down the hallway.

"Hey sailor, belay! I've got news that's hotter than sex."

"Ivanova?"

"She's coming to us! Turning the trick, we just need to follow her lead.

Grace recounts the setting and events of the afternoon, including every detail of their meal and its presentation at Tea and Sympathy. Mike starts sitting on the edge of his chair, but slowly sinks back as the narrative wends its way through the minutiae to the punchline. When she reaches what Ivanova said, she gives him a signal to not respond. "I need some fresh air. Let's go for a walk honey."

Mike gets it. Despite their checks, the apartment might be bugged. On the street the wind has a sharp edge. Trash is flying past in its race to dive into the East River. Grace pulls her jacket around her neck and leans into Mike to share what Ivanova revealed.

"I'm astounded. Do you mean she's ready to disclose confidential data from the IPI files?"

"Not only data, but she somehow hacks into communications between petroleum executives. Apparently she programmed in a secret access that allows her to bypass the firewall."

"Wow, a back door into OPEC."

"Frankly, Michael, I'm astounded. This is more than just data. This is espionage in its truest form. It could dangerous. We have to plan how to put this together before we approach Phil."

"Sweetheart, you're right. This is a once in a lifetime bonanza. Let's take it a step further. Is there some way we can get a cut of this for ourselves? Honestly, of course."

She laughs, "Michael, now that you're sleeping in my bed, you're talking like a Chinaman."

"Let's start with the facts. We have a person with a privileged, extremely useful, on-going information flow. She's interested, even eager, to trade that for some compensation. Our *quote* client—the USA—is more than willing to have such information. Even eager, if they knew it existed. In effect, we are ready to broker a sale."

"You're pretty clever, Sherlock."

Mike pauses for a moment, looking down at his shoes. "So, how do we structure this without betraying Ivanova or our country? I don't want to spend the rest of our lives looking over our shoulders.

"Yes, but America's interests come first," Grace adds. We're providing America with a competitive advantage as loyal citizens. Still it's reasonable to share the data with our allies and their companies, so long as we give our government good lead time with it."

"Grace, let's start with what we have. We'll keep phase two in mind once this is up and running. We need to be certain that Ivanova can deliver as described, and on a consistent basis. Would you agree?"

Grace nods and picks up the pace. "It's getting too windy. Let's go to that coffee shop around the corner. I'm hungry, but I'm so excited I don't know if I can eat. But I need to get warm."

Monday they enter Phil's office with smug smiles. "We've recruited Ivanova. She trusts us and is interested in providing privileged data. In return for some compensation."

They outline the basic data Ivanova has to offer. Since this is preliminary, they don't go into the details of her offering.

Mike poses the key question. "Phil, are you sufficiently interested for us to go back to Ivanova and talk about how this can work from her side? For example, should she provide monthly benchmark data with details a level below the IPI means?"

Mike holds back on the hacking. They can sweeten the deal later, if necessary. Phil sits still, his fingers laced over his little belly. He appears to be mulling. Deep down he's revved.

"Wow." He jumps up and paces the office, looking out at the Manhattan skyline and laughing to himself about the CIA. He tugs his pants up and chuckles in an unnerving way. This is a big feather in his cap. He's getting more than his salary out of this. "We would probably pay a fee in any form she wants. The amount depends on the quality and utility of the data. I can't make a commitment regarding even the range of compensation at this point."

Grace opens the gambit. "Try this for openers. Ivanova provides a sample of the data and we pay $2,000. It's a pittance, but to her it will look substantial. If the data is of sufficient interest, we negotiate a longer term arrangement. Where and how we give her the money is up to her."

Without committing, Phil agrees that might be workable.

When they return to Grace's office, Mike exclaims, "What did you think of that, Madam Liu?"

"Very cool, Mr. Holmes."

"He's clearly excited about the prospect, but I don't think he really knows how to proceed. He's not CIA, so he's not used to this kind of business. My view is, we take control at this point. First we make sure Ivanova is not a double agent. Why was she sent here if she wasn't too happy at home? Is she really upset about her husband's death, or is that just a concocted story? How come the CIA couldn't recruit her? That's their job. They're the experts at it. Phil has to get someone to check her out. I mean, really check her out. If they have a dossier on her, we should see it before we go any further. No deal until then. I don't want us to get played for suckers. If Phil asks why we're bringing this up now, we tell him that she's acting a little strange lately."

"Good idea. Assuming they clear her, we'll make Ivanova a tentative offer. If she accepts, and I'm certain she will, we go back to Phil with the deal. If she's legit, he has to put up or shut up."

"Right. If he waffles we know he's in over his head, and we withdraw the offer. It'll be up to him to come back with a concrete proposal he's committed to."

Four days later Ivanova calls Grace. Over lunch Grace tells her the plan of starting with a test run for $2,000. Ivanova is thrilled.

"I can download a recent month's benchmarks, including the raw data from one of the countries. When would you like it?"

"Give me a week to get a commitment from the client."

Grace shows no emotion as she comes back to the office. It wouldn't be cool for people to see her excitement. As they walk home, Grace can finally update Mike. "Two thousand is a good amount for her. She has no idea what this type of information is worth. A couple thousand dollars is a nice bonus for her."

It's taking too long for Phil to get clearance on Ivanova. They almost barge into his office. "Phil, you've had a couple weeks to think it over. We can't keep this simmering on the stove much longer. She's not a double agent, so we have to move. For all we know she's talking to another party as well. Do you want to take the chance of losing the deal to China? Or even the Brits?"

Grace has laid it out this way to Mike: "Fear of loss is often a greater motivator than the possibility for gain. People are insecure about their job, their relationships, their future. They may not have the courage to take a risk, but the prospect of losing can push them to overcome their fear."

Phil seems a bit uncertain, yet he says, "Let's go ahead with the trial. I can fund the 2k myself. If she delivers what she claims to have, I can take it upstairs and develop a long term plan."

* * *

When Ivanova calls Grace from an outside line, reports, "It's a go from our side. Two thousand for the first data set."

"I can't thank you and Michael enough. This makes up for many hurts. I can put together a sample in a couple days. If you like what I have, can we arrange to do this on a regular basis? Where can we meet?"

Mike suggests, "The most common place for two women to meet is the ladies room. The KGB can't follow her there, unless the agent is a woman also. Meet in the cafeteria and then go off to powder your noses. Take a big purse."

Thursday Grace walks past Mike's office. "On my way to lunch. Wish me luck."

"Go get em, tiger."

When she returns she plops down in a chair and starts laughing. "You wouldn't believe how it went. The entire UN delegation was in the ladies room. We have to find another place."

"But did you make the switch?"

"Yes, but it took a half hour in there for the coast to clear. Finally we found a little alcove with a baby changing platform. This project gave birth there." She almost falls off her chair laughing at her little pun.

"Great, can I see what the tyke looks like?"

Grace hands him a manila envelope. "This is about half of the file. Ivanova will deliver the other half in a day or two."

There are about thirty sheets of paper, income statements, balance sheets, equipment manifests, daily production runs, all sorted by country. This is much more than he'd imagined, and it's only half of the data she claims to have. He passes several sheets back to Grace, "Did you see this?"

"Of course not. I put it in my purse and came right up here. Oh my goodness. The scope and level of detail is amazing."

"It's the jackpot, sweetie, the Holy Grail. Wait till Phil sees this."

"Wait a minute. Do you realize what we have here? With this we know more about the world's petroleum production than anyone. Than a-n-y-o-n-e. In the right hands this isn't worth 2K—it's worth millions, to a bank, a petroleum company, a government, even a futures trader."

"You're right, Michael. This is truly gold. And imagine getting this once a month. It's overwhelming."

"Hang on there, old girl. Once the brass gets their hands on this, we can get blown out of the water. Their heavy hands could grab Ivanova and scare the hell out of her. We've made her truly vulnerable. With no protection, they can blackmail her, she continues on their terms or they turn her in to the Soviets. We need to think on this.

"But first, I'm going to have my apartment debugged one more time and install a scrambler. I want to make sure that we can talk unheard by CIA, KGB, NSA or other big ears. I'll call in sick and have someone on this first thing tomorrow. I'll supervise while they do their job. If you'll bring dinner there we can talk this over."

"Good idea. I don't think I'll sleep tonight."

"We've uncovered a bee's nest. We have to be very careful getting the honey without the stingers."

Next evening, Grace let's herself into Mike's apartment.

"It smells like Chinese," he says.

"What were you expecting, Fatburgers?"

The table is set, cartons opened. "My love," Mike says, "We have a great opportunity. Imagine what we could do with information like this. I'll hit twenty in a couple years and can retire. We could develop a group of agents around the world. On their own, or on assignment from us, they could develop intelligence that we would sell to corporate clients. I have some ideas about how to organize this and where the money would come from. But for now what do you think? Can you picture us being in this business?"

"It sounds great, but I have questions. it's not as simple as ordering fortune cookies and starting a Chinese restaurant. I'm all for it, but for starters, how would we find agents like Ivanova?"

"Good questions. You're not just a pretty face either. For agents we might start with Jiang Gao. I know a fellow in England who might be interested, Hugh Phelps. Also, Khaled in Dubai and Emre in Turkey are possibilities. Certainly Ned is a candidate. We're sitting in the middle of a field of potential agents at the UN. Whenever you put money on the table, ethics takes second place to greed. We need to work Asia Pacific first. That'll be your territory.

We need to start checking possible future agents in all developed countries.

"What types of intelligence do you want on our menu?"

"When you start a brokerage you offer whatever you can get your hands on. We would ask our agents to look for private data in finance, politics, military, technology—anything that is saleable. There are thousands of plans, projects and developments all over the world whose details are not well known.

"Think about the USSR satellite states. I've heard a couple of them have found promising oil properties. If I'm Standard Oil or Shell, I want the inside information before my competition learns of it. Of course, we share it first with the State Department."

"Slow down, my dear entrepreneur. Let's just get Ivanova running smoothly. Then we can take on the rest of the world."

"Sure, but just think of the scope, the possibilities. What's going on politically and militarily in Iran and Iraq? How about the area of Syria, Lebanon, Israel, Egypt and the other Arab Gulf states? Don't forget your countrymen. Have China or the Soviets developed space capabilities that we don't know about? Think about Vietnam. Now that we have withdrawn, what is China planning? Will it go for Laos and Cambodia next? Would we risk all-out war to save little Laos? How about their internal economic development plans and strategies? There's no end to useful intelligence. We just have to develop a network of agents."

"It's a bit scary, but also exciting. You need a drink before you explode."

"Absolutely. But the more I think about it, the more intriguing it becomes. Let me give you an example of something we weren't expecting from this. I'm scanning Ivanova's report and see a small item about a shipment of oil well drilling sand and fertilizer. It's leaving Vladivostok for Caracas next week. That doesn't make sense to me. Why ship oil field supplies and fertilizer all the way from Russia to Venezuela when there are sources in North and South America? Unless the Soviets are giving it away, it's not economically feasible to ship it all the way across the Pacific and through the Panama Canal to the Caribbean. We should ask Ivanova to check with her petroleum pals about what is behind that. That's a good test of her capability. Does she really have contacts in the industry? Or just access to the IPI system? Again, we'll pay her if she digs up something useful."

"I'll take her to lunch on Saturday."

* * *

While waiting for Ivanova to find out about the drilling supply shipment, Mike turns his attention back to Jiang Gao. They opened a door by inviting him to their engagement party. Now they need to increase the contacts. All they know is his title: Commercial Attaché, and that he spends a lot of time on trade issues. This means close ties with Chinese banks, exporters and perhaps manufacturers. Phil told them in the beginning that his soft spot had to do with Taiwan, but he was wrong. Jiang Qing is his itch. How can they scratch it?

From his comments, Grace thinks he's angry at Deng Xiaoping and Hua Guofeng for their opposition to her. He might be interested in a little revenge. He's due to complete his assignment at the UN in a couple months. He likes them both enough to confide in Grace. Every man has a weakness. They'll find his soon.

Every day about 1230 Mike goes to the employee cafeteria and the Delegates Dining Room. Jiang never shows, so Grace goes to the Chinese delegation to find out when he goes to eat and where. She makes up a story about Chinese restaurants on Long Island. Because she's Chinese, the staff welcomes her, except for a few hardline communists. They invite her to stay for a birthday party for one of the staff. Jiang attends and speaks to her briefly. She tells him, "Mike would like to have lunch with him but doesn't want to be too forward." Three days later he calls Mike suggesting they meet on Thursday.

"That would be fine. Would you like to go to the Delegates Dining Room or some place in the city?"

Maybe you like Mexican food?"

Mike answers, "*Si, me gusta mucho. Esta muy delicioso.*"

Jiang laughs for the first time since they've met. They agree to meet at 1330 at Pinalito City on Houston Street. Mike arrives a few minutes before Jiang and waits in the lobby. Rule number one: Always be first in new situations. Scope the physical facility. Watch how the person is received. Waiters greet Jiang enthusiastically and offer a corner table where they can talk. They chat easily during tapas, margaritas, and enchiladas. As they relax over Mexican coffee and flan with coconut ice cream, Mike asks, "What's happening with China's new leadership? Rumors are that Mao is sick. A successor must be waiting."

Jiang's mood suddenly turns black. He scans the room for any Chinese people nearby. Then he takes off on Deng and Hua, speaking quietly in Mandarin. "If I had a chance I would kill them!"

This is a traitorous statement. To make it to a westerner is even more astonishing, and risky. Either the margarita has gotten to him or he's playing Mike, or he trusts Mike. Mike tries to act concerned.

"I understand your feelings, but you wouldn't really kill them, would you?"

"Yes I would."

"Aren't there other ways to take revenge? Ways that are safer for you, but still very painful for them?"

"Of course. I could cause them great grief with what I know."

"What could you do to them that wouldn't harm you?"

Jiang lights up, then looks furtively around the room again. He waves his arms. "I have information that could drive them from office. It will shock the world if it is known."

"Financial information?"

"Financial and political. Personal bank accounts outside China. Secret trade agreements. That's why they sent me, to negotiate them on behalf of Deng. Hua is a weakling. Deng will get rid of him soon."

"So how can you do it in a way that's advantageous to you personally?"

"I've been thinking about that."

"I may have some ideas. Do you want to meet again?" Jiang agrees. Mike picks up the tab. Jiang doesn't miss the gesture.

After work Grace and Mike walk through the cool spring evening to a neighborhood Greek tavern, with visions of a hot omeletta: fried egg cooked with spinach, peppers, onions and cheese. Mike devours his. Grace nibbles on the edges of a Greek salad.

"My dearest, you must have been ravenous. Half of yours is already history, before I've even organized mine," she says.

The night sky is cloudless and the breeze is gentle. Spring is clearly on the way. Mike loves strolling and talking with his sweetheart. With his arm around Grace he kisses her neck. "I'm crazy about you, but I'll stop kissing you if it bothers you."

"Don't you dare. I never had much romance with Jerry. I love it with you."

After walking a short block in silence Grace asks, "Are you going to tell me about your lunch with Jiang or do I have to beat it out of you?"

"Oh, would you please?"

"Not until you've told me everything."

"You didn't notice that I told you the whole story, but I'll hit the high points again for you."

Grace is very quiet. Then she says, "That is a most extraordinary thing for a Chinese man to say, especially to a Westerner or someone who's not a lifelong friend. Chinese are mostly reticent to speak of feelings. Do you think he's sincere, or just testing you?"

"I wondered about that. To a Westerner you people are, as they say, inscrutable. I think we have to meet him alone in a comfortable setting with both of us to see if he opens up again."

"Good idea, Sherlock. We can invite him for dinner at your place that we know is secure. I'll cook him a Chinese dinner that he'll love."

"I think it's best for you to invite him. He really likes you, and you're a kinsman."

* * *

Next day Ivanova calls Grace and asks her to meet in one of the empty conference rooms. She hands over a short but enigmatic report. The main cargo of the ship from Vladivostok is drilling sand, along with a large amount of fertilizer. The name of the ship is the SS Gonzales. It's of Lebanese registry and owned by Pactic, S.A., a French holding company that's a wholly owned subsidiary of another investment management group. Not uncommon to have a string of companies ultimately controlled by an invisible someone somewhere. To Mike, it's highly suspicious. Why ship fertilizer thousands of miles, when it is abundant locally? He calls Ron, a CIA agent whom he sort of trusts. It takes ten days for Ron to learn through an agent in Vladivostok that the cargo report is accurate. However, it's also carrying a very small amount of high explosives not on the manifest."

It's starting to make sense. Ammonium nitrate—the fertilizer—is a component of bombs: inert until mixed with other chemicals or ignited with a small explosive charge. But what does someone want to blow up?

Ron's sources go to work full time. The sailing plan shows the first landfall is the Panama Canal. Final destination Maracaibo, the heart of Venezuela's oil business. Sounds like they might try to sink the ship in the locks of the Canal.

"That's a foolhardy scheme, Mike tells Grace. 'It's almost an act of war. The explosion would sink the ship and dump a massive amount of drilling sand into and around the locks, totally disrupting shipping to and from the U.S. for years."

"Who would be behind this?" Grace asks. It's not a typical Soviet strategy. More likely some dissident lunatic group. Blocking the Canal would affect U.S. shipping, but Russia can ship through their Black Sea ports of Odessa, Yalta and Sebastopol to the Mediterranean. And through Vladivostok to Pacific ports like China."

Ron follows up. The CIA is planning to intercept the ship with a Coast Guard frigate as it approaches the Canal. There'll be protests about boarding a vessel at sea. But it's worth the risk given the apparent intent.

Mike advises Grace against sharing the intercept with Phil. "We want his attention focused on the IPI intelligence. Besides, it's not within his jurisdiction or mission. But what this confirms is that Ivanova has live contacts and wide capability. She's more than an IPI hacker. Most important, it demonstrates she's not a Russian double agent."

They move on Jiang inviting him to dinner on a rainy April evening. Grace welcomes him in Chinese and hangs his wet rain coat on the hall tree by the door. It's a chance to check his pockets for eavesdropping or recording devises. None.

"An aperitif?" Mike asks.

"Do you happen to have scotch?"

Mike serves him a large tumbler of the Macallan farms—Elchies Scotch, and watches as he sips it. Gao's eyes light up.

"This is the best Scotch I've ever tasted." Gao swallows a second large mouthful, confirming the value of Mike's investment.

"I can see you're a connoisseur. Is this brand available in China?"

"I've never seen it there, even at the best restaurants. Is it expensive?"

"And hard to find. It's made in small quantities. I'll see if we can find a bottle for you."

"That would be most appreciated." Jiang sets down the glass, the ice rattling in the empty tumbler.

Mike pours him another and they chat about world politics and China's movements since Mao's signs of illness. As expected and hoped, the second scotch loosens Gao's tongue. He becomes very vocal about Jiang Qing. They empathize and he takes off, expanding his views.

"Neither Deng nor certainly Hua are worthy to succeed Mao. They've both been in the party since the beginning, but Deng has had several disagreements with Mao, and Hua simply is not capable of leading our country. I'm very concerned about what will happen when Chairman Mao is gone."

"You're due to return to the homeland this year, aren't you?" Grace asks. "What do you think will be there for you when you return?"

"I'll be going back around year end. I don't know what scheming is going on behind the wall, but Deng is quite clever and very ambitious. He may not take Mao's position as General Secretary of the Communist Party, but he's the strong hand that guides future changes. When he was young Deng spent several years in France and one in Russia. He came away totally committed to communism, yet convinced that China has to join the world market. Mao has never been overseas nor seen western industrialism. President Nixon's visit to China last year opened a new door. I expect eventually, if he comes to power, Deng will move China toward a market economy by opening the country to foreign investment. China has the resources to grow at an astronomical rate. It will raise the standard of living for tens of millions. In the next twenty-five years China can become a global economic power, both exporting and importing. Imagine a market of over a billion consumers. People don't realize that the PRC and the US are becoming more aligned. As this progresses Russia will feel threatened. That may bring new problems regarding the balance of power around the world."

Grace smiles at him. "Then there should be great opportunities for you when you go home. I'm very happy for you."

"But I'm torn between my career goals and my anger over Jiang Qing's treatment. Like I told Michael, if I could kill Deng and Hua I would."

"My friend, we Chinese know better ways to take revenge. If you wish to devour the animal, it is safer to work from the inside where he cannot see you or kick you."

"What do you mean?"

Grace is rolling. Mike sits back and takes mental notes on a seminar in manipulation. *Clever and gorgeous. Worth every day of the five year wait.*

"You'll have access to sensitive information. How you use it is up to you."

"Please go on."

"You can use it first to set and reach your career goals, but simultaneously you enrich yourself. There are people who'll pay generously to know Deng's economic and military plans."

"I imagine you're correct. But one must be very careful that the animal doesn't find a way to kick him."

"He can't kick what he can't see. With the right connections you can be highly successful, as well as quite safe. Oh, excuse me, I hear the timer. We can eat now and talk more later."

Gao is a bright young man, but not experienced in the ways of the world. He hasn't learned the machinations that go on behind the scenes. But they can see that he's thinking. After dinner and dessert they relax in the living room with a glass of port basking in the sweet lull that immediately follows a good meal.

Finally, Gao perks up. "Thank you, Grace. That was an exceptional dinner. I would like to hear more of the ways you and Michael mentioned before dinner."

"My friend, tell me what your dream is for five years from now. What do you envision for yourself? Do you want political or financial power, maybe both?"

"I know I can grow up through the system, but I would like to have more money. In a communist state only the very top people are wealthy. The managers work for reasonable but not enriching income."

Grace steps in, "You're a very intelligent young man. Perhaps we can help you reach your financial goals. We have connections with people who would like the type of private information that you could supply. They'll pay handsomely for it. If you want to know more, we can talk about it another time. It's quite late now and we all have to go to work tomorrow."

"Oh yes, excuse me. I didn't realize how late it is. Again, I thank you both for a most delightful evening. You've given me much to think about."

After he clicks the lock bolt, Mike pulls Grace into his arms. "You never fail to amaze me. How can someone who is so beautiful also be so clever? You even left him wanting more by saying it was late. I'm going to have to watch you, so you don't manipulate me."

"Too late, Yankee imperialist."

Chapter 8

NEW SHIPMATES

April 1974
New York

Ivanova is delivering the IPI data regularly, gradually adding comments regarding its implications. Phil is eating it up. He increases her payout. She's delighted to be building a secret bank account that will secure her future. Periodically, Grace and she go to lunch or shopping. Their friendship is genuine, not confined to business matters.

"I notice you're wearing more lively colors, Ivanova."

"Yes. It's fun. I'm feeling more energized and optimistic."

"Capitalism does have some benefits," Grace teases.

"I've been thinking about that. The longer I'm in America the worse the Soviet Union looks."

"I understand. I feel the same way about communist China. Capitalism isn't perfect, but in practice, it's a more humane political system."

"Yes, when I was growing up in Russia life was difficult. Living conditions were bad. We never had enough good food. Our clothes were boring. They were cheaply made and wore out quickly. We lived in constant fear of the government. You never knew who you could confide in. I'm thinking, maybe someday I might want to change sides."

"My dear, if you ever decide to do that, we'll help every way we can."

Meanwhile, Gao meets with Mike and Grace several times before he returns to China. Shortly after his departure he sends a letter telling he's been promoted to Deputy Director of the Bank of China's Foreign Exchange Center in Beijing. This is a major promotion for a man so young. Obviously, he's well regarded by China's leadership, whom he despises. In their last visit he confirms his interest in their proposal. Should the opportunity ever present itself they can call on him. He's firmly in their camp, if and when they need him. Phil was told they couldn't recruit him. Because of the great success with Ivanova, Phil barely notices.

* * *

As the New Year blossoms, Mike and Grace start planning their wedding—set for Saturday June 2, 1974. 1974 is the Year of the Tiger which is Grace's birth sign. Tigers are tolerant, strong, valiant, respected, deep thinkers and capable of great sympathy. But also short-tempered and have conflicts with people in authority, as Mike's learning.

The wedding will be a small affair, only a couple dozen of their best friends, mostly UN staff, including Ivanova. Neither of them have family except for Mike's brother Bob, who's on duty in Germany and can't get back. They talk to the rector at The Church of the Transfiguration East 29th Street. It's also known as The Little Church Around the Corner for welcoming people of all denominations. The charming sanctuary fits their wedding party, a multi-ethnic mix. Grace has asked two of her friends, Laurie and Denise, to be her bridesmaids. Ned will be best man and CIA Ron will be in the party. The wedding is scheduled at 11 a.m. with the reception and lunch following immediately at the Seville Hotel, a Beaux Arts style gem, charming yet modern, just a block away.

Other than the local bureaucratic requirements, it's all about the bride. Mike is glad to be left out, but he can't resist telling Grace, "You could have a cardboard image of me at the altar and few people would notice."

"Let me think about that."

Grace's friends organize a shower before the wedding. Mike stays as far away as possible. Her après affair report is sufficient for him.

Grace will wear a softly flowing pale blue dress in the Chinese custom for widows. The cake is alternate layers of chocolate, white, and yellow—symbolic of the racial groups who will be attending. Grace will have her hair held by decorative Chinese hair pins. The flowers are mostly bouquets of orchids and gardeniasbe mostly.

The hotel bnquest manager suggests a spring pear salad with orange blossom vinaigrette, entrée choices of chicken piccata or grilled salmon in butter lemon sauce, with a medley of Chinese delicacies and desserts, plus decoratively draped bowls of mixed grapes. Mike asks Grace about a Chinese musical group, but she says they would be too loud for their event. Instead, she opts for a string quartet playing in the background.

No wedding rehearsal is necessary. Still, they invite the wedding party to dinner. Each person makes a short toast and Ned promises to have a special one delivered at the wedding luncheon.

For rings they go to Chinatown where Grace has found a jeweler she likes. He makes identical rings bearing tiny symbols of their respective birth signs. Grace's ring is embellished with several diamonds and rose zircons, her Chinese birthstones. Mike's is simple with only the carved design.

They decide to write one integrated nuptial, partly in English and partly in Chinese to express their unity. They practice in harmony just once so it will be fresh at the ceremony.

By 1045 the guests are assembled At the stroke of 1100 the organ begins Mendelssohn's Wedding March, and Grace comes down the aisle on the arm of an old friend of her father whom she has flown in from Hawaii. She's exquisite.

At the altar, on a sign from the minister they look at each other and speak their wedding vows together, Chinese first, then English:

"One beautiful evening many years ago we met for a moment and then were lost for what seemed would be forever. But God was good to us, bringing us together again. Now, in this moment, we are united forever, never again to be separated, pledging our love for eternity."

The minister is an old man who has worked and lived here on the edge of Chinatown for many years. He speaks some Chinese. When they finish he adds:

"Love is of all passions the strongest, for it combines simultaneously the head, the heart and the senses. You have the destiny to meet across a thousand miles. Lovers' hearts are linked together and always beat as one. In lovers' eyes beauty is perfected."

He repeats it in English. Mike's heart is so overwhelmed with tenderness, he can hardly keep his balance on his tortured knees. Grace is smiling so radiantly that he has to close his eyes to maintain his composure. Taking her gently in his arms he kisses her lightly. Then he reaches for her left hand and kisses it just as he did the first night in Hawaii. Nearly everyone has a handkerchief at their eyes.

The guests strike out for the Seville, a fifteen minute stroll on a luscious late spring morning. Mike has arranged a limo to carry the wedding party for a short champagne ride around lower Manhattan. They stuff themselves into the limo and head toward the East River. They turn south onto the FDR, under Battery Park, around and north on the Westside Highway to 28th Street, and work eastward across town back to the Seville. With no traffic problems they make a quick circuit and a grand entrance for the guests who are already into their first glass of champagne.

Everyone is talking about their wedding vows and the minister's proverb. Small toasts are offered around the table. After they've all had several tastes of the hors d'oeuvres, Ned stands to deliver the best man's toast. In this case, Aussie style.

Gidday everybody,

I feel as flash as a rat with a gold tooth being asked to propose the toast to me mate Mike and his new missus, Grace. This toast is on behalf of Bridesmaids Laurie and Denise, Groom Ron and all of yous in the audience. Mike has been busier than a blue-arsed fly getting this bun fight organised. Fair dinkum he's been flat out like a lizard drinkin. I wouldn't give you a bum steer about this—he has been.

Good onya mate but cripes, between you, me and the gatepost, I didn't think a Yank, who seems to me to have a few roos loose in the top paddock, could pull it off. For an Intelligence Officer, he strikes me as slow as a month of Sundays sometimes."

Hey Waiter—how about some grog? I'm as dry as a drover's dog. Good onya mate, thanks. I won't bash your ear for long but crikey! he's landed a ripper sheila in Grace. I'll be buggered, no way in the bloody world did I think he would get hitched. Anyway, you look good Grace, not fat at all and blue suits ya. Everyone, please stand, charge your glasses and drink to Mike and Grace.

Thank yous all.

Nothing can top that. Everyone lets out a couple notches and has a grand time. The string quartet gets in the mood and switches from Bach to Swing and C & W. Soon they're all dancing and frolicking with abandon.

Chapter 9

BERMUDA

June 1974
Bermuda

Next stop Bermuda, a one week honeymoon. After clearing customs and immigration they taxi south to the Fairmont Southampton. The hotel is perched on a ridge overlooking Bermuda's southeast shore and its pink sand beaches. Its nearly one hundred acres include an 18 hole par three golf course and access to a the pink sand beach several hundred feet below. Their room has a balcony on the east side with a view out over the course and the Atlantic Ocean. After checking in they decide to play the par three course in the afternoon.

On the first tee Mike's in traditional tan Bermuda shorts with a white polo shirt. Grace looks great in a blue visor and golf shirt, white shorts and white shoes. From the vista point of the tee it's hard to concentrate. The first tee is about 110 yards above the green. Mike walks over to Grace, gives her a hug and tells her, "I'm so happy that I'm about to burst. Now you're fulfilling another of my dreams, playing golf with my wife."

"I'm so happy that you're so happy."

Grace tells Mike to tee off first. His shot is straight for the flag but lands a yard short of the green. Her's stops dead about two feet left of the hole. She taps in a birdie and looks at him with her coy smile as they get into the cart and start down the hill. "You're one down. Are you still so happy?"

"I'm not as happy as I was five minutes ago."

The course is very hilly, with elevation changes on every hole. There is also water on several holes. The ridge shelters the course from the wind. Mike never quite catches up on the lost first hole. The afternoon is filled with smart remarks going both ways. In the end Grace wins by two shots. Mike's one down in the Holmes Family Bermuda Championship.

After turning in the cart and clubs they head to the patio bar. A couple of pina coladas and they're back to their room. It's too late for romance. They shower and get ready for dinner. Down the elevator and across the lobby to the pink stone path that leads to Bacci's restaurant behind the hotel. Grace is wearing a red high collar, long sleeve silk blouse over crisp white cotton pants and white pumps. As they pass through the lobby everyone stops to look at her. He's in a white linen sport shirt and blue pleated slacks. His jockey shorts are having a problem restraining him, but no one gives him a second look. As they exit and start up the path he asks, "Do you ever get tired of being the center of attention?"

"Are you kidding me?"

Mike orders a glass of champagne to celebrate followed by a capellini appetizer of butter, parsley and a sprinkling of parmesan. Grace opts for John Dory seared and drizzled with lemon and just a touch of ginger for her Chinese palette. Mike orders North Atlantic salmon. Grace actually cleans her plate and amazes Mike with a little gelato dessert.

Monday, it's quite breezy, so they decide to pass on the golf and go into the capital city of Hamilton. Front Street, running along the harbor, is lined with the spikes of sailboat masts. Here most of the island's major shops, restaurants and The Bank of Bermuda are located. Wealthy people sometimes have accounts at the Bank where they can maneuver money from overseas ventures without sharing their activities with Uncle Sam or other tax entities. Something to keep in mind if they hit the lottery or their business model takes off some day.

The morning is just wandering along, stopping in shops and sampling some of the quaint bakeries. Crisson's is the major jewelry and watch store. Bermuda is a duty-free port. Accordingly, this is the place to pick up some bargains. Mike's a watch junky, so this is nirvana to him. He salivates over the gorgeous selection.

Grace goes for the diamonds. Several pairs of diamond earrings light up her eyes. He still has much of the pay he accrued while undercover. While Grace is occupied he talks to the saleswoman about two carat diamond earrings set in platinum. Good discounts and duty free; the deal is done. He slips the box into his pocket and says to Grace, "We'll be here for another five days. Maybe we should think about it before we jump."

She agrees. By midafternoon they've exhausted Front Street and its tributaries. Returning to the hotel they turn in for a nap. Despite all this activity around the wedding and reception, they're still energized. As they change out of their street clothes, Mike comes up behind Grace. Their bodies blend. Love matches passion and the next hour is bliss.

At seven o'clock they're ready to head for dinner at The Waterlot Inn in town. Before they leave Mike repeats the invitation he made to Grace the night they met in Hawaii, "May I obtain a libation for you and invite you to accompany me to the lanai where we might separate ourselves from the flock? Once there we may be able to converse without megaphones."

"You are one sweet hunk." He looks at her for a long minute. How lucky he is to have this extraordinary woman as his wife. He repeats his proposal in Chinese.

She smiles lovingly. "Yes, I will."

Mike pulls the earring box out of his pocket and hands it to her. "Here's your wedding present, sweetheart."

She's surprised. Opening the box she starts to cry. "Michael, you're so wonderful, but you can't afford this. Please, you must return it and get your money back."

"Don't worry, sweetheart. I'm not just a pretty face. I have hidden wealth. Just enjoy wearing them."

With the earrings firmly in place, they take the elevator to the lobby and the shuttle that runs to The Waterlot. The restaurant is nestled dockside on Jews Bay, in an historic house dating back two hundred years. Undoubtedly one of the top eateries in Bermuda. Besides fantastic steaks and seafood, its wine list is excellent. The setting offers breathtaking sunsets as well. Late in the evening as the crowd is thinning, the maitre d' asks if he can bring them a drink on the house. He asks about their backgrounds. Grace gives him the short course of her time in China with Chiang. Mike follows with the high points of his time in Shanghai and Hong Kong.

"Wow. I've met some interesting people passing through here, but you two are extraordinary. The next time you visit Bermuda you're my guests."

On Tuesday they sleep late. Midmorning they wake to clouds wind—a sign to stay in be and enjoy themselves. By noon they've loved, dozed, loved again.

"Sweetheart, you are such a sensitive lover. I believe I would like a rain check on another session until after dinner."

"Madam, you do indeed fulfill my dreams, quite. I shall make a note to accommodate you with another visit on my return."

When the squalls have passed and the sun breaks through to crystal blue skies, they decide on sightseeing. A guide recommended by the hotel starts with basic background information. Bermuda was settled by England in 1609 and became the Royal Navy's base in the Western Atlantic. The Dockyard houses wide parade grounds surrounded by a nineteenth century wall.

Then he takes them the length of the island to the north shore, the site of the Bermuda Aquarium, Museum and Zoo, home to more than 300 species of birds, reptiles and mammals from the islands and more than 200 species of fish. By the time they travel from the Dockyard to BAMZ and back it's almost dinner hour. This leisurely time is much needed. They dine in again at Bacci's.

Wednesday is golf day. They start in the south end at Port Royal, an exquisitely maintained, hilly and challenging course. Mike figures he has a chance of beating Grace here because of its length off the tees. He has to give her four strokes a side handicap so he needs some advantage somewhere. She's turned out to be a formidable player. *How is it that one person can have so many gifts?* He's very competitive, but almost doesn't mind losing to her.

The most interesting part of the course is the three finishing holes. Sixteen is a par 3 with a small tee on a cliff jutting out over the ocean. Not comfortable for acrophobiacs. Across an inlet the green is set on a bluff barely wider than the green.

"There's no bluffing on this shot." She glares at him and cracks up. "Sorry for the pun." They're even at this point. Grace's shot is safely over the inlet just short of the green. His is on the green about twenty feet past the pin. She chips on and one putts. Mike two putts. They're still even. Seventeen is a very long par four running down a shallow valley somewhat sheltered from the ever present wind. For amateurs it plays like as a par five. A long drive leaves you next to a lake on the left side, with a very long second toward a highly elevated and well bunkered green. It's the number one handicap hole, so Mike must give her a stroke on it. Most amateurs can't reach it in two shots. Grace leaves her third shot short of the green and by the time she pitches on, Mike's in for a five and she two putts for a six. Mike wins. He's one up with one to go. Eighteen tees off from a very high tee box into a strong wind and down to a deep valley. Then it's up to a blind flag on the elevated green. They tie the hole and he wins the match, one up. This makes them even in the Holmes Family Bermuda Championship.

Thursday, they leave for Tucker's Point on the west side of the northern coast. It's interesting and scenic like Port Royal, but not as difficult. Holes ten through eighteen have spectacular views of the ocean. Once on the course they're caught in a sudden, small squall that lasts about ten minutes. The cart partially protects them, but they still get wet. Mike's complaining that he has to give Grace too many shots based on their handicaps.

"Stop whining and hit the ball." No sympathy there. She's a very tough opponent. She wins one up and takes the 1974 Holmes Family Bermuda Championship. The prize: he has to buy drinks and rub her feet every night before they go to bed. Best second place finish ever.

They decide to make their final day, Friday, a beach day. At the sheltered pink sand beach below the hotel they pick a sunny spot and do absolutely nothing except, talk, have a snack, drinks and doze.

Saturday is getaway day. It's been a revitalizing week. Breakfast buffet at Windows on the Sound affords another beautiful view and fine food. Afterwards they take a last stroll around the hotel. On the second floor are a few souvenir and clothes shops, and Crisson's. Mike finds a beautiful yellow sweater with a small Bermuda symbol on the left breast at the clothing store. Grace has a hard time finding something she really likes and finally settles for a hand painted scarf.

Crisson's shop is run by a charming Indian lady. Mike and Grace are the only patrons. The merchandise, jewelry and watches, is gorgeous and expensive. Mike's eye goes to a blue-faced Rolex with gold numbers. It's ONLY $6,400! The lady sees that he's taken by it but reluctant. She begins offering discounts. Grace steps in. Little does the lady know that she is dealing with a Chinese bargainer. The two cultures begin jousting. It's fascinating for a westerner to watch. The lady gets down to $5,250 including tax, of which there is none for tourists. Grace looks at Mike. "It's yours!"

"Sweetheart, it's too much."

"It's less than you paid for my earrings. Besides I too have a little hidden away. Daddy didn't leave Taiwan empty-handed. Case closed." She's fulfilled one of his dreams, owning a Rolex.

Sunday morning they fly home to a cool early July day in NYC. It's been one of the greatest weeks of both their lives. Come to think of it, it's probably number one.

Chapter 10

BACK TO SCHOOL

July 1974
Washington D.C.

From JFK the cab drops them in front of their apartment. The short elevator ride is blissful. Stepping out they find a large, long-haired white cat with green eyes and an imperious manner sitting by their door. No collar.

"How did that thing get up here?" Mike asks.

Grace stands frozen, looking intensely at the cat. "This is Cixi," she says.

"Tits-she? What's that?

"No, cts-shi. It's a difficult sound for foreigners to make, even those who think they speak Chinese. She was the Empress Dowager of China from 1861 until 1908."

"Sorry, darling. Whatever you call her; this is just a fat cat."

Cixi stands up, raises her tail, steps stiff legged toward Mike and yowls.

"You've insulted her. She's not fat, just furry."

Mike squats down and puts his hand out. She swats at it with claws out.

"You see? You'll have to apologize to Cixi."

"Wait a minute. How could a cat get up three stories to our door?"

"That's irrelevant. She's here. She's come to live with us. We can't throw the Empress out, not after what happened to her."

"May I carry my bride across the threshold before my lesson in Chinese history?

"Okay, but Cixi is important. Grace wraps her arms around Mike's neck whispering, "She led the Qing Dynasty during the fight against the foreigners around 1900, the Boxer Rebellion. In 1928 warlord Sun Dianying's troops looted her magnificent tomb of rich decorations and exhumed her body. It was still intact. They ripped the large pearl from her mouth that was to keep her body from decomposing. Cixi is very angry. She demands respect. We have to care for her and treat her as the empress she is."

There is no point in fighting a battle that is already concluded. "Welcome, your highness," Mike says with a deep bow and deposits Grace in the apartment.

Cixi sits down, licks her paw and wipes her face with dignity. She looks apprehensively at Michael and appreciatively at Grace. *Who does he think he is? I am royalty.*

A few days later Mike's instructed to report to ONI in D.C. He knew he would probably be sent to a new duty station within the year. Why don't they just send him orders and travel documents? Both Mike and Grace love Washington, so they decide to take some vacation days in D.C. Cixi has already established herself and can be left alone. With food and water dispensers and a large cat box she is quite content. From the back of the sofa she can survey her Manhattan realm. At night, or whenever she tires from her responsibilities as empress, Cixi retires to a dog bed large enough to accommodate her majestic body. A couple drops of Bailey's Irish Cream in her milk help her sleep peacefully through the night.

Mike and Grace check into a small hotel not far from Union Station a couple blocks off the Capital Mall. D.C. is its typical sultry self, with the temperature and humidity competing to create discomfort. That evening the newlyweds choose room service in the hotel.

Next morning Mike's in his summer tan uniform and off to ONI while Grace walks the shops in the area. Captain Samson greets him, "Congratulations. I hear you recently married a State Department Agent. Have you known her a long time?"

"I met her when I was stationed in Hawaii nearly seven years ago. I lost track of her until we met again eighteen months ago at the UN."

"That's great. It must be fate. The reason you're here is to give you your next assignment. It's Top Secret. You're going back to Hawaii. The necessary initial documents are in this envelope. I'm headed for a meeting in a few minutes, any questions?"

"Thank you sir. I need to wrap up some loose ends and handoffs at the UN. That won't take more than a few days. I can be here on the job Monday the 24th, if that's satisfactory."

"Good. My aide will fill in the details when you report. If I don't see you before you leave, good luck."

Mike finds an empty room to read the mission details before cabbing back to the hotel. How will Grace feel about this sudden change? Once in their room over a cup of tea he asks, "Sweetheart, how do you feel about Greenland?"

"I've never had the pleasure of visiting that icecap. I hope you and the polar bears will be quite happy together."

"It's going to be cold there without you to snuggle with."

"Buy a hot water bottle. I promised to be with you forever, but that didn't include Greenland. You should have read the fine print." After pausing she says, "So, okay Yankee, where ARE we going?"

"How about Hawaii?"

"YES," she yells jumping into his arms.

"Besides the assignment they've arranged for me to enroll in the Political Science doctoral program at UH-Manoa. They've composed a letter to a Professor Ling petitioning him to take me on to complete my degree. Ling defected from communist China three years ago. Suspicious signs have been reported. The FBI's watching, but can't pin him down. My job while studying with him is to discern his loyalty. Given my knowledge of China and your heritage, I was the obvious choice for this mission. We have to be in Honolulu no later than 1 September. I'll report direct to Samson. CINCPAC (Commander-in-Chief Pacific) is not aware of this."

Grace is intrigued. "We've had good experiences with Ivanova and Gao. There's no reason why you can't find this fellow out."

Samson had told Mike that ONI recommended to State that Grace accompany him on the mission, since she is Chinese and has shown her talent at the UN. Mike decides to wait to see if State follows through. He doesn't want to get Grace's hopes too high. Interagency politics are known to subvert even brilliant ideas.

The next month is spent researching and planning for Hawaii. One afternoon Grace says, "Mike, a letter from the State Department just arrived in the mail. I'm a little nervous about opening it."

"Go ahead. Open it."

There's a thirty second silence then, "Mike, Mike, they want me to stay active. They're assigning me to ONI as a Special Agent to work with you in Hawaii. Oh, sweetheart. This is fantastic. You and me, a spy team. Better than The Thin Man. Wait, did you know about this?"

"I knew they were considering it, but I didn't want to say anything in case they didn't go with it. Congratulations Special Agent Liu."

Cixi looks at the two and thinks, *How nice for two young people to be so happy together. But how long will it last with this yang guizi (foreign devil)? And what about me?* she growls.

Chapter 11

SHIPPING OUT

August 1974
In Transit

Mike writes to Ling describing his prior studies and explaining the navy wants him to complete his Ph.D. under Ling's direction. Mike also notes he has access to documents regarding Chiang Kai-shek's rise to power, which will be the basis of his dissertation—these documents are the bait.

Next are plans for living in Honolulu. "Michael, we should rent something for the year we'll be in Honolulu. Who knows where we go after this adventure."

"I forgot to tell you about the Watsons."

"Who are the Watsons?"

"Two years before I met you, I met them. They're multimillionaires. James, everyone calls him Jimmy, although he's at least sixty and owns half the Pacific Ocean, he's the great grandson of the man who founded what became Watson Lines during the Gold Rush. Jimmy is Chairman Emeritus of Watson Lines. He and Joanie had three children when I met them. The oldest daughter tried for years to make it as a singer, but she can't carry a tune in a bucket. George was a couple years younger. He was a bum, never worked in the business or anywhere else, drank, gambled and contributed nothing to the family but worry. In his twenties he got involved in ocean racing. The third child was Maureen."

"Wait a minute. Why do you keep saying *was?*"

"Be patient, my anxious associate. I met Maureen at a party and, due to my irresistible charm, she invited me to a luau at the family condominium complex. They own a large development just west of Diamond Head above Kapiolani Park. They occupy the top floor. It's a gorgeous place looking south to the Pacific, with Diamond Head on the left and Waikiki on the right. Carmen, housekeeper and cook, travels with them between Honolulu and their main residence in San Francisco's Sea Cliff. Basically they've adopted Carmen. In Honolulu she lives in a unit just underneath the Watson's. She's a fabulous cook.

"Maureen was a nice girl, but basically an airhead, somewhat like her mother. She had the body of a goddess and the brain of a cuckoo. I seldom saw her. The year I was in Shanghai George took her out on his racer. In the channel between Maui and Oahu the boat flipped and exploded. They both drowned."

"Oh my god, how terrible. The poor parents to lose two children at one time, they must have been devastated."

"Yes, especially Joanie. She almost had a nervous breakdown over it. When I returned from Shanghai and found you gone, I called them just to say hello, and learned of the tragedy. Jimmy and Joanie had always been very nice to me. Although I was in town for just a few weeks after that, they really leaned on me. I spent all my free time with them. I was happy to be able to provide some comfort. When I left for New York they wanted to give me one of the condo units, as a present. I thanked them but refused it."

"That was extremely generous. They must really love you."

"I believe so. The bottom line is that I sent them a short note about being stationed in Honolulu. They replied that they had moved back to San Francisco and would like to see us, especially to meet you. They said we could live in one of their condos while in Honolulu free. No rent, no HOA's. This is no big deal for them. I didn't want to respond until I talked to you. What do you think? I forgot one thing. When I turned down their housing offer before I left for the UN they gave me a check for $25,000, a little pocket money they called it, to thank me for being a comfort to them. Now I'm like their son. They're like my family too. We're very close."

"I'm stunned. I've never heard of people like that. I've got to meet them."

*   *   *

July first they give notice to the landlord. On the night of the fourteenth they taxi to Dulles Airport to spend the last night in the Hyatt Dulles and catch an early flight to SFO. Their travel allowance covers only coach, but they agree to upgrade to first class. It's a worthwhile treat. Cixi has a few drops of Bailey's Irish Cream in her milk so she can sleep through the flight in a large carry-all box.

They've booked a small suite on the northeast corner of the 9th floor in the Fairmont Hotel on Nob Hill. They have a view from the Bay Bridge north and west over the Bay, past Treasure Island, Alcatraz and Angel Island clear to the Golden Gate Bridge.

The suite is well worth the cost for the few days they'll be there. When Cixi recovers from her nap she inspects the room, views San Francisco from the window sill, and promptly goes into the bedroom to preen her fur. That night they have dinner at Trader Vic's to get in the mood for Hawaii.

In the morning Mike calls the Watsons.

"*Carmen, como esta?*"

After a short pause she almost shouts, "*Señor Miguel, es usted?*"

"*Sí como esta?*"

A pause. "*Señor Watson*" she yells, "*Esta Señor Miguel.*"

In a few seconds Jimmy comes on the phone. "Michael, are you in The City?"

"Hi Jimmy. Yes I am."

"It's so good to hear your voice again, son. How are you, and your wife?"

"We're doing very well, sir, thank you"

"When can we see you?"

"We're going over to Sausalito tomorrow for the day. How about Wednesday?

"I know we're free that afternoon, will two o'clock for tea work?"

"That's fine, sir. We'll see you then."

"No, I'll send Ramon. Where're you staying?'

"We're at the Fairmont, but that's really not necessary."

"Nonsense. It'll give him a chance to see you also."

"OK, ask him to pick us up at 1:45. We'll be waiting out front."

"Excellent. Joanie's out now. Wait till I tell her. She'll be overjoyed to see you and meet your wife."

Chapter 12

THE WATSONS

July 1974
San Francisco

After spending the day walking Sausalito, they have a quiet room service breakfast before visiting the Watson's. Cixi has planted herself on the window seat. She's fascinated with the views over the city, her head following the darting sea gulls. Grace asks the basic question, "What should I wear?"

"The Watsons are regular people. Dress comfortably, like you're going to visit friends." She perks up her ensemble with patent leather red low heels, red skirt, white blouse embroidered with flowers on one shoulder, white cardigan and a light blue jacket. Mike selects grey slacks, an oxford cloth blue shirt, no tie, a light grey sweater vest and a man's standby, a blue blazer.

1340, they're in front of the Fairmont with Cixi. Ramon is standing by the car with a smile that lights up the world. *"Ay, Madre de Dios, un gran gato,"* he exclaims looking at Cixi.

"Ramon, cómo está, amigo?"

"Muy bien. Señora Holmes?" he asks taking off his cap and giving Grace a slight head bow.

"Mucho gusto, Ramon," putting out her hand.

For a moment he is taken aback. A Chinese person speaking Spanish surprises him. *"Muy bien, muchas gracias señora."* shaking her hand hesitantly.

In fifteen minutes they're under the portico on El Camino Del Mar. Carmen rushes out the door ready to give Mike a big hug. She sees Grace and doesn't know what to do, so Mike hugs her. Then he introduces Grace. Grace puts her arms around a hesitant Carmen. Cixi steps down from the car and stares at Carmen with a quizzical look.

"Que magnífico gato!" she exclaims as she leads them into the house.

Ten steps inside Joanie comes flying to them, arms outstretched. "Oh Michael, I'm so, so happy to see you. This beautiful girl is your bride?" She turns to Grace hugging her, "I'm very happy to meet you, my dear. This is a wonderful man you've chosen. And what is this magnificent creature? I've never seen such a large beautiful cat."

"This is Cixi. I hope you don't mind our bringing her. She let us know she didn't like being left in the hotel yesterday. She's quite mellow, will probably just lie down at my feet."

Jimmy arrives and gives Mike a bear hug. Jimmy's a big man, well over six-two and probably 250 pounds, he's brimming over with happiness. "Michael, so good, so good. This elegant lady must be Grace. Welcome." He hugs her, but gently. "Please come in and bring your furry friend with you."

Jimmy throws his arm around Mike's shoulder and heads into the house. Grace follows, arm in arm with Joanie. Cixi is inspecting everything as she pads along beside Grace. The sitting room looks left to the Farallon Islands and right to a piece of the Golden Gate Bridge. The afternoon sunlight bounces off the ocean giving out white and gold flashes that almost sing. Mike picks up Cixi so she can look out the window. Her neck swivels following the soaring gulls and the bouncing light. Back on the floor she inspects all corners of the room, then sits next to Grace, watching each person as they speak.

"Does she understand what we're saying?" Joanie asks.

"I'm sure she's taking notes," Grace responds. "How long have you lived here?"

"We've had this house for over thirty years. We used to shuttle between here, Carmel and Honolulu, but San Francisco is our home."

Carmen appears, "Would you like something to snack on?

"Carmen, do you still make those great tapas?"

"Sí, le gustan las tapas?"

Everyone nods and she goes off almost skipping toward the kitchen.

"How about a drink to celebrate your arrival?"

It's a little early for martinis so they settle for club sodas and juices while waiting for Carmen's treasures.

Grace turns to Jimmy. "Mr. Watson, Michael told me a little about your company. I lived in Honolulu for almost fifteen years, so I'm familiar with Watson Lines. Mike told me they've been plying the ocean since the Gold Rush?"

*   *   *

"Yes Grace. My great-grandfather, George, was one of the early gringo settlers in California. He was a man who looked ahead. He didn't stake a mining claim. Instead he saw a better future in transportation than mining. He started a boat service between San Francisco and Sacramento hauling people and freight. The early bird catches the worm. There wasn't much competition and he gradually moved up to a larger paddle wheel vessel.

By 1865 when the commission came from Washington to plan the transcontinental railroad, Watson had the best organized land and water service in the region. Almost all building equipment for the western section of the new rail line had to be shipped from the east coast around the Cape of Good Hope or hauled overland through the Isthmus of Panama. George won the contracts to move it all up river to Sacramento. By 1869, when the transcontinental railroad was completed, he's a very wealthy man. He started investing in San Francisco real estate and deep draft vessels to haul people and freight up and down the west coast from Alaska to Mexico, and eventually out to Hawaii. In 1896 when gold was discovered in the Klondike, George was there again. Three generations later it's a billion dollar enterprise. I'm chairman emeritus and the major stockholder of Watson Lines."

Jimmy turns to Mike and asks, "Tell us Michael, what were you doing at the UN?"

"As fortune would bestow, Grace and I were assigned as partners. She's a Agent for the State Department. We've been working on classified intelligence projects," his voice drops, "that we're not at liberty to discuss."

Joanie chirps up asking Grace the classic woman's question, "Where did you and Michael meet?"

Grace looks at Mike and gives them the short version of meeting at a party at Pearl Harbor. He was shipped out two weeks later. We kept in contact until we met again about two years ago at the UN. It must have been fate."

"You're right. Are you from Hawaii originally?"

While Grace is spinning her tale of family intrigue Carmen brings in a large tray of tapas. The conversation pauses as they dip in.

When they resurface Joanie says, "We'd love to have you stay for dinner but we've made a previous date. Are you free tomorrow evening?"

Mike looks at Grace and she nods.

Jimmy jumps in, "We'll take you to the Carnelian Room on the top of the Bank of America building. It's three blocks down the hill from the Fairmont and has a fabulous view. We'll pick you up at seven o'clock, if that's satisfactory."

Grace suggests they leave and let the Watsons prepare for their event. Cixi rises and stretches. She's heard enough. Joanie kneels down and strokes her luxurious fur. "What a beautiful animal, so well behaved. It looked like she was interested in our conversation."

After more hugs, thanks to Carmen and promises for tomorrow, Ramon takes them back to the hotel.

In their room Mike asks, "What do you think of the Watsons?"

"Given the heartache they've had, I think they're remarkably kind and thoughtful. I like them very, very much. What did you think, Cixi?" The cat looks at Grace, purrs and goes into the bedroom for a nap.

1900, Mike and Grace are standing by the front door of the Fairmont as the Watsons arrive. Cixi has been given her touch of Bailey's and has mellowed out on the sofa. As Grace gets into the car she says, "I truly appreciate how you received us yesterday. You are an amazing couple. I love you already."

Joanie begins to tear up and reaches out to touch Grace. Jimmy also has a problem seeing. In five minutes they're in front of the red granite monolith of the Bank of America. The high speed elevator sweeps them directly to the restaurant. The receptionist greets them, "Good evening, Mr. and Mrs. Watson. So nice to see you again."

Once seated, Grace and Mike are entranced by the view in the late afternoon light. They can see from the Golden Gate eastward past Alcatraz and northward out over the hills of Belvedere into Marin County. They all watch ships entering and leaving the port. In another hour dusk approaches and the ships' running lights reflect off their wakes.

In lieu of cocktails they agree on wine. The sommelier greets Jimmy and Joanie in personal tones.

Jimmy says, "Henri, please bring your best chardonnay. Wait. Make it Dom Perignon. This is a very special occasion. After we order we'll decide what to have with dinner."

Grace and Mike are mesmerized by the view. It's difficult to drag their attention to the table. Jimmy laughs at their dilemma, "It's the same for everyone who comes here the first time. There is nothing like it that I know of in the whole world. Considering the elevation, the water, the bridges, it's incredible isn't it? To be truly honest with you, the cuisine here is not the best in The City. But the view more than makes up for it."

The Dom goes down easily and relaxes everyone. The conversation between Joanie and Grace is continuous and filled with laughter. Jimmy turns to Mike and says *soto voce*, "This is the happiest I've seen Joanie in over a year. It makes me feel very good because my poor sweetheart has had a horrible couple of years."

By the time dinner, dessert, and coffee are finished, a nearly full moon rises over the eastern hills and bounces silver and gold shards off the water. Jimmy asks, "Michael, are you enjoying being in the navy."

"Yes, it's good. Best of all Grace and I worked together on intelligence projects at the UN. They went well. We've become a skilled team that's quickly making an impression. It's directly responsible for our new duty station in Hawaii, and probably will affect the next assignment as well."

Grace adds, "He's being too modest. He's the leader. I just follow along and try to keep him out of trouble."

"We truly are equals," Mike responds. "Grace is a brilliant and insightful partner. Her background adds so much to what we do. Without her I would struggle, and probably fail."

"Stop it you two," Jimmy interrupts. "I can see that you're a great team and I don't even know what game you are playing."

Joanie chimes in, "Can you tell us what you are going to be doing in Hawaii?"

Grace says proudly, "The navy is sending Mike to the University to complete his Ph.D. in Asian Political Economics.

Joanie is impressed and Jimmy leans forward, "A fascinating topic. I'm not in your league, but I've studied it for years. It has a bearing on our business, of course. I'd like to hear more what you have to say about it. Will you have time while you're here to come and educate me?"

"Sure Jimmy. You pick the time and I'll bring my partner who has a very interesting personal history on the region. Right partner?" he asks turning to Grace.

"I'd be happy to talk with you about it. I'd also like to spend some time with my friend here," Grace replies, gently touching Joanie's arm. It looks like she is going to collapse with emotion.

The evening ends on this high note. They decide the day after tomorrow they'll go to the Watson's for lunch.

"Wonderful. I'll have Ramon pick you up at noon. Bring Cixi with you. She's a real queen."

*   *   *

When they arrive, Carmen's at the door with a mile-wide smile. After a few minutes to settle and revisit dinner at the Bank, Joanie announces that it's time for lunch. The dining room table is set beautifully in a Mexican theme. Carmen is going over the top on this opportunity. There is *albondigas* (meatball soup), *arroz con pollo* (rice with chicken), plus refried beans of course, bowls of sour cream and sliced avocados, hot tortillas on which they can spread anything from shredded beef or chicken, to beans, sour cream or *mantequilla* (butter). As they dive in Carmen hovers over them, smiling as they savor each dish.

After lunch they go to the sitting room with a cup of Mexican coffee topped off with whipped cream. The wind is churning the Pacific churns with rolling white caps. Sea gulls, terns and an occasional albatross soar by to complete the scene. Cixi is preoccupied keeping up with the flying circus. Every few minutes a fluffy white cloud rolls through, casting a moving black shadow across the water. The kaleidoscopic changes of sun and shade add another dimension to the sight.

"I could easily spend the day watching the constant changes flowing across nature's oceanic palette," Grace says to Joanie.

"Some days I have that luxury," she replies.

Cixi finally gives up following the hundreds of birds flying past. She takes a place next to Grace's chair and contentedly dozes.

Jimmy asks Mike to fill him in on what he'll be studying.

"We should have Grace provide a base for understanding what Asia is really about."

"In order to understand China you have to start with the family. That's the center of life. Confucian philosophy is explained by four virtues, loyalty, respect for parents and elders, benevolence, and righteousness. Although Confucianism has been modified in recent times, it's still the foundation of the way we think. Everything springs from the hierarchical structure of family and social life. There's a premium put on self-restraint, obedience, hard work and achievement. Children are taught that elders are to be respected. It's assumed that if the family thrives, everyone within it will also.

"Education is highly esteemed. It comes from the Confucian concept that 'he who excels in learning can be a leader.' This is why you see Chinese, Japanese and Korean students work so hard in school.

"There are many aspects of our culture that are too complex to go into now. But one example is our attitude toward colors. Red is considered good luck, and is for celebrations. Pink and yellow mean prosperity. White, gray and black are funeral colors. Another is about lucky numbers. People like to live in houses whose address contains the number 8, considered a sign of prosperity. I feel like I am babbling."

"No, this is most interesting. Please go on." Joanie nods.

"If we look back to the beginning of the modern era, during the nineteenth century China was humiliated by the Western powers. Germany, Britain, Russian, France and Japan carved up the country to suit their needs. Nevertheless, western ideas of social, political and economic organization began to shift China toward the twentieth century. Sun Yat-Sen was the most prominent politician of the early 1900s, with his Three Principles of the People: nationalism, democracy and welfare. Sun said that the line from Lincoln's Gettysburg address, 'of the people, by the people and for the people,' was the inspiration for the Three Principles."

Jimmy breaks in, "I remember my dad talking about Sun. He thought Sun was the best thing that had happened to China to that point. Our company was getting more and more active in China and Japan then."

"Yes, Sun was very influential. In 1920 he started an effort to unify the country. When he died in 1925 his protégé Chiang Kai-shek took control and succeeded in bringing the north and south together. Then he turned on the small communist party and drove them north. Under Mao's leadership they survived. In the late 1930s allying with Chiang's Nationalists, the Kuomintang Party, they fought the Japanese who were occupying eastern China. After the war, the communists defeated Chiang, and he fled to Taiwan. You know the rest of the story. The important point is that from 1927 to 1945 China had a small market economy. There's every reason to believe that sooner or later it will return to a market economy."

Mike steps in, "Jimmy, my focus will be on what to expect from the CPC (Communist Party of China) going forward, principally on the economic front. Of course, this is tied together with the political leadership. Is your company experiencing anything unusual in China?'

"Yes, that's why I'm interested. Since I'm no longer in daily management, I'm mostly concerned with long term strategy. I'd certainly like to know which way the wind is blowing."

"That opens up another topic. Grace and I have developed some talent and connections that allow us to uncover information that's not readily available to the public. Let me give you a couple examples. Suppose you had access to inside information on the international petroleum market. Would it be useful for you to know what is going on behind OPEC's doors?

"Or would it be valuable to know China's policy and intent to build deep draft vessels for foreign trade? There are government and private reports on this that anyone, including your competition, can access. Therefore, there is no competitive advantage to anyone there. If this is true, how do you get your hands on what's behind that?"

"Exactly what I'd like to know."

"So how much would something like that be worth to you? A thousand dollars, ten thousand, a hundred thousand?"

"If it is accurate, with sufficient detail, the sky's the limit. Success is all about competitive advantage. And that stems from information, what you might call *intelligence*. Of course, we also have to have the ability to execute."

"Agreed. Here's why we brought this up. In five years I'll be able to retire. That's my intention, although the navy doesn't know it. In the meantime, we've already opened a small back channel into Russia and possibly China. We already have a back door into OPEC, if and when we get our business set up, we could get that type of info for you. We wouldn't know the price or how long it might take until you give us detailed requirements and we contact our agents in the USSR and the PRC. Obviously they're going to have to work behind the scenes to locate and extract this information. Sound interesting?"

"Of course. The oil data would help us hedge our future diesel fuel purchases. We might be able to save millions. On the ship-building data, I could give you the specs quickly."

Mike looks at Grace and sees that she supports this foray into their future. "After retirement, we plan to start a business focusing on what people call *business intelligence*. There are already people doing that, but not to the depth that we intend to dig. You seem to be interested in playing some part in that plan, yes?"

"I'm interested, but I need more details of course."

"Exactly. Given that the world is now one marketplace and everyone is in it, there is great opportunity for someone who can provide the type of intelligence we're talking about. We're not going to do anything that directly harms people or the United States. We're not spies or counterintelligence agents in any sense. If the request will lead to someone being exposed or harmed, such as an intelligence agent or politician, we'll pass. Secondly, we'll also be a confidential business dating service. What I mean is, if you were our client and wanted to talk to someone regarding a given topic but can't risk being seen or known to be doing that for competitive reasons, we can set up a one hundred percent guaranteed confidential transportation and meeting place, for your discussion. Or we can be the back channel to move information between the two of you, out of sight. Did I miss anything, Grace?"

"You've covered the basic idea and long range plan. If we tell him anymore we'll have to kill him."

Jimmy hesitates for a second then bursts out laughing. Joanie has left the room so they needn't worry about her getting the joke.

"To be honest, Jimmy, we don't know until we try. Right now we have to focus on our current mission. Time permitting we'll work on the concept. When we're ready to go, we'll let you know."

"Good. If your concept proves out and you need funding to grow quickly, come talk to me about it."

Jimmy calls Joanie back to the room to say goodbye. Grace gives her a warm embrace. "Are you free to do a little shopping together tomorrow? I'd like to check out San Francisco fashions."

"Delighted. Ramon and I will pick you up at the hotel at ten o'clock when the stores open."

Cixi stands up and stretches, walks over to Joanie and rubs against her leg. "She likes you, Joanie." Cixi sits down in front of Jimmy and raises her paw, as if for him to kiss it. Jimmy squats down and shakes it. Ramon drives them back to the Fairmont. They had planned to leave in a couple days and hadn't expected to see the Watsons again. Grace's move changes that. Grace says, "I believe she'll love to have a girlfriend day."

On getaway day, they call Jimmy and Joanie to thank them for their hospitality and promise to keep in touch. A Bailey's-relaxed Cixi goes into her travel box without a fuss. The visit was a very healthy experience on all counts. Without having to sell Jimmy, they have a client and a partner when the time comes.

Chapter 13

CIRCLING THE PREY

August 1974
Honolulu

Honolulu puts them in two minds. On one side they're thinking and talking about their business intelligence project. On the other, their primary business is to meet Mr. Ling and test his allegiance.

By mid-August they've settled in the Watson's spectacular condo. Hawaii's climate, the comfort of the spacious condo and the view over the endless Pacific add up to nirvana. Cixi has inspected all corners and purrs her approval. She chooses the top of a sofa looking out over Kapiolani Park as her throne. Mike takes a seat on the sofa and talks to the Empress. "I know you don't like me, but I want you to know I'm going to take good care of Chan-juan and of you, forever." Cixi looks at him and purrs, *"We'll see."*

Ling is easy to locate. His number is in the UH phone book under Asian Studies. Mike reaches him on the first call. "Professor Ling, this is Michael Holmes. I wrote to you regarding my doctoral program.

"Yes, I received your letter. Are you in Hawaii now? Whenever it is convenient for you I'll be happy to discuss what you plan as your course of study. I recall you mentioning you have access to some private papers from Chiang Kai-shek's time leading the Kuomintang. That would be most interesting to see."

"It's true. I have the papers through my wife, Liu Chan-juan. She's the daughter of General Liu. You probably know he was on Chiang's staff."

"Oh yes, he was highly regarded by both sides during that period. When would you like to get together?"

"May I suggest the three of us meet next Tuesday about 11 a.m.? We can discuss my program and if you're available we can take you to lunch."

"Excellent. My office is in the Asian Studies building on the third floor."

"Splendid. We'll be there."

Grace will be a key part of this. Ling will certainly ask about her father's documents. Mike can tell from his tone he's salivating to get his hands on them. They'll hold back until they get his study plan worked out. Mike wants Grace's impression. Women have that intuitive sense to size up a person's basic personality and integrity rather quickly. Grace has that gift, squared.

The first week they're in town they buy a near new red Toyota convertible. As long as they're in Hawaii they may as well enjoy the sun. The trunk can hold two sets of golf clubs, one of their requirements. Cixi loves to hold court in the back with the top down, fur flying in the wind, viewing her dominion as it flows by.

The campus is a short drive from their condo. What a campus. Huge banyan trees provide shade from the tropical sun and a plethora of flower beds covered with hibiscus, lotus, plumeria, kukui, and yellow ilima in a glorious spectrum. It's less a college campus and more a botanical garden. The place is like a hive of bees each seeking their cell in the comb. Grace knows the UH-Manoa campus, since she studied there. She guides Mike to the Asian Studies Department.

Ling's office is located on the southwest side of the building overlooking the city and Pearl Harbor. From there he can see ships going in and out of the port. They knock on his door. He responds, "Come in."

"Professor Ling, I'm Mike Holmes and this is my wife Liu Chanjuan." He shakes Mike's hand while looking at Grace. Sometimes it gets a little tiring for Mike with people ignoring him when Grace is present. But, he's not complaining, he understands why.

Ling and Grace exchange greetings in Chinese. "Professor, I'm called Grace by Westerners."

"Please have a seat." There are just two chairs in his office, in addition to his own. Against the sidewall are a locked two drawer file cabinet and a bookcase with a vase on top. The flowers look like they have not had a great deal of attention. Unlike most professors' offices, Ling's is very neat. No messy pile of books and papers occupying the floor, desk and bookcases. Is this fellow a real teacher?

"Professor, I've read your curriculum vitae" It's most interesting. You started your college education at Xian during the Japanese occupation. Was that difficult?"

"I was born in Henan Province, but since Xian was outside of the occupied zone there was little or no interference. However you may have seen the gap in my education from 1939 to 1945. I was inducted into the Nationalist army during that period to fight the Japanese, though I had no allegiance to Chiang or the Kuomintang. When the war was over I was accepted at Shanghai University to continue my studies. The period right after the war with Japan was difficult. The Kuomintang and the communists resumed their civil war. You know what happened. I avoided the conflict and was able to complete my degree by 1949.

Ling continues, "I'm teaching a graduate seminar on the relationships among China, Korea and Japan. These three nations dominate Asia, and their interactions have been anything but pleasant over the last century. Please join the seminar. It is a good class for you, a summary of the region."

Mike already has enough credits for his degree picked up through directed study correspondence, but this will give him a chance to spend more time with Ling.

"Professor, I'll need to spend the next few months reviewing the core subjects. It's been a while since my last class. I should be able to take the written qualifying exam by the end of the year. I'll formalize my dissertation proposal during that time as well. Then, if you agree, I can use the spring to write it and take the oral exam before the end of the term."

"When do you expect you'll begin your study of the Liu papers? You said in your letter that they'll be the base for your dissertation."

"Yes, they'll be the core documents on which the dissertation will be built, but I don't need to get into them until I've taken the written exam." Mike can see his disappointment. He's aching to see the documents, but can't show his desire.

"I understand. My seminar starts two weeks from today. Go to the registrar's office and sign up for it. Here's a slip indicating you've been accepted. The class will be held in a room on the second floor. I don't know the number yet, but the registrar will have it. Is there anything else you need at this point?"

"No, sir. Thank you. I'm looking forward to working with you."

He shakes hands with them and says something Mike doesn't quite catch when Ling turned toward Grace. "I would enjoy having lunch with you, but things are quite busy now. Perhaps when we settle into the semester routine we can get together."

As they leave the building Mike asks Grace, "Well, what's our first impression?"

"I don't have one yet. We didn't have any time to talk. When we have lunch with him, or maybe invite him for dinner, I'll have a better opportunity to feel him out."

Chapter 14

REELING HIM IN

October 1974
UH-Manoa

In early October there's a tea for new grad students. Ling is in attendance along with about twenty students. While Grace mingles, Mike and Ling come together on the lanai and engage in a lengthy conversation. When Grace joins the conversation Mike asks if Ling would like to have dinner with them. He accepts.

"There is an excellent Chinese restaurant called the Golden Buddha." He offers directions, but Mike suggests they take him. They can bring him back to the school to get his car or take him home afterwards. Ling replies he never learned to drive in China and the traffic here scares him. He has a small motorbike to ride to school and on local trips. He lives on a ridge overlooking Honolulu.

A week later they pick up Ling. He's correct in his selection of the Golden Buddha. "I think it's the best Chinese food I've tasted outside of China," Grace says. "It reminds me of some of the dishes we had when I was a child. Where in Henan were you born and reared?"

"I'm from Kaifeng along the Yellow River."

Grace exclaims, "I'm also from Henan Province, but in a small town a little closer to Shanghai. What do you remember about growing up in Kaifeng?"

"Actually I don't remember much because we moved to Xian when I was starting middle school."

Grace doesn't find that very suspicious. However, she points out that his accent is not typical of the Kaifeng region. Still, she doesn't have a strong feeling about him yet.

*　*　*

Besides attending Ling's seminar, Mike schedules a regular semi-monthly meeting with him to discuss material. He doesn't need to see Ling that much, but it's an excuse to get close to him. His seminars are surprising in the amount of attention paid to military matters. They don't seem to be very useful. When students ask him questions critical of the Chinese communist leadership, he goes off the deep end chastising Mao, Deng, Hua and others. Mike thinks he protests too much. Yet, on the issue of Mao's wife and attempts at succession, he's uncharacteristically noncommittal.

On one visit to Ling's office Mike has a few minutes alone when Ling has to deal of another matter outside. He takes the chance to look around. Mike's struck by the number of military magazines and reports on his shelves. While none of them are classified, he does have "tell all" magazines about military and governmental matters. Perhaps it's reasonable, since he's teaching governmental and military topics. Mike notices Ling has a spotting scope on a tripod. He can see Pearl Harbor from here.

Grace suggests they look for topics of common interest as a reason for social contact. Ling has commented that he's an aficionado of Asian art, so when a traveling exhibition arrives in Honolulu, they invite him to join them in viewing the Avery Brundidge and John Paul Getty collections at the Honolulu Museum of Art. They have an enlightening afternoon as he shows off his knowledge. Occasionally, when a gallery is showing some interesting local artists, they plan a visit followed by dinner. Ling doesn't seem to have made many friends on the island in the two years he's been here and readily accepts their invitations.

He mentions that he's a big fan of surfing. He's never surfed but has become fascinated with it. From November to February the huge, glassy winter waves pound the seven mile north shore beaches at Waimea and Haleiwa. They can grow to thirty or forty feet and easily wipe out even a professional surfer. When Grace sees publicity regarding the contests, they invite Ling to drive north to watch. He's very anxious. When they pick him up he's dressed in typical tourist beachwear, big straw hat and sun glasses, wild Hawaiian shirt, baggy tan shorts covering his chubby hairless legs, and multi-colored sandals. They insist on taking his picture to commemorate the event, and he poses proudly.

The beach is crowded. There's a strong breeze from the north that's piling up the waves. The sun is blazing over a cloudless sky. Ling's very excited. He constantly runs up and down the beach to find better viewing sites. As the big waves break, he jumps up and down with joy. By the end of the day he's burnt a fire engine red, worn down, and blistered by his sandals and beach sand. Yet he's as happy as can be. On the drive back to Honolulu he falls asleep.

Once Grace feels that they're firmly settled in the Watson's condo, she goes back to the Chinese Community Center where she used to volunteer. They're very happy to see her and she quickly sets up volunteer hours for herself again. She asks Ling if he would like to visit the center. He quickly accepts. It's his chance to get into a comfortable community. If he's a spy he's certainly not an aggressive one.

Near the end of the Fall term, Mike and Grace have grown close to him. He invites them to dinner at his place, a modest apartment with a good view all the way across Honolulu to Pearl Harbor. They notice he has a mounted telescope pointed toward Pearl. The meal is nothing special, but the conversation opens new doors. Grace has commented in passing that Mike's not too happy with the navy or with the way American leadership is running the country.

After dinner Ling asks him, "How do you like being in Hawaii?"

"It's like being home again. I was stationed at Barber's Point about seven years ago. I met Grace there."

"How do you like being in the navy? Are they treating you well?"

"They are paying for my Ph.D., so I can't complain."

"I mean, do you like your duties? What was your assignment before you came here?"

"I worked at the United Nations in the U.S. delegation."

"Was that interesting?"

"Yes, but I don't feel it advanced my career."

"Where will you go from here?"

"I don't know, but it will probably be to another desk job. I don't expect to have a sea command. This degree suggests I would go to an embassy or a fleet command center here or in Westpac."

"Wouldn't you like to command a vessel?"

"Of course, but that's highly unlikely. I'm pretty sure I will be pushing paper somewhere. It's frustrating at times."

Ling has planted a seed and doesn't push further.

When they're home the first thing Grace says, "The little bastard is going to try to recruit you."

"You may be right. If he's really doing that it's confirmation he's an intelligence agent. We may be in a chess match to see who checkmates who."

*   *   *

A month later they invite Ling to a Saturday drive around the south and west sides of Oahu. There's not much development west of Pearl City so the traffic is light. They drive northwest along the coast to the Pali Cliffs enjoying the sun and sea air. By late afternoon the sun is starting its race to meet the horizon. There are some high cirrus clouds. The sky is gradually shifting from pale blue to yellow,

112

which means they should have a spectacular sunset. They look for a restaurant to have something to eat and wait for the sunset.

The faded and chipped sign says, Kaliki's Tiki Shack. It's rightly named; a collection of flotsam and jetsam perched rather unsteadily on a bluff fifteen feet above the surf. In the breeze the shack groans and shudders. If this was on the windy east coast it would have joined the fishes. They have seafood accompanied by a fresh fruit salad of mangos, papayas and pineapple, washed down with a cheap tequila margarita that scalds their throats. The bartender must be a surviving kamikaze pilot. As the wind picks up, the shack trembles a bit more. Eventually the sun nears the horizon. The guests hurry outside to find a seat among the nondescript collection of chairs, recliners, benches and a couple of weather beaten church pews. The great yellow ball seems to flatten and grow as it gradually stretches for the line. For the next twenty minutes nature's fireworks are on display. Yellows, pinks, red shafts and vermilions meld into each other as the sun slides into the ocean. Beams of golden light slip between the clouds. Each second the movement of the disappearing sun changes the palette. It's breathtaking. After they exhale, it's time to head home.

"Professor, would you like to come in for a drink?"

"Thank you, but it's getting too late."

"How about dinner next Saturday?" Grace offers.

He accepts.

Saturday Ling arrives on this little yellow Kawasaki motorcycle. Visualize this short, rotund Chinese man with a Hawaiian shirt flapping in his slipstream and a big grin on his sunglass covered face. He hops off and gives them a loud "Aloha." When he comes in Cixi walks all around him, shakes herself and retreats to her sofa perch. Clearly she doesn't like him. They start with a mai tai before dinner along with Chinese appetizers that he consumes as though food hasn't passed his lips for a month. The conversation is general;

some discussion about the school is mixed with local events and his comments about the big surf on the north coast.

During a lull, Ling asks again how things are going with Mike.

"Just about the same. I feel like I'm topping out in my career. I'll never command a deep draft vessel. That means I'll most likely never make captain. In short, my career has hit the wall. Now, it's just waiting out the next few years until I can retire. It's not a pleasant prospect."

"Grace, how do you feel about this? Do you think Mike is not being dealt with properly?"

"I definitely do. I've seen his work at the UN and I've seen his record of achievements in the past ten years. He's definitely not being treated with respect."

"It makes you angry to see a man so talented be so underpaid and unappreciated, doesn't it?"

"It definitely does. It's not fair, but what can you do about it?" The navy has all the power."

"Well, perhaps not all the power. You speak of retiring in a few years. Does the navy provide a comfortable retirement package?"

"I'd say it's minimal, but then the pay has never been great either. My army officer brother describes it as *genteel poverty*."

"What does genteel mean?"

"It means refined, courteous, well-mannered."

"I see. That sounds very nice, but is it financially comfortable?"

"Hardly," Grace interjects. It's a shame how poorly retirees live, after giving their lives in service to their country."

"That is shameful. Is there anything you can do to increase your income?"

"Well, I'll probably have to go to work in a company in order to stay even middle class. I have a lot of knowledge about how the military works, especially the navy. There are companies who would benefit from knowing that. In addition, I also know a lot of naval officers who can add to what I know."

"This may sound offensive to a man of your high standards, sir, but have you ever considered trading some of your knowledge for additional income while you are still in service? A lot of people do it, you know."

"What do you mean?" Grace asks pointedly.

"Please don't take offense, I only meant that many military personnel in all services find ways to trade their knowledge for additional income, sometimes a great deal of income."

"Do you mean becoming a spy?'

"That's too harsh a word. I refer only to sharing some information that you may have access to."

"Wait a minute," Mike says, getting up and leaving the room.

Ling looks at Grace and shrugs his shoulders questioningly. This fellow is cool. He's been well trained by Beijing.

When Mike returns he hands a document to Ling and asks, "Is this what you mean?"

It's a report that is labeled *Secret*, but actually isn't. Ling takes it and flips through the pages. "Is this the type of information you have access to?"

He handles it casually, but they see he's excited, "Yes."

"I believe you could trade such harmless information for a sum of money. It's a common practice among military men in all countries. I'm surprised no one has approached you before. A man has to think about his family's welfare, doesn't he? Loyalty is nice but you can't eat loyalty or pay bills with it. I know. Living in a socialist society one learns to lookout for himself."

"How would I go about trading my knowledge? Who would I deal with that I could trust to not get me in trouble?"

"I know people who are interested in recent developments by the navy. They would pay handsomely for this."

"I don't know if I'm comfortable doing that. What do you think, Grace?"

Grace pauses for a moment, looking as though she's giving it deep thought. "Actually, I don't see how it can cause harm. There are probably people inside our government who are already collecting this type of information. You read about them in the newspapers. I've also heard some gossip from other wives about such things. I wouldn't be surprised if their husbands aren't doing it already."

Mike pauses for a moment deep in thought. "Well, I don't know. Maybe it's harmless. In our open society you see diagrams in military magazines showing some of our latest weaponry."

"I think we should thank Mr. Ling for the idea. Let's consider it."

"You should think about it. If you have any questions, please just ask me."

"Ready for dessert, gentlemen?" They nod. Shortly, she returns with Ling's favorite, macadamia ice cream, and coffee. Cixi has left her perch and is circling Ling, looking him over very carefully.

When Ling roars off on his cycle, they turn to each other with big smiles. He thinks he has them and they know they have him. Grace looks at Cixi. "Cixi doesn't trust him. She had a great deal of experience with political and military people. Did you notice how she was sniffing him? She can smell when someone isn't honest."

A week before the Christmas holidays Mike meets with Ling to talk about taking the qualifying exam. If he passes, the only thing left is the dissertation.

Ling asks, "Are you ready for the exam?"

"I believe so. It's a long time since I took classes in those topics, so I feel a bit nervous about them. But overall I think I can handle it."

"You can expect questions on political, economic, military and philosophical topics. For example, you might be asked about the modern history of politics in China from the time of Sun Yet Sen to date. In economics, the questions could be about China's traditional markets versus moves toward a market economy. In political matters, the main question could be contrasting the Nationalist and PRC positions on international relations. Philosophical questions could address how traditional Confucian philosophy is being transformed to meet modern life. You should be prepared for questions such as those," he says smiling.

"Professor, I appreciate your guidance. I'll see you after the holidays."

Mike can't believe it. The little man just gave him the exam. Mike expects he's using this as part of his campaign to get into his good graces and build confidence in him.

* * *

In January, Mike sits for the qualifying exam. It is no surprise when he sees the questions. They are almost word for word what Ling outlined. Since Mike figured that is what he was doing, he prepared for them. He has no doubt he aced the exam.

Afterward Mike starts outlining his dissertation. The primary source is Grace's father's papers. His title is "The Political Economic Theory of Chiang Kai-shek." It's a sensitive exposition, since Chiang is still alive. Yet if it's like most dissertations, no one beyond his committee will ever read it.

General Liu left notes and documents regarding Chiang's theory of politics and economics. Many came from personal conversations with Chiang. Within the immediate staff there was a division of attitudes. In one case an individual was not discrete about his feelings. Shortly afterward he disappeared. Chiang had little concern for the average person, seeing people merely as economic units. Although he did not espouse this publicly, his actions proved it and Liu's documents support it. The best example was in Taiwan where he and sixty thousand of his Kuomintang followers fled after their defeat by Mao on the mainland.

Chiang's philosophy was a mix of Confucianism, Christianity, nationalism and, most notably, authoritarianism. Liu noted that in private Chiang is a neo-fascist. He rejected western democratic values and opposed western forms of social justice. Liu pointed out how out of touch Chiang was with the suffering of the general population. This is exemplified by his suppression of political dissidents following the 228 Incident, a protest against the government in Taiwan on February 27 and 28, 1947. It was violently suppressed by Chiang's government, resulting in the massacre of from 10,000 to 30,000 people. No one really knows how many perished under the guns of government forces. Martial law has been in effect in Taiwan since. Over 140,000 Taiwanese have been imprisoned during this period, at least 3,000 executed. Still, America continues to support his despotic regime. What will happen when he's gone is unknown.

Ling is intensely interested in General Liu's documents. When he asks about them, Mike tells him he's working with other historical documents and will use them once he has the foundation prepared.

Easter and spring breaks are mid-April. Ling leaves town for several days to attend a conference in San Francisco. Mike and Grace have a chance to get into his office, although it's locked. The lock picking class at DIS comes in handy now. There are several ways. The easiest for a simple office or house lock is what's called "bumping." No need for picks or wrenches. You just insert a bump key, pull it out a sixteenth of an inch, tap it lightly and pull. This pushes all the tumblers up for a split second, enough time to turn and retract the bolt.

Sunday morning they go to his office. The office lock is old, nothing especially secure about it. While Mike works at it Grace keeps watch. In a few seconds they're in. Mike manages the locks on the desk and file cabinet. They go through his papers very carefully to not disturb anything. There are Chinese language files inside a folder tucked behind a false front in the back of one drawer. Grace skims the file since she can read Chinese faster than Mike. She gasps.

"What's the matter? What did you find?"

"This file folder has several documents from The Western Nations Analysis, Bureau of Military Strategic Intelligence, Beijing. A paper notes the usefulness of his most recent report and urges him to learn more about the navy's plans for deploying vessels to WESTPAC. They're most anxious to obtain classified data on our new submarine weapons systems."

"That does it. I'll get in touch with Captain Samson. We've got him. There's no question he is a Beijing agent. Still, we need to go as deep as we can before we bust him. I'll ask Samson to have someone bug his office and home and tap his phones before he gets back on Saturday."

Mike calls Samson. Samson says he'll have someone from JAG get a court order to bug. This way they won't have a problem if they go to trial with him. Mike says he also wants to wear a wire the next time they discuss the navy document turnover with him. He suggests to Grace that she also wear one.

"Can I have one that's red? It's my favorite color."

"Your face will be red if he discovers it on you."

"I assure you he's not going to get that close."

In record time the spooks have bugs in place at Ling's office, house and phones. They provide Mike and Grace with wires. It's a couple weeks before they hear anything worthwhile. One day he's overheard talking to a Chinese man at his house. The man works at Pearl within CINCPAC, and feeds classified data to Ling. It's an unexpected dividend. Time to close the trap.

* * *

2 May, Mike and Grace call Samson. "Captain, we have a chance to do more than capture a couple spies. The one at Pearl we can give to the FBI. But we have another idea for Ling. Rather than arrest him for espionage; we can use him to our long term advantage. Think about this, sir. Suppose we recruit him? We can arrest him and deport

him with the understanding that he will work for us when he gets back to the intell function in Beijing."

"You mean he'll be our agent? What makes you think he'll do it?"

"We've gotten to know him quite well. He seems ready to go whichever way the wind blows."

Grace adds, "I'll explain in a way only a Chinese person can. If he double crosses us, we will expose him to Beijing or kill him. If *we* don't kill him, they'll execute him as a traitor. Whichever way, he's a dead man. He'll believe me."

Mike steps in, "Sir, you can further ensure he comes over, if Grace and I are assigned as attachés to the US Liaison Office in Beijing. There we can get the most intell out of him and ensure against a double cross."

"It sounds like you've got this all figured out," Samson ventures, with a note of sarcasm.

"Sir, it makes sense to optimize the situation. Why imprison or deport him? In prison he's a useless expense. If we deport him without some reciprocity, we don't realize any further benefits. Having him working for us is the best return on our investment."

"I'll think about that. What do you have in mind for the sting?"

"We'll invite him for dinner—like a Last Supper. We'll confront him with the evidence. He's a dead man with no options. We'll tell him the FBI is outside waiting to arrest him. We'll have locked down his office and house. There's no way out. But before we turn him over, we'll give him the option. He'll have about one minute to accept it. If he accepts, he will be arrested and deported as quickly as possible. We'll remind him if he accepts and does not perform, we'll have him killed. He's not brave. Put in this situation, he has no choice. It's prison or a new job."

Samson interrupts. "I don't like the FBI part. As soon as those people get their hands on him, we've lost him. Instead, you have Shore Patrol pick him up and put him on ice in the brig at Pearl with the other man. Treat both the same. If we recruit and then deport him we should deport the two of them together. I'll think about the other option. When do you want to pull it off?"

"We need a few days to assemble our case against him. We have tapes of the telephone surveillance. Grace can get him out of the office next Sunday for a tea at the Chinese Cultural Center and then dinner at our house. I'll get back into his office and pick up the incriminating files."

"Breaking in without a court order is illegal you know."

"I wouldn't think of it, sir. If JAG get a court order, I'll go in."

"You want to do this Sunday?"

"Yes, sir. We'll tell him Grace will have General Liu's documents ready for him to view. There is no way he is going to pass up that opportunity. He's been salivating about them for almost a year. If you can talk to the local SP command and have them call me, we can set up the arrest."

"Very well. Proceed."

"Are you saying to offer him the option?"

"Yes, it makes sense."

"Are you also supporting the posting to Beijing for Grace and me? It might be considered an assignment through the Kennedy Irregular Warfare Center."

"You just set up the arrest and let me take care of that, Commander. It'll take time to arrange and I don't know if I can get the boss to go for it."

*　*　*

Next day Shore Patrol, Lieutenant Commander Brock calls. "Commander Holmes, I just got off the phone with Captain Samson at ONI. He explained the sensitivity. There'll be no leaks on this end. I'm fully prepared to support the sting. I'll be there with my best man to make sure this goes smoothly. We'll take him directly to the brig and put him and the other man in solitary confinements awaiting further instructions."

"That's great. Here's my home address, 2814 Malii Drive. It's a white house on the Mauka side of the street. Stand by outside at 1700 day after tomorrow. As soon as I have a court order I'll get into his office and pick up the evidence. This will not be a difficult arrest. He's a small, nonviolent man."

"Yes sir, 1700 it is. Will there be other parties in your home? How will you signal us to come in?"

"There'll be only three of us. Me, my wife who is a Special Agent of the State Department, and Ling. We'll turn on the porch light and unlock the door. That is your signal to come in. If something is wrong, we will flick the light on and off. Should that happen call my house phone 808 935 8767. "

"We'll be standing by."

That afternoon Mike stops by Ling's office. "Grace would like to take you to a tea at the Chinese Cultural Center and then dinner at our place. Also, she will have her father's papers for you."

"That would be wonderful. What time?"

"Grace will pick you up at one."

"I'll be ready. Thank you."

1530, Grace and Ling arrive to find cold pina coladas ready. Ling's almost hyperventilating about seeing General Liu's papers.

"Come in professor. I have your favorite cold drink ready. After lunch Grace will bring the papers out."

Cixi's fur stands up when she sees him. She retreats to the bedroom with a low growl.

Lunch goes somewhat hastily because he is so anxious. They clear the table and Grace spreads the papers on it. They watch amused as he digs in. Some papers he passes over and others he studies slowly and carefully. He asks Grace if he can take one or another back to his office to copy. Grace says nicely by firmly, "No."

There's no reason to let him see all the papers. This is the moment of truth. He's a nice man, but he's on the wrong side, at least for now.

Mike stops his examination, "Professor, I have some bad news for you. I'm a naval intelligence officer. My reason for being at UH is to learn if you're engaged in any, shall we say, competitive intelligence activities? We've had you under surveillance for several months. We've obtained search warrants for your office and home. We have sufficient data to arrest you, which we are going to do now. There are two Shore Patrol men waiting outside to take you to Pearl Harbor. We are also picking up your associate who works at CINCPAC. We will hold you until we arrange to try you for espionage or deport you."

The little fellow looks like a balloon that's deflating. Mike thinks he's going into shock. He goes over to him and pushes his head down to his knees to get blood flowing to his brain. After several seconds Mike pulls him back up. Grace moves around behind him to apply Chinese massage to his neck and forehead. Gradually, he starts breathing normally.

He came to look at something he's wanted to see ever since he knew it existed. It turns out he's losing his freedom instead. They give him a couple of minutes and a shot of Macallans to get over the shock. After he relaxes Grace offers the option.

"Professor, rather than throw you in jail for the rest of your life, we have a choice. We can deport you to China. How do you think you will be received? Do you expect to be returned to the intelligence service? Or have some other fate in store for you?"

He pauses for a minute to gather his composure. "I've never thought about it. I never expected this. I expected to live and work here for many years. If I go back I believe I'll be well received, as I've done what has been asked for the past two years. There is no reason to dishonor me.

"People in our business are well known within the intelligence community, so we cannot easily circulate. I'll either be retired or more likely given a desk job. My case will be an example for other agents who will see that they are well taken care of when they return from clandestine duty."

"Assuming that you're well received, you can earn your freedom by becoming an agent for us." She stops to see what effect this has on him. He's stunned.

Grace repeats the deal in Chinese to make it more palatable for him, "Professor, this offer can make you a very wealthy man as well. If you work with us you'll be paid for your information. The money can be put in a bank account off shore or paid to you in gold if you choose."

Ling is silent for a long time. It's a very important decision, jail or freedom. "I need time to think this over."

"Professor, you don't have time," Mike interjects. There are arresting officers waiting to come in here as soon as you make up your mind."

"What will happen to my things, my personal effects?"

Grace assures him, "If you accept our offer, we'll personally see to it that whatever we can release and send will be shipped. We can't treat you too well or the people in Beijing will believe that you've gone over. The most important issue is, what is your decision? We need to know that now. One thing I have to add is that if you double cross us, we have ways to deal with that and they aren't pleasant. As an agent you understand how the game is played."

Again for a minute he's thinking. Mike asks if he'd like another drink.

"That will be wonderful. It might be the only one I'll have for a while," he says with a rueful smile.

"Does that mean you have accepted our offer?"

"I don't think the other option is very agreeable."

"Very well. Your associate will not be offered a deal. He'll just be deported or traded, probably at the same time as you."

"I understand."

Grace leans toward him and says in a comforting voice, "You've made the right decision. We'll do everything we can to handle this matter carefully, so you're not exposed."

With that Mike turns on the porch light and cracks the door open. "The Shore Patrol will be here in a minute. If you give me the keys to your motorcycle, house and office we'll handle them carefully. We'll donate your motorcycle, clothes and furniture to the Chinese Cultural Center. We want you to know that we've honestly enjoyed our time with you. We're sorry that this happened, but it probably would have sooner or later. Hopefully our offer will work out for you."

There is a knock on the door. Brock and his man come in, handcuff Ling, and take him away.

First thing next morning Mike calls Captain Samson. "Sir, the deal is done. He's in the brig at Pearl. The Shore Patrol picked up his associate last night as well. I agree with you. Rather than treat them separately I believe we should treat them exactly the same way. Otherwise there could be suspicion regarding Ling."

"Yes, I'll get in touch with the FBI and let them know what's happening. We'll hold them as long as we can. Then they can take the lead on deportation or trading of both parties."

"Thank you, sir. We'll clean up the loose ends here over the next week. After that, I'll submit my dissertation, take my final exam, and be finished here and ready for reassignment."

"Very good. I'll expect to see you here by June 30. We'll talk about your Beijing idea. Holmes, you're a smart man. Just don't lose your head and become a smart guy."

Too late, he thinks, winking at Grace.

Chapter 15

MURDER AT MOFFETT

July 1975
Honolulu

By the end of June the dissertation is submitted to the Dean of the Asian Studies Department. Normally the next step is the oral defense conducted by the faculty advisor, Professor Ling, and the dissertation committee. The Dean is utterly embarrassed about Ling, so he and Mike go through the dissertation together. The Dean signs off on it and it goes to printing.

Mike bursts into the condo. "Mission accomplished you can call me. You can all me Doctor Holmes, my ravishing princess. How about a bit of ravishing before we start packing for Washington?"

As they're making final arrangements to fly to D.C. Samson calls.

"Michael, there has been a slight change in plans."

He's thinking, "*When isn't there a change of plan?*"

"You're going to Moffett Field in California. A naval officer was murdered there on Saturday, 26 June. You and Grace are assigned to investigate and obviously find the killer. Your orders are on the way. Report to Captain Metzger, CO of Moffett. He's expecting you ASAP."

They decide Mike should go ahead while Grace finishes packing. She'll follow as quickly as she can.

Wednesday, 7 July Mike checks in at Moffett and makes an appointment with Metzger for 0800 the next morning. Norman Metzger is an imposing man. He's a poster model for the ideal naval officer. Tall, firmly built, short well-groomed gray hair, steel blue eyes and a firm chin.

"At ease, commander. Glad to see you. This is a tragic thing. Excellent young naval officer, Lieutenant Commander Larry Winslow, family man, cut down by some low lifes. It's a damned shame. When we catch them they'll probably have a battery of fancy attorneys and get off on some technicality."

"Sir, do you think that navy personnel weren't involved?"

"You bet your life, Holmes. Navy people wouldn't blow up his car. That's a coward's way. I'm pretty certain it's a mob hit."

"What brings you to that conclusion, sir?"

"Gambling!"

"Gambling? Was the Lieutenant Commander Winslow a gambler?"

"Yes, I first saw it at the opening of the racing season at Bay Meadows, a track about 15 miles north of here in San Mateo. Two weeks ago we had a party at the track for some of the officers and wives. Someone mentioned that Winslow seemed to be betting heavily. He lost a bundle. I called in Commander Taylor, his boss, and told him to counsel Winslow about gambling. I've since heard that he bets on just about everything. Gambling can be an aaddiction, as you certainly know."

"Yes, sir, it can be."

"You may also know that the CO is compelled to report the addiction and take away his security clearance. A commanding officer who fails to report the problem risks his own career. I know Taylor talked to Winslow. Last Saturday my wife and I attended a dinner for a local charity at Bay Meadows. I saw Winslow at the window in the Turf Club. That means he was a frequent attendee and probably a high roller. Monday morning, five days before the incident, I told Taylor we had to remove Winslow immediately. Saturday he was killed in Santa Cruz at the Beach Boardwalk. He had taken his family and a young civilian engineer from the Blue Cube to the beach. Whoever did it had the decency to wait until he was in the car by himself before they acted. I'm certain it was a mob hit because they respect family. Maybe it was an impetuous bookie who forgot that dead people can't pay their debts."

"That's very interesting, sir."

"The Santa Cruz PD is on the case and the FBI was called in as well. I told them my theory. Holmes, get on this immediately. Protect the interests of the navy, and keep the press from turning this into a circus. Make sure the culprits are brought to justice."

"I'll start immediately, sir. Who has the case file?"

"My assistant outside will give you the material we have so far. You'll want to talk to his wife; a very nice young woman. Probably don't need to upset his daughter. She's only about thirteen. It's a terrible thing for a child to go through."

"Yes sir, I agree. I'll be discreet, but thorough."

"Keep me updated on your progress and whenever you have some breakthrough I want to know about it before the press gets to it. Good luck. Wrap it up as quickly as you can Holmes."

"One last thing, sir. Special Agent Grace Liu, my wife, will also be working this case with me. We're a special investigative team set up by ONI and State a year ago. We've just completed our assignment in Honolulu. She's wrapping that up and will be here in a couple of days. I'll start the investigation and bring her up to date when she gets here."

"ONI and State cooperating, that's a new one! Very well Holmes, Carry on."

* * *

Metzger's yeoman hands him a key to his new office and Winslow's 201 File, an officer's file that contains copies of every incident during his career. It includes not only duty stations, but also promotions, awards and decorations, facts such as weapons and skill qualifications, and even records of leaves. The yeoman tells Mike that Commander Taylor has the case file and the preliminary police report. First step is to find his office and read the 201. Then he'll make an appointment to see Taylor.

The 201 isn't especially interesting. Winslow was 34, a lieutenant commander, married to Eve Winslow, nee Newell, age 36, and has a 13 year old daughter from Eve's first marriage. His service record is good, but not outstanding. His current assignment is at the Blue Cube. That's the nickname for the large windowless building painted blue on the south side of the base. It is a super-secret satellite tracking operation under the direction of the National Reconnaissance Office. There's no mention of any disciplinary action about gambling. Mike calls Grace, gives her a short briefing and asks when she'll arrive.

"I've booked a flight for Cixi and me to SFO on United for Sunday. My ETA is 1710."

"I suggest we don't mention her just now. I don't want to have a hassle with the housing people."

Grace arrives on schedule. They make up a place for Cixi in their quarters, which she ignores in favor of their bed.

Monday morning they walk into Jeff's office to find a lanky, seemingly easy-going, ex-farm boy. He moves slowly, but Mike senses that beneath the aw-shucks look there's a hard core. "Good morning, Jeff. I'm Mike. This is agent Grace Liu, also my wife."

"Welcome to Moffett. Nice to meet you, Grace."

"Jeff, it's a pleasure. Have you been here long?" Grace asks.

"Yep, I'm near ready to be reassigned. I figure it's about time for embassy duty in Rio." He leans back laughing.

"Sorry, Jeff. That's my billet, replies Mike. We'll send you a postcard from Ipanema Beach."

"Well, that figures. I'll probably get Kodiak Search and Rescue next."

"How about NAS Mojave? Do you like warm weather and rattlesnakes?"

"I'd rather have NAS Lincoln. It's not far from Hays where I grew up."

"Well, we'll keep our fingers crossed for you."

"Thanks. Winslow was a dirty shame. He was a good ol' boy. Sort of the All-American type. Tall, good lookin', athletic, smart, always laughin' and tellin' jokes. We played on the base basketball team. Ready to party anywhere, any time. Everybody liked him. Well, almost everybody. Sometimes he went too far. Liked to pull tricks on people, and he was a topper, you know, always had a story that topped yours. Good officer and good family man though. Nice wife, a bit bossy at times, but pleasant. She's from Nebraska."

"How did you learn that?"

"Anyone working in the Cube has to have a TS clearance. They run background checks on relatives and even some close friends. Mrs. Winslow, her name is Eve, was born in North Platte. It's west of Omaha about 250 miles and north, northwest of my home, about 200 miles. They've got a really cute 13 year old daughter, smart as can be."

"I understand that Captain Metzger told you to remove Winslow. How did that go down?"

"The boss was really pissed, excuse me ma'am, cause despite our talk Larry kept on gambling. Had no choice but to call him in and tell him we were removing his clearance. Advised him to resign his commission. Left him no future in the navy. Told him I would talk with the boss about whether this will be an honorable or general discharge.

"Larry took it real hard. Assume he told Eve that afternoon. I told him to come back the next day and clean out his desk. Started on the paperwork. Security was there when he came back to take his personal effects. With a TS clearance, you have to be extra careful. But now things have changed. Cause we had no resignation letter from him yet, he's still on active duty with all rights and privileges. Since he was killed while on active duty, all benefits accrue to Eve and daughter."

"Tell me what you know about the murder. It's a very strange case."

"Police report is slim at this point. Here's the case file. All it says is family drove to Santa Cruz Beach Boardwalk on Saturday and took along Ethan Winesoff, a young engineer who works in the Cube with Larry. About 1600 Larry goes to take their gear back to the car so they can go to dinner on the Pier. He leaves Eve and Abigail on the Boardwalk. Ethan follows Larry. Next thing there's an explosion in the parking lot. Larry had just gotten to the car when it blew up. Explosive was in the trunk. Apparently went off when Larry either approached the car or opened the trunk. Bomb was a small one and didn't destroy the whole car. Some damage to several cars nearby in the lot. Mostly small dents and paint chips. Ripped Larry's head off his body. Ethan was several yards behind him and wasn't hurt."

"Where did you say his wife and child were when the bomb went off?" Grace asks.

"Somewhere on the Boardwalk."

"Is there anyone under suspicion at this point, or any motive?"

"Don't know. Boss thinks it's a mob hit cause Larry was deep into gambling debts. You'll have to talk to Santa Cruz PD. Believe an FBI agent has just arrived also, to look into this since it involved a naval officer and two staff with TS clearances."

"Thanks, Jeff. We'll pay a visit to Santa Cruz."

Mike and Grace go back to their office and call SCPD. This is a big event for Santa Cruz. "Detective Gallacher, this is Commander Mike Holmes of the Navy's Defense Investigative Service. My partner,

Special Agent Grace Liu from the State Department, and I have been assigned to work the murder of Lieutenant Commander Winslow. I understand you're handling the case. We need to come to Santa Cruz and talk with you as soon as possible."

"Commander, I'm available any time. Most of my time is being allocated to this case. When would you like to meet?"

"How does 10 a.m. tomorrow suit you?"

"Come ahead. I'll be at the station. Do you know where that is?"

"No."

"Come down Highway 101 from Moffett to 17 south. Take it West over the hill to 1 North, then one mile on 1 North, left on Chestnut, left on Laurel, 2 blocks, right on Center."

"Got it. Thanks. We'll be there at 10."

*　*　*

When they enter the Santa Cruz Police Station they're greeted by a large Scotsman with a ruddy complexion and a ready smile. Behind that smile is toughness. He's 6'4" and 240 pounds with hands large enough to crush your head, and a semi-visible attitude that says, *don't tempt me*. After a few minutes getting acquainted and going over the basic points of the case he says, "Let's go to the crime scene." The beach parking lot is just a couple blocks west of the station. The crime scene is still cordoned off with yellow tape and barricades. The wrecked car has been removed to the police impound building, and what is left of Larry has been carefully taken to the morgue. There is a couple, a man and a woman, examining the ground and looking at samples taken from the tarmac. They're looking for remnants of the explosive that they might have missed the day of the explosion. There's another man. Craig introduces them, "This is Ken Mason from the FBI."

Mason nods. Craig asks the woman if she has found anything.

"With a sly smile she replies, "You betcha, Craig. We don't know what it is yet, but there are some unusual traces of powder on the ground and in the trunk. That's why we're taking another look. Once we're back in the lab it won't take long to find its signature."

Mason's already seen the car, so he heads out to San Francisco to file a first report. Next stop for Mike and Grace is the police impound building to see the car. It's a smelly, damp, dark, moldy place.

Craig told them the car is actually recognizable. "The bomb must have been a small one," he says. "Front half of the car is untouched."

He's right. There wasn't a fire that consumed everything, which is unusual. Explosives start fires, and a decent size one like this should have ignited the gas tank. No telltale black marks of the explosive. Whoever did this knew what he was doing. Also, he must have designed it so it wouldn't blow up vehicles all around Larry's car. There's something fishy here, and it's not the Boardwalk. There's nothing else they can do until they get the lab reports. They thank Craig and ask him to call when he has something. In the meantime they're going to contact Mrs. Winslow and Ethan Winesoff. They need to hear their version of what happened.

On the way back to Moffett they stop in Saratoga to look at the Winslow house and neighborhood. Along the short main street of this small upscale Silicon Valley village there are several fine restaurants. Grace says, "I'm hungry. Let's have lunch here. Maybe we can pick up some gossip about the Winslows from the local people."

Chapter 16

NO SMOKING GUN

July 1975
Saratoga

Set back from Big Basin Way, the main street, is a small retail nook. It houses a jewelry shop, Hong's Chinese restaurant, a sushi bar and Florentine's Italian. Grace pulls Mike away from Flortentines and says, "Let's go talk to the people in Hong's."

Lunch time is almost over. Only a few people linger. Most are local housewives enjoying a break before the kids and husband descend on them. They hardly notice Grace, but for once Mike gets the look over.

Grace asks the waiter if he speaks Mandarin. He nods and says in Mandarin, "Also Cantonese," with a big smile. After a few words they order. The waiter asks with a sly look, "Chop sticks or fork for the gentleman?"

Mike surprises him with, *"Kuaizi, ruguo ni yuanyi."* (Chopsticks, if you please).

The teapot is delivered by a middle-aged woman in a Chinese dress. Grace smiles, says "Thank you," and chats with her for a moment. "Just warming up the team," she says quietly to Mike after the woman leaves.

Every time the staff comes by asking if everything is okay, Mike answers, *"Shì de xiè xiè."* (It's fine.) They grin and nod. It becomes a game.

The check comes with a question from the manager about their satisfaction. The place is empty except for Grace and Mike. She asks the man if he knows the Winslows.

He nods gravely, "Terrible, terrible."

Hearing that, the tea lady slides up and nods, "Nice family, terrible."

"What were they like?"

They all nod and repeat, "Nice family. Wife is boss. Little girl very nice. Husband always smiling." That's the extent of the intell they'll find here.

Thursday morning Grace calls the Winslow residence. A woman answers. Grace introduces herself as Special Agent Grace Liu and asks if she's talking to Mrs. Winslow.

"No, I'm Vivian Camp, a friend of Mrs. Winslow. I'm staying with her as long as she needs me."

"That's very good of you, Ms. Camp. I'm certain she appreciates you. We need to speak with Mrs. Winslow as soon as possible, so we can get on with the investigation. Would you please ask her when would be the earliest convenience?

"We, who is we? I hope you're not going to bring an army in here and upset her and Abby."

"No. I promise we will be discreet. However, my partner Lieutenant Commander Holmes and I, are committed to finding who did this horrible thing. The sooner we talk to Mrs. Winslow the better."

After a minute Ms. Camp comes back on the phone, "Mrs. Winslow will be happy to cooperate in any way to help you find the people who murdered Larry. She'll be available tomorrow morning at ten. Would it be all right if I'm here to support her in case she needs me?"

"Tomorrow is fine. Thank you. However, we need to speak to Mrs. Winslow alone, and in private. I'm certain you can understand."

Saratoga is home to about 30,000 people tucked into the wooded foothills of the Santa Cruz Mountains. The house is a white Cape

Cod bungalow surrounded by a huge blue spruce and two large redwoods along the driveway. There are flagstone steps leading up to a small stoop and a beautiful heart of redwood door, with a artfully crafted, stained glass window. *How can a lieutenant commander afford a place like this?*" Mike wonders. He knocks and in a few seconds they're greeted by a tall, fortyish, bleached blonde woman.

"I'm Vivian Camp. Come in. Mrs. Winslow is waiting for you in the living room."

They follow her into a room with polished wide-plank oak floors, redwood paneling and an arched ceiling supported by redwood beams. The fieldstone fireplace confirms this was built decades earlier; probably when Saratoga was a summer retreat in the country hot springs like its namesake in New York.

"Eve, this is Special Agent Liu and Commander Holmes. I'll be leaving now. Eve dear, if you need anything just call, anything at all. Nice meeting you," she says as she turns abruptly and leaves with her nose slightly elevated. The petite brunette stands to meet them. She's quite well dressed for this occasion. She watches Mrs. Camp go. When the door closes she says, "Don't mind her. She's just very protective of me."

"No problem, Mrs. Winslow," Grace replies with a smile.

She shakes hands firmly. "Please sit down", she says motioning them to a sofa. She chooses a wingback chair to their right.

"Thank you for seeing us so quickly Mrs. Winslow."

"Please call me Eve. Can I call you Grace and Michael? After all, we are shipmates, so to speak."

"Of course. You have a beautiful house. How long have you lived here?"

"We bought it soon after Larry was stationed here. Since we were told this would be a lengthy assignment we decided to buy rather than rent. Are you two married?"

"Yes," Grace replies with a smile at Michael.

"Then you know what it's like to be constantly renting someone else's house. I imagine you're wondering how we could afford this neighborhood and this pretty house. Actually, I bought it. I'm certain you already know I was married before. My late husband was from a wealthy family in Omaha. Now I guess I have to say, my previous husband. When he died I inherited a significant estate. Would you like to see the house?"

"That would be very nice."

"The place was small when we bought it, just two bedrooms and one bath. We've done extensive remodeling and expansion to bring it up to the neighborhood. Please, come this way. We totally updated and expanded the kitchen and added a family room. They didn't have family rooms when this place was built in the 1920s."

The kitchen and family room with wet bar are large, with state of the art décor and top brand appliances. The walls are adobe white and the backsplash and counters have hand-painted tiles.

"The living room was small but featured a large bay window and heart of redwood paneling that's no longer available. We left it as is, because it's so charming. We put sky lights in the dining room and kitchen. The big trees are gorgeous but really provide more shade than we like in the winter months. Finally we added to the master bedroom wing." They walked down the hall to the bedroom suite that includes a sunken tub of custom made tiles and a beautiful view of a large California live oak holding court in the center of the large back yard.

"I love your decorating, Eve. This is a showplace."

"Well thank you, Grace, not everyone has an eye for beauty like you. Would you like something to drink? It's a bit early for martinis but I have coffee or tea."

"You're very gracious. No thank you. I appreciate what you are going through, Eve. I lost a husband and I know the feeling. We'll try to keep this short and to the point. Then we'll leave you to take care of the many things that come up at a time like this. I presume that Larry told you what happened on Tuesday."

"Yes, I was devastated. I'd told him over and over that he had to cut out his gambling or it would catch up with him. Those gambling people don't like it if you can't pay up, and I'm guessing that Larry was deep into debt with them. Of course he never mentioned it to me or I would have had a fit."

"I was referring to his resignation. You think it was a gambling payback?"

"Absolutely. What else could it be? Larry was very popular with everyone. He must have owed the mob a lot for them to go this far. Maybe it was a lesson for other gamblers."

"Please describe what happened Saturday starting with your preparations to go to Santa Cruz."

"Well, nothing special. Abigail, my daughter, and I prepared the food for the beach and gathered the serving items into a couple baskets. Larry got drinks and put them into a cooler. He organized blankets and four small beach chairs, you know the ones without legs that sit right on the sand or blanket. About that time Ethan arrived and we packed the car."

"Excuse me. Who packed the trunk?" Mike asks.

"Larry and Ethan did, I suppose. Why do you ask?"

"Someone put the bomb in the trunk. The question is: who did it and when? But continue, please."

"I suppose someone did it while we were at the beach. We'd have seen it if it was there before, wouldn't we?" she remarked. "But anyway, we all got in the car and drove to Santa Cruz. We parked and went down to the beach. After we set up Abigail wanted to see the Boardwalk, so she went off while we lounged. All day we played around in the water and on the sand. About quarter to four I suggested we pack up and go to The Grill for an early dinner. That way we could get out ahead of the crowd. Larry and Ethan picked up our things and headed back to the car. Abby and I walked to the Boardwalk to wait for them.

The next thing I heard was an explosion from the direction of the parking lot. We waited to see what was going on. A few minutes later someone said that a blue Ford station wagon had blown up and someone was hurt. We began running toward the parking lot. As we got closer we could see the signs of the explosion, lots of dust, but no flames or smoke. We couldn't get through the crowd. There were police and beach security people around the car. I could see that it was ours. I started screaming. Abby too. Ethan heard us and came through the crowd. He looked dazed and rather upset, but not bleeding anywhere I could see.

"When he got to us he hugged us and said, Don't go any farther. There's been an explosion and Larry was hit. He's dead.

"I didn't faint, but slowly sat down on the ground. Abby did too. She was terrified and started crying. One of the policemen pushed through the crowd. He said, "Ma'am, you don't want to go over there," motioning in the direction of the car. "We'll take you home."

On the way back to Saratoga the policeman asked me a few questions, but since then no one has come to talk to me."

"I'm very sorry that you've been put through this. How is Abby taking it?"

"She's too upset to go to school. She's gone to her best friend's house down the street this morning. Do you need to talk to her?"

"We'll probably want to see her, but for now there's no need to upset her more. If we find a need to talk to her I'll call you."

"By the way, her name is Abigail Evans, not Winslow. We kept her father's name when I married Larry."

"I understand," Grace said. "We'll be going now. We'll probably want to talk to you later."

As they went down the stone walk to the car, Mike said, "She's certainly a strong woman, isn't she? You've been through this. The feelings must be horrible."

Grace simply nodded.

Ethan Winesoff is a civilian engineer working for the NRO (National Reconnaissance Office) in the Blue Cube. They meet at 0900 on at the headquarters building located at the end of the long parade field. It's northwest of the giant dirigible hangar that is Moffett's trademark.

"Good morning. I'm E—Ethan W—Winesoff', he said with a slight stutter." He's early thirties, five foot seven, one hundred eighty, with already thinning black hair and glasses.

"Good morning, Ethan. Make yourself comfortable. This is Special Agent Liu. I'm Commander Holmes. We want to hear from you what happened last Saturday in Santa Cruz. I understand that you're a friend of the Winslows and were with them at the beach."

"T—that's correct, sir. I work, worked, in the same section as Commander Winslow. It…it was a terrible thing. I'm having nightmares about it."

"I'm sorry to hear that. It's a terrible thing to happen to anyone, much less a popular fellow like Larry. Let's start at the beginning. When did you arrive at the Winslow residence?"

"It w—was five minutes to nine. I make an effort to be punctual."

"After I said hello and played with Abby for a few minutes, we s—s—s-started organizing the gear for the trip. I had brought a small cooler with my drinks and meds. I have a tendency to stutter in certain occasions such as this when I'm nervous. I always carry a relaxant that calms me down so the stuttering goes away."

"Ethan, there's no need to be nervous. We're not here to trap you or accuse you of anything. We're just trying to get everyone's story of what happened so we can find the people who did this terrible deed."

"I-I-I-I understand, sir."

"What next?"

"We left for Santa Cruz at 0945 and arrived at 1030. We were at the beach all day. At 1535 Eve said we should pack up and go to The Grill for a quick dinner to beat the crowd back over the hill. There are a lot of people who come from Silicon Valley on weekends, so the drive over the mountain can be very slow. Larry and I picked up the gear and went toward the car. He was about ten feet in front of me when all of a sudden there was a big explosion that knocked me down. My glasses fell on the sand. When I put them back on I saw Larry's head lying in the sand about five feet from me. It was h-h-horrible. That's the n-n-n-nightmare I keep having over and over - his h-h-h-head near my feet and his bloody f-f-f-face staring at me."

"Would you like some water or coffee? Take your time."

Ethan leans forward, head down, shaking and crying. His back is heaving and he's sobbing. It's clear he can't go on.

Grace says, "Ethan, let's stop for now. We can get together later and continue."

"T-t-t-thank you, ma'am. I think I b-b-b-better go home for a while. Will you tell Commander Taylor that I w-w-will be in later today?"

"Of course. Take care of yourself. Can we talk Monday at 0900, here again?"

"Yes, ma'am. I'll be here. Sorry for—"

"Don't worry about it, Ethan. We'll see you on Monday. Have a relaxing weekend. You're not in trouble."

Mike calls Gallacher to learn if the lab has come up with anything.

"They're having a problem. The results don't make sense. There are traces of some substance that is not an explosive. They're continuing to run more tests. I'll let you know when they have something."

"Okay. But on the gambling suspicion, have you turned up anything yet?"

"Since Winslow lived in Santa Clara County, we've asked the sheriff's office and the police to look into the gambling allegations. They're checking their sources to learn the word on the street. If I don't hear soon, I'll check if they have anything. One thing they will certainly do is get his home phone records to see if there are repeated calls to a gambling connection. You're probably doing that on his phone at the base, right?"

"It's part of our investigation here. We want to learn what he was doing both on and off the job. We've started talking to people who worked with him at the Cube. I'll let you know if we find anything unusual." Mike hangs up and they start making notes on next steps. The rest of the day is spent running possible scenarios and developing a work plan.

Thursday morning, they call Jeff again to pick his brain on the Blue Cube, someone who worked with Larry and anything else that seems relevant.

"Well, it is very top secret work related to satellite tracking. I can't go into it very far, as the work is on a "need to know" basis. I can tell you that the people there are very smart and dedicated to their mission."

"Tell me about Ethan Winesoff."

"He's a very bright chemical engineer. I think he has a Ph.D."

"What does he work on?"

"Among other things he tracks navigation and propulsion. His job is to work with the team that keeps our satellites in the right orbit and the right attitude."

"Do you know if he has a gambling tendency?"

"Not that I know of. He's been here about four years and is highly thought of. He does tend to get nervous under stress and stutters sometimes."

"Yes, we've seen that. I'd like to see his personnel file."

The file shows he's a twin. His brother Aaron's background check shows he works for a venture capital firm in Palo Alto. The brothers share an apartment in that nearby city, home to Stanford University. They grew up in Woodside, a wealthy community in the foothills a few miles northwest of Palo Alto. Both attended Stanford. Aaron has an MBA in finance and Ethan a Ph.D. in chemistry. They're members of Mensa Society, the high-IQ organization that requires members to score in the top two percent of standard intelligence tests. They agree they need to meet Aaron.

Monday, Ethan arrives exactly at 0900. "Ethan, as part of the investigation we're looking at personnel files. You have a twin brother Aaron?"

"Yes, he's the smart one. He works for a VC in Palo Alto. He's doing very well. You don't need to talk to him do you?"

"I think it would be a good idea eventually," Grace says. "You two are obviously very close and you might have said something to him about Larry or Eve that would be interesting. But right now, let's go back to Saturday to the point just after the explosion. I understand you have a Ph.D. in chemistry. Do you have any ideas about the explosive that was used? Have you been back to see the car or the scene?"

"I have been back. The police asked me to come and answer the same question you have. I didn't see anything unusual, except there weren't clear traces of an explosive that I could see. The explosion wasn't that loud for the power that it gave off. Whoever did it must be pretty smart not to leave trace elements."

"Well, if it wasn't normal, what do you think it might have been?"

"I don't know, but those mob people are pretty experienced at getting rid of people. They must know a lot about car bombs."

"So you think that it was a gambling related hit?"

"I'd bet on it, if I were a gambling man, w-w-which I'm not."

"Tell me, what did you do Saturday after the police brought you home?"

"They dropped me at Eve's because my car was there. I stayed with Eve and Abby for about five hours. We talked and cried and talked some more. Finally, at a quarter to ten Eve said they needed to go to bed and try to get some sleep. I volunteered to stay with them if they needed me. Abby thought it was a good idea, she was really shaken. But Eve said they would be all right, so I went home, showered and went to bed. I didn't sleep much that night or any night since."

"Was Aaron home when you got back?"

"He came in late from a date. He's the lady's man. I'm the book worm. I was still awake when he came in, so I told him what happened. We talked for several hours until I couldn't keep my eyes open. I went to bed at 0320."

"I think we should talk to him. Can you have him call me and we can set up a date?"

"S-s-sure. What's your number?"

Mike gives him their office number and sends him off to work. He leaves looking rather nervous, but there's no reason to suspect him.

Tuesday, just after lunch Aaron calls and says he has to go out of town with a client on a road show this week. They set up an appointment at his apartment for Wednesday of next week at 1800. Grace especially wants to see how he and Ethan live.

Wednesday night they drive the few miles to Palo Alto and find their modern luxury apartment building. Obviously they can afford the best. Aaron answers the door. For a moment he's taken aback by Grace. He knew she was coming, but her beauty always knocks men back. As he recovers he sweeps them in as if they were old friends. He's certainly not like his brother.

"Commander, ma'am, please come in. I've been looking forward to meeting you. Ethan has been talking about your investigation and his conversations with you. Do you think Ethan is the bomber?"

"Whoa. That's pretty fast," Mike says. We have no idea who the culprit is at this time."

"Forgive me folks, would you like a drink?'

"Do you have scotch?"

"Sure, how about on the rocks with a water back? What would you like Grace?"

"I think some fruit juice would be nice. Do you have grape?"

"I believe we have some white grape juice."

"That would be splendid, thank you."

"Commander, what's your preferred brand of scotch?"

"Macallans, if you have it."

"Aha yes, a discerning drinker. I like that. Of course we have Mr. Macallan farms—Elchies 21 year old. Do you think this is some sleazy roadhouse?" he laughs.

"This is quite a nice building and location," Grace says when Aaron returns with the drinks. "How long have you and Ethan lived here?"

"It's been over three years. When Ethan was hired at Moffett I decided that it was time for the boys to be on their own. Now I think it's time to look for something a bit more permanent. Maybe a house. Neither of us seems to be near a serious relationship, so we could be together for a couple more years at least."

"Ethan is pretty quiet. Does he have a girlfriend?"

"My god no. You might have sensed that we're not like two peas that came out of the same pod. I have a Porsche. Ethan has a Buick sedan. I collect girlfriends, he collects incunabula. That's where he is tonight, at his book club meeting."

"What are incunabula?"

"Forgive me for being a snob. Incunabula are books or ephemera, pamphlets, broadsheets, et cetera printed before 1500, although that is a loosely agreed upon date. That's only sixty years after Gutenberg came along. Some bibliophiles accept 1540, the centenary of the printing press as an end date. Ethan is an authentic book worm. He has a start on a pretty decent collection already. His nose is almost totally into the topic. I don't think he's ever been close to a naked woman, excuse me, Grace."

"No girlfriends or steadies?"

"No, but he does seem to have a crush on Eve Winslow, which is absurd. She's almost ten years older than him, and she'd eat him alive. She's small, but one tough cookie."

"We've only met her once, briefly. What makes you say that?"

"I've only been around her a couple times myself, but she runs that household like a drill sergeant. She strikes me as a bit of a narcissist."

"How's that?"

"Everything is about her. I think she came from backcountry stock and is trying to crack into society. Her clothes, her house, her furnishings, her car are all top of the line, although not always, in my opinion, very chic. It's clear that Larry doesn't, didn't, make enough money to support her dreams."

"She told us that when her previous husband died she inherited a lot of money. That's how she can afford her lifestyle."

"Fine, ennaways, as my grandma used to say, she and Ethan are not an item, except maybe in his mind."

"Ethan told me the night of the murder you two talked for several hours."

"That's right. I came in from a late date with a stewardess and he was still up. Couldn't sleep. I got him to take a drink, he seldom drinks you know, and let him vent about the bomb mostly. He told me about Larry's head being blown off and almost landing in his lap. That image is haunting him still. He kept going over and over it."

"Did he talk about it technically?" Mike asks. "Such as what kind of bomb it might have been, any after effects like smoke, burning pieces, smell? I thought his chemical background would intrigue him. What has he said about Mrs. Winslow and her daughter Abby?"

"He didn't talk about the bomb, just the force of the explosion and Larry. He was really shaken up, still is. He's feeling pressured by your repeated questioning. He did spend some time talking about Eve and Abby, asking what will they do now? Will they move back to Nebraska or what? Whenever he mentions them, it's always in the most affectionate terms. That's why I say he has a crush on her. He really likes playing with Abby and teaching her. He'll be devastated if they leave, but I doubt they will."

"Why do you say that?" Grace asks?

"Eve could never fulfill her ambition in Omaha. She needs a stage like the Bay Area and Silicon Valley."

"Have we missed anything that we should have asked you?"

"I think you've asked enough. You have nothing on Ethan and I'm very tired of your gestapo tactics. Your attempts to intimidate Ethan, and now me, are way off base. If you don't back off I'm going to the authorities to put a stop to this harassment. You need to leave right now. I've got to get ready for a date."

Suddenly, Mike's entire persona changes. He leans forward into Aaron. Mike's face turns crimson and hardens into granite. His dark eyes transform into two large black cannons aimed directly at his target. "We'll leave when we are *ready* to leave. If you don't change your attitude you'll be spending the night in jail. That is, if I don't beat the shit out of you first."

Aaron cringes and slides back into the deep recesses of the sofa. He tries to speak, but nothing comes out. "S-s-sorry. No offense. If I think of anything I'll be in touch with you immediately, honest, I will.

Mike doesn't move. His glare is still intense—penetrating. It's thirty seconds before he says, "Don't you dare think of doing anything other than fully cooperating, sonny boy." He nods to Grace. They stand up and leave with Mike never taking his eyes off Aaron.

"It's the mask again. That's really scary, you know."

"It's supposed to be. That punk kid thought he was in control. I needed to bring him back to reality."

Thursday, Craig calls with two interesting bits. Santa Clara County Sheriff's office has found a fellow, apparently a bookie, who has something he is willing to talk about regarding Larry's gambling. The coroner has completed his autopsy and the lab is also finished their search for clues. Both have similar findings. The coroner says that the body has many tiny nylon fragments embedded in the chest, throat and face, the focal area of the blast. He also found microscopic pits in the skin containing what appear to be chunks of corn starch, but he can't be certain. The lab corroborates: nylon microfibers in the trunk along with traces of corn starch.

"What kind of bomb contains nylon and cornstarch?" Grace asks? "Sounds like a homemaker, any little old ladies on the suspect list?"

"I have no idea, sweetheart, but we better get to the bookie before he changes his mind."

Mike calls the number Craig gave him and sets up a meeting for coffee on Friday at a bakery in the Stanford Shopping Center.

Grace recommends that he go alone. "He's more like to open up if I'm not there."

Mike is waiting in front of the small bakery when a sharply dressed small, 40ish fellow walks up to him, "Holmes?"

They order coffees and sit down at a table out on the concourse. "They tell me you have some information about the Winslow case that might be helpful."

"Could be. Larry is—guess I need to say was." There's a slight snicker in his tone. "He was well known around the neighborhood. He'd bet on anything including if the sun would come up tomorrow if you gave him good odds. Rumors around the big boys in Reno and Vegas wouldn't take his action no more. He owes em' and they was puttin' some heat on him. Locally he's worked with a number of boys, including me. Fact is he's into me for over 20 Gs. When I hear that the Bigs have closed him out I figure I better get mine fore something happens to him, ya know? They're soft soft pedalin' it cause he's a navy officer, but I figure it ain't goin' to last forever, no matter how patriotic they are. But, if you think they did it you're wrong buddy. They don't like to lose money, but they also don't like to make news, if you know what I mean. If they were goin' to do somethin' it would be more subtly. Maybe like rig an accident, not blow him up for chrissakes. But some local yokel might not be so cool. Either way, time for me to make a move."

"Go on."

"I stake out his house and see the Mrs. go out one morning. I follow her to the mall here, introduce myself as a friend of her husband. Right quick she tenses up. It's like she knows what's comin and it ain't gonna be good. To make a long one short I lay on the bad news without leanin too heavy on her I let her know I want my 20 Gs. Clearly, she don't want no trouble for Larry. But she says she can't get it all at once, raise questions ya know. She promises three weekly drops. She keeps her word and to date has made two payments. But, I'm still short about six grand. Given recent event, I figure I'll just have to eat it. I don't want no one thinkin I'm involved in what happened in Santa Cruz. That's why I told the dicks I had some info. I want to be straight from the gitgo with you guys."

After some small talk about "the business" on the Peninsula, Mike thanks him.

When he returns Grace says, "I have a feeling that the corn starch thing is at the heart of all this. I don't know why or how, but I'm feeling somehow this has to be the hook. Cixi agrees and says to keep asking questions. Anything as weird as this has got to be a pointer. We better talk to Craig to learn if he has anything more on it."

Grace makes the call and puts on the speaker phone. "Craig, can you tell us any more about this corn starch thing. It's very strange. How can it fit in?"

"Damned if I know. The lab just says there is only a tiny dark burn spot that could have been produced by a common explosive. Not enough to generate that mess. But Larry, the car trunk, and the area around the car all turn up corn starch. Corn starch is not an explosive no matter how you treat it."

"Still, it must have been involved, maybe even accidently. Perhaps there was a box of corn starch in the trunk left over from a shopping trip."

"Could be."

"We've got to go back to the Winslow house to talk to Abby. It will give us a chance to check that out."

Grace calls Eve and tells her some new developments have occurred and they need to ask her a couple more questions and have a short talk with Abby. She mentions that they have a fluffy white cat that Abby might like to play with. Eve invites them for dinner the following Wednesday at 6 p.m. and tells Grace to bring the cat along.

As they drive through Saratoga, Grace remarks on what a beautiful wooded area it is. Cixi is very attentive, her nose almost stuck to the car window. Many of the houses were built forty years ago and recently remodeled. But the original rustic charm with large redwoods, spruces and eucalyptus is still pervasive. It's quiet and the aroma of the trees fills the air. They turn into Eve's circular driveway and walk up the flagstone path. Abby opens the beautiful redwood door. She's about five feet tall with long straight black hair and dark eyes like her mother. "Hi, I'm Abby. Oh, what a beautiful cat. Please come in."

"Abby, this is Mike, I'm Grace and this is Cixi."

"Wow, you're pretty", she says to Grace.

"Thank you, honey. You're beautiful yourself," Grace hands her the flowers they brought.

"Oh, pink roses, my favorite! Come in. Mom's in the kitchen with Maria. They're making dinner."

Eve comes out and smiles. "Grace, Michael, nice to see you again. Please come into the living room and have a seat. Oh my, your cat is gorgeous." Cixi seems to acknowledge the compliment by looking Eve up and down. It isn't clear if the cat approves or not just yet. "I've prepared margaritas if you would like one."

"That would be splendid," Grace replies, looking around the paneled living room. This is extraordinary. I love this room. "Everything about it is wonderful; the floor, fireplace, ceiling beams. What a gorgeous place, so warm and comfortable."

"Thank you. We love it too."

"The beams and paneling are more than fifty years old. The wood is from the heart of the tree. So sad that the old growth trees have been cut down. Abby, why don't you show Commander Holmes and the kitty the back yard with the beautiful oak tree and your garden?"

Abby nods and leads the way through the sunken family room and out to a gently sloping backyard. "I have a garden on the far end of the lot. Would you like to see it?"

"That would be fun. Have you been gardening very long?"

Cixi decides to sit it out on the back patio. An empress does not soil her feet.

"I started when I was ten. Ethan has been helping me with the chemicals and minerals that the plants need. He's a doctor of chemistry, you know."

"Yes, he's very smart. I'll bet you and he get along well. I know he likes you a lot."

"I like him too. He's a little shy, especially when daddy's around. Daddy liked to talk and make jokes all the time, and Ethan is quiet and polite. Mom says you wanted to talk to me about Santa Cruz, is that right?"

"Yes, how upsetting it must have been. Can you talk about it?"

"I'm over the shock. What would you like to know?"

"Can you tell me what happened after Ethan arrived here on Saturday morning?"

"We packed everything in baskets and put it all by the car in the driveway. Then mom told daddy to check the back windows and doors. While he was doing that Ethan packed the car and we left. The traffic was heavy, but we got there in about forty-five minutes. Ethan unpacked the trunk and each of us carried things to the beach."

"Was Ethan the last one to leave?"

"Yes, he had the picnic basket and a little cooler. I carried the little folding chairs. Daddy carried the umbrella and a big basket. Mom carried the small basket and a shoulder bag. We spent the day on the sand and playing at the edge of the water. The water's always so cold that I don't like to go in very far. Neither does mom. About four o'clock mom said, 'Let's go have some fish and chips at the Grill.' That's the name of the restaurant by the pier. 'I want to get out ahead of the traffic'. So daddy and Ethan picked up the gear and headed for the car. Mom and I walked over to the entrance to The Grill to wait for them. You know what happened next."

"It was a terrible thing and we're working to find out who was responsible. I promise you, we'll catch whoever did it. I understand that the police brought you home and Ethan stayed with you for a few hours."

"He was very nervous because he was almost killed too. The car blew up right as he was coming up to it behind daddy. When we got back I went to take a shower while mom and Ethan went into the kitchen to have a drink. When I came out they were hugging each other. When they heard me they stepped back. Daddy was only gone a few hours and already mom was hugging Ethan. I didn't like it. It made me cry."

"I'm sure it was just to comfort each other."

Inside they joined Eve and Grace in the living room. Eve looks at Abby, "Are you okay? You look a little off."

"I'm fine. I'm going to my room. Can the kitty come with me?"

"Certainly. See you at dinner."

"Michael, you said you had something to talk about. Was Abby helpful? Do you have some questions?"

"She's fine. She just repeated what you and Ethan had already said. I have another question that may sound strange. Do you recall, was there a package of nylons or a box or bag of corn starch in the trunk of the car that day?"

"Corn starch? Goodness no. I haven't bought any corn starch in months. And there weren't any nylons in there either. Who wears nylons in the summer? See, my legs are quite tanned. Why do you ask?"

Grace interjected, "It's just that there were nylon fibers and traces of corn starch around the site and in the trunk of the car."

"Well, you've got me on that one. I can't imagine where they came from."

Maria calls them to dinner.

As they're driving back Grace observes, "There's something wrong in that house. Some tension. Didn't you feel it?"

"Yes, some. But remember it's only a month since the accident."

"It's more than that. The house is not set up right."

"What do you mean?"

"The energy flow is all wrong. In China we're concerned with the positioning of things to enhance and not block the flow of positive energy. In a house it's mostly about the placement of objects to divert energy in positive directions. In that house the forces are all wrong. The energy is conflicted. I could feel it as soon as I walked in. The worst place was in the master bedroom. The people living in that space could not be happy. I don't trust that woman. She has very bad *chi*, personal energy. Cixi agrees with me. She didn't like the home at all. I think Eve is at the heart of this whole case."

"Okay, how do you account for the corn starch?"

"I don't know yet. Do you want me to solve the case for you already?" she asks mockingly?

"There's one thing that doesn't smell right. The first time I talked to her Eve told me that Ethan and Larry packed the trunk together. Abby says that her mom told Larry to check the back doors and windows while Ethan packed the trunk. He was the last one to unpack the trunk too. She also says she saw Eve and Ethan hugging the night of the murder. Maybe when we put all this together we'll have something to go with. I think I'll have the D.A.'s office run a check on Eve's background in Nebraska before she married Larry."

Chapter 17

ALL ABOUT EVE

August 1975
Saratoga

Two weeks later the D.A.'s office calls them to look at Eve's background report. This is what they learned:

Eve was born in 1942 and baptized Evelyn Everley in North Platte, Nebraska.

Three years later her father Ernest, bought a dealership for Chevrolets and also one for Harley Davidson motorcycles. There was a brother five years older named Edwin. The family was prominent in North Platte's small social circle.

Having the dealership in two of the most popular vehicles brought prosperity without a great deal of effort. Evelyn's mother died when she was eight years old after a long battle with cancer. From then on she and her father became inseparable. He called her his little wife. Unlike most young girls Eve passed on the typical early social life of a girl, and instead spent nearly all of her spare time at the dealerships near her dad.

When Evelyn was twelve, her father married again. She was not happy with this new arrangement. The new Mrs. Everley felt the relationship between father and daughter was much too close. She tried to turn Evelyn towards normal preteen activities of a young girl. Evelyn wasn't interested. When she was sixteen her father and stepmother were killed in an automobile accident. Their car ran a stop sign on the highway and a semi-trailer hit them broadside. The car erupted in flames from a gas can in the trunk.

There was evidence that the brake pads on the front of the car were excessively worn. It was strange that Ernest would have let his brakes wear out or have a can of flammable gas in the trunk. Nevertheless, it was ruled an accident.

Brother Edwin was a motorcycle racer and Evelyn often went with him to races. A year after their father's death Edwin got engaged, which drove a wedge between the siblings. The fiancée went with Ed and Evelyn to the races. Ed and his fiancée planned a fall wedding in 1958. Late that summer Ed died in a race when the front tire blew and he went over the handlebars. No reason could be found for the tire failure. He had severe brain damage and chest wounds from the handle bar broke some ribs and punctured a lung. After five days in the hospital he died. Evelyn, now 20, inherited the family business. She ran it for one year, sold it, and moved to Omaha.

Since she had inherited an estate of just under two million dollars, Evelyn was able to buy a very nice house in an upscale neighborhood. She was an attractive and determined girl who moved easily into the social life of Omaha.

In a short time she met the son of a prominent meat packing family. After a whirlwind romance they were married, and she became Eve Newell. She legally changed Evelyn to Eve saying she got tired of having to spell it for people. Abigail, was born eight months after they were married. Eve claimed she was premature, but a check of hospital records showed the baby was full term.

The marriage was not a happy one. Eve's string of bad luck continued. In 1964, Eve's husband died during a labor dispute at the packing plant. His car was tampered with and blew up when he started it. It was suspected that an employee or union rep was involved, but no one was ever charged. The case is still open a dozen years later. Larry and Eve met when Larry was stationed briefly at the base in Lincoln, Nebraska. In 1968, they married.

Over dinner, Grace comments, "What a coincidence. Poor Eve has a lot of problems with the men in her life, doesn't she? Dad—brother—first husband, even Larry has a gambling addiction. The question is: When did Eve find out and when did she share that with Ethan? Didn't Aaron say Ethan had a crush on Eve, but that Eve was much stronger than him? Do I have to spell it out for you?"

"Yes, all the evidence is pointing in that direction. But how did he do it, if he did it?"

"Don't worry. I'm here to figure it out for you. Isn't that why you married me?"

"Ah, a problem solver with benefits. I'm very relieved."

Next week they spend hours with Craig going back over the evidence. Based on Abby's description of the trunk packing, it certainly makes Ethan out to be the guilty party. But they still don't know how he did it, if he did. They ask the D.A. to look at Eve's phone record again for June 22. Grace wants to know if she called Ethan or he called her shortly after Larry told her he was being booted out of the navy.

The D.A.'s office said they would check, but apparently the request got lost, or deliberately set aside. No response for a week. Tuesday, the twenty-third Grace takes a call from Detective Lopez who's assigned the case at the D.A. He wants to know what she has so far. She's thinking, *They want me to do all the digging and then they come in to grab the gold at the last minute.* "It's going very slowly. We just want to look at the relationship of Eve and Ethan."

Lopez says, "See if this helps. There was a call the morning of June 22nd from the Winslow residence to the Blue Cube exchange at Moffett. It could be a call to Ethan. The internal records should show where the call was routed."

Grace has Mike call Security regarding the routing of the call. They call back with the news the call went to Ethan's number. Bingo!

"It looks like we may have a conspiracy going on. I bet they have a tape of that call. Because of the extreme security at the Cube they probably record all calls incoming and outgoing."

"Yes, Commander, we tape all calls. What was the call again that you wanted? I can't release the tape, but if you come to my office I'll have it played for you."

The next morning the tape is played for them.

"Hello, Ethan Winesoff here."
"Ethan, I need to talk to you right away. Something terrible has happened. Larry is being forced to resign because of his gambling. This is disgraceful. I need to do something. We need….
"Wait a minute. Calm down. Can you meet me for lunch today, the usual place?"
"Yes, hurry please."
"I'll be there at 11:30."

End of call.

"We've got 'em! We don't know how he made the bomb or what it was, but he did it or arranged for it. It's time to drop the hammer."

Mike calls Jeff. "Jeff, we're sure that Ethan did it. We need to bring him in with someone from Security and put it to him. He's a nervous little man and when I tell him about the phone call I think he'll crack. At first he'll deny it, but as we build the case, including Abby's seeing them hugging, I believe he'll collapse. Give us a couple days to put this together. Then, we'll go see Captain Metzger with you and tell him what we have. If he agrees, we'll bring Ethan in and put it to him."

That night they go over all the evidence. Grace says, "Yes, but the smoking gun, the bomb, is still a mystery. But I suspect Ethan will solve that for you if you set him up properly. His ego will compel him to tell you how smart he is. Remember, he is the weaker twin. I'll bet throughout their lives Aaron has run the parade and Ethan has followed. You know there's a tight relationship between him and Eve. Probably no hanky-panky. She's too strong and controlling, just uses him as needed. He's the one in love, not her. Not much evidence she can love a man. Cixi concurs. Men haven't met her needs —they've disappointed her and she's taken care of them. Larry is just the latest in the series. If the police in Nebraska were a little more diligent they would have seen through her long ago. Perhaps she may have had accomplices there. This time she provided the target and got Ethan to pull the trigger."

Monday, they go with Jeff to Captain Metzger with the evidence and suspicions. He agrees to confront Ethan. Metzger wants this case solved quickly and successfully. It's been two months since Mike and Grace arrived and he's getting impatient. He doesn't know that these things often take many months. Sometimes they're never solved.

Wednesday 1 September, they call Ethan into the same room in HQ where they met before. Jeff and Lieutenant Young from Security have joined Mike and Grace. Ethan's startled to find four people waiting for him.

"Commander, w-w-w-what's this? W-w-why are these m-m-men here? J-J-Jeff, what's happening?

Mike goes right to the point. "Ethan, we have substantial evidence pointing to the fact that you placed the bomb in the trunk of Lieutenant Commander Winslow's car."

Ethan reels back in his chair. "What evidence? I d-d-didn't do anything. I didn't p-p-put a bomb in L-L-L-Larry's trunk."

"We also have evidence that there was a conspiracy between you and Eve Winslow to murder her husband."

Flinching, he almost knocks his chair over. Ethan bobs his head, looks at everyone quickly hoping to find some support. His face is flushed. He closes his eyes, bobs back and forth moaning softly. Finally, he stops and looks at everyone, "Y-You're crazy. You don't have a-a-any evidence that I or Mrs. Winslow were in any way responsible for W-W-Winslow's death. You're just looking for a-a-a scapegoat."

"No, Ethan. We do have very strong evidence." Step by step Mike lays out the story. Unfortunately, it's all circumstantial. Hitting each point hard, Mike moves closer to him, looking for reactions. He deals the ace. "Abby said you packed and unpacked the trunk."

Ethan is stunned. He's mute. After a long pause he whispers, "I don't remember packing the trunk by myself. She's confused. I'm certain Larry helped me and was there when we unpacked it. If there had been a bomb he would have seen it."

Grace says quietly, "Ethan, the bomb was in the cooler you brought from home, wasn't it? He wouldn't have suspected anything when he saw that. Just figured it was your picnic stuff. Isn't that the way it was? He saw it as part of the gear in the trunk. He didn't question it."

"How could I put something that big in a little cooler?"

"We hear your cooler wasn't so small. How big a bomb did you make?"

"I told you I didn't make a b-b-bomb…any bomb."

"How do you explain the phone call from Eve to you on the morning after Larry told her that he was being kicked out of the navy? Didn't she say this was a disgrace she couldn't live with and she needed you to do something right away"

He hesitates, trying to collect his thoughts. "Yes, she called me and she was upset. Of course, any wife would have been. She just needed someone to talk to and I'm a close friend."

"How close are you and Eve, Ethan?" Grace leans forward and presses. "Are you lovers? How long have you and Eve been having an affair? Abby saw you and Eve in a passionate embrace the night of the murder. How do you explain that?"

"Don't talk that way about Mrs. Winslow. We-w-we w-were not loers. She's a fine lady."

"Ethan, did you know that your fine lady has been involved in four deaths? First, her father and step-mother. Then her brother. Then her first husband? It looks like Larry is number five. Maybe you'll be number six."

He looks down, silent. Finally, "I've said enough. I'm going to get a lawyer."

"That's a good idea, son," Jeff says. You're going to need one. By the way, don't try to leave town. We have you under surveillance. While we've been talking, your office and apartment have been searched."

Nothing turned up in his office at the Blue Cube by the end of the day, but they've not heard the results of the search of Ethan's apartment. Grace admits, "I thought he would crack when you told him about Abby saying he packed the trunk. He sounded shaken. Once he hires an attorney it's going to be impossible for him to admit his guilt. What do you think of that, Cixi?"

The cat's been sitting on the sofa next to Grace. At the mention of her name she looks up as if to say, *"It's so easy. I handled situations much more complex than this in my day. Just look into the bomb."*

The next morning the Palo Alto police report shows nothing incriminating in Ethan's apartment. Mike thinks, *It's time to go back to Aaron and dig deeper. He's certain to protect Ethan, but he might give us more background that will be useful.*

Aaron's very upset. "What are you doing searching our apartment? Did you have a search warrant? Those mugs tore the place apart. It's a mess. They didn't find anything, and didn't even apologize when they came up empty. Now what do you want?"

"Aaron, sorry that they made a mess of your place. They had to be thorough. They did have a warrant. We need to talk to you again, tomorrow after work."

"I've got a date tomorrow night."

"Cancel it. Your brother's in trouble. We're pretty sure he planted the bomb that killed Lieutenant Commander Winslow. Make it easy on yourself. Cooperate with us and we'll make it brief. Otherwise we'll have to have you brought to the police station for our talk. I'd rather do it at your place."

"That's absurd—Ethan and a bomb. Don't make me laugh. He's the most nonviolent person in the western hemisphere. Sure. Let's talk. You don't have anything on him."

They plan for Grace to take the lead. Given Aaron's obsession with women, she might break his concentration. He'll want to impress her. He's liable to say something he wouldn't otherwise.

Aaron opens the door and steps back, giving Grace, who's wearing a tightfitting red dress, the full floor to ceiling examination.

Graciously, he welcomes her, "Ms. Liu, please come in and have a seat here. It's the most comfortable chair in the place."

Grace nods and with a quiet, "Thank you," she sits.

He doesn't know how to act. He's so used to turning on the charm and having young women fall all over themselves that he can't figure this one out. "Can I get you anything? A drink, juice, water? How about you, Commander?"

"No thank you. This isn't a social call." He steps back.

"Aaron, I understand you have to protect your brother," Graces starts. "However, if you give us any false statements or misinformation you'll be in trouble yourself. So let's play this straight up, okay?"

"Certainly. What do you want to know?" He's twitching nervously.

"Let's go back over Ethan's activities. What does he do besides work at Moffett, socialize with the Winslows and collect old books? Is he involved in other activities in the community?"

"Not really. He's pretty quiet, rather shy. Other than the Winslows, and the book club, he pretty much sticks to himself."

"How did he feel about Winslow? Were they as good friends as it seems?"

"To tell the truth he didn't like Winslow all that much. Just hung out with them because of Eve and Abby. Winslow was a blowhard who razzed Ethan a lot. He thought he was being funny. But Ethan certainly didn't dislike him enough to kill him."

"Are you sure he wasn't involved in other activities in the area? He doesn't seem like a recluse."

"Oh yeah. He does belong to a kite flying group. I think it's called the Big Kite Club or something pretentious as that. They make these huge kites and fly them up on the summit where the winds are strong enough to lift them."

"How big are these things?"

"I've only see pictures, but some look like they're at least six feet from top to bottom. They're huge."

"What are they made of? Certainly can't be paper. It wouldn't have the strength to hold up in those conditions."

"I don't know for sure, but I think Ethan said they're made of a synthetic."

Without reacting Grace continues to focus on the kites. Once they wrap up that topic Aaron doesn't give them any other leads nor do they need them.

Walking to the car, Grace says, "There you are Sherlock. He's your boy all wrapped up in nylon. Ever hear of a kite being a smoking gun? Do you want anything else from me?"

"A little humility might be welcome, although your imperious smile turns me on. Can we schedule a play date after work?"

In the morning Mike tells Craig about the kites. They'll get samples of the nylon used in the kites. If it matches the bits found on Larry and in the trunk, they should have enough to indict. Mike calls the fellow running the kite club and tells him they need a sample of the nylon. When he asks why Mike warns it's confidential, he's not to mention it to anyone. In two days Mike receives a large piece of nylon by express mail. He divides it and sends samples to the labs in both Santa Cruz and Santa Clara County. He figures its better to be on the safe side.

When the lab results come back Grace calls Ethan for another meeting. She mentions the kites, but he stands firm. He says he has an attorney and has been advised to say nothing. His stutter tells them he realizes they're closing in.

With the case assembled, they inform Metzger and, along with detective Gallacher, they take it to the District Attorney in Santa Cruz, who has jurisdiction for the case. Armed with arrest warrants signed by a local judge they prepare to arrest Ethan and Eve the next morning.

The night before the arrests are to be made Grace calls Eve. "Eve, this is Grace. You probably know that an indictment was handed down in Santa Cruz naming you and Ethan for having taken part in Larry's murder."

"Yes, I am aware of it. My attorney told me this afternoon. It's too preposterous to believe. I can't imagi….."

Grace cuts her off. "I understand. I'm only calling you to give you time to prepare Abby for the news and to have your friend Vivian come to stay with her. The police are planning to have you and Ethan arrested tomorrow morning. Michael and I will be with the arresting officers to ensure that you're treated properly. You're not flight risks, so we expect bail in some amount will be set for each of you. Once that occurs you can arrange for it and come home to await the trial. It will probably be at least three months before the trail can take place."

"You can't do this! Is anyone considering how this will harm Abby? I've got to think how to tell Abby so that she doesn't believe

I was involved, or worse, that I could be going to prison. We don't have any relatives, so I don't know what I'm going to do with my little girl while all this is working its way through the court system."

"I understand, Eve. We'll do whatever we can to support Abby through this. We're aware of Abby's concern and we will be over in the morning to do whatever we can to help."

Wednesday October 29, 0900. Mike and Grace are parked in front of Eve's house to wait for the police. Within fifteen minutes, with two police officers and Eve's attorney, who insisted on being present, they knock on the door. Vivian opens the door looking. "This is shocking. How can anyone believe that Eve was involved?"

They walk past her into the living room. Eve is dressed and ready to go. "Thanks for the heads up, Grace. I told Abby I have to go explain things to the police. I sent her to school so she wouldn't see her mother being arrested. Vivian will pick her up and take her to her house until I return."

At the police station Eve's cool demeanor is shattered by the reality of being finger-printed and photographed. She starts screaming at the booking sergeant, detective Gallacher, the assistant D.A. who's handling the case, and everyone within hearing distance. "I'm outraged. This is preposterous! Absurd! I'll sue all of you for this. Each of you! This will devastate Abby. She's lost her father and now you tell her that her mother was responsible for killing him. I'll see to it you pay for this."

There is a demonic look in her eyes. They glow, protruding as if they will explode from their sockets.

"That goes for you too Michael and your Chinese bitch in heat! You pretended to be my friends when all the time you were setting me up. I'll get you good for this."

Her attorney attempts to quiet her, finally dragging her off in a corner and silencing her.

Ethan arrives with his attorney in the middle of her tirade. He looks beaten.

"Ethan, what did you tell these people? Did you tell them I put you up to this? What did you say? Why do they think I was involved with you in a plan to kill Larry?"

"N-n-n-no," he says quietly. "I d-d-d-didn't say anything. They m-m-m-made it all up themselves. I love you Eve. I wouldn't d-d-d-do a-a-a-anything to hurt you."

Ethan's attorney takes him aside telling him, pointedly, to shut up.

The attorneys both demand a judge be summoned and bail be set for their clients. "You knew this was coming. Do you have a judge ready to hear the evidence and release them on their own recognizance so Mrs. Winslow can get back to her daughter? You know there's no flight risk."

The Santa Cruz Assistant DA replies, "There will be a hearing in a couple of hours. You don't run the system here, so I advise you to cool it. Everything will be handled properly and on a timely basis."

At one o'clock the bail hearing commences. The judge tells the defense attorneys to state their position. As expected they point to the character of both defendants noting, they are not a risk to the community. In Eve's case her attorney makes a strong statement regarding the welfare of her daughter.

On the prosecution side the DA points out that this is a capital crime, but agrees there is little risk. However, he insists the defendants be under house arrest. If they leave they should be arrested and held until their trial.

The judge takes that into consideration and releases the defendants on their own recognizance without posting bail, but requiring they each call the DA's office daily and not leave their home.

Since the crime was committed by residents of Santa Clara County, the District Attorney would like a change of venue. He sees it as a political plum, knowing there's a better chance for conviction here than in very liberal Santa Cruz. But, the Santa Cruz D.A. won't cooperate. He wants to keep the case since it is an unusually high profile case for his jurisdiction—he can build a reputation on it.

While that's being considered Ethan and Eve's attorneys are talking about plea deals. While the evidence is strong that Ethan had the skill and motivation to build and plant the bomb, the conspiracy angle will be difficult to prove beyond a reasonable doubt. Although the defendants cannot be compelled to testify, under protection of the fifth amendment of the Constitution, they are not sympathetic parties. Still, Ethan would probably come across as a pawn of Eve and might have his charge reduced to manslaughter through a plea bargain. If they can keep Eve's past out of the trial, she has a chance for acquittal or at least a lesser charge since she can claim that Ethan over reacted and took it upon himself to make and plant the bomb. The specter of Abby having to live with the stigma of a mother who is a murderer might be enough to get Eve off. The local oddsmakers are calling it even money, pick' em.

Thanksgiving Day, the world comes to a crashing halt. In the middle of the night Ethan drives to Eve's house. He posts a love letter with blue tape that won't mar her beautiful redwood front door. Then he sits down in her front yard and blows himself up.

On Friday, Grace receives a letter from him posted on Tuesday. It says briefly he can't stand to go through the trial, dragging Eve with him. He's certain they would be found guilty. He states Eve could not stand the disgrace of her husband being booted out of the navy. So, under her direction, he acted before Larry could be discharged. Now he feels betrayed. She just used him and really doesn't love him. The letter also contains a description and a diagram of the bomb that he built and used on Larry, and now on himself. It's a prototype of something called an air bag. His letter explains:

You're probably wondering what caused the explosion. It is an air bag or cushion. The concept was patented in 1951 by

John Hentrick, an industrial engineer employed by the navy. His design was based on his experience using compressed air for torpedo launches. The aerospace program has been experimenting with it since the 1960s to protect pilots of space craft. I've read his work and looked at the chemistry and mechanics of it.

An air bag, made of nylon, is ignited when a sensor triggers a very small amount of sodium azide (NaN3). My sensor, prompted by opening the trunk, was rigged after everyone had headed for the beach. It took only a couple minutes to rig it to the trunk lid, so I wasn't missed.

I used a large dose, 200 grams, to insure inflation. The decomposition of NaN3 under high temperature burns extremely rapidly at up to 300 °C, a temperature that produces a large volume of nitrogen gas to inflate the bag. The bag bursts from its storage box at up to 200 mph. Once a standard airbag deploys, deflation begins immediately as gas and dust escape through vent(s) in the nylon fabric. Most of this dust consists of cornstarch used to lubricate the inside of the bag. This is why your labs found traces of it along with nylon microfibers. However, in my system there are no holes in the nylon bag, allowing for deflation. The bag explodes with its full capacity as it strikes the victim, scattering dust throughout the scene. I wanted the full force of the bag to hit the victim. The victim is punched by a surface as hard as a granite block crushing his torso and, in Larry's case, tearing off his head. He never felt it because it is so fast. And he deserved it for the way he treated Eve.

I built this in the Big Kite Club workshop in the middle of Wednesday and Thursday nights after meeting with Eve on Tuesday noon. We planned the trip to the beach to provide the opportunity for dealing with Larry's disgraceful behavior. I didn't have time to test it so I linked two bags together to *increase the odds that it would work. I believe you have to give me credit for designing and building an ingenious solution in just 48 hours. Who is the smart twin now?"*

Chapter 18

BEIJING AT LAST

December 1975
In Transit

December 20 they've finished with the details in the case report and given Captain Metzger a copy. He's grateful that the case is closed, especially that a navy man didn't do it.

Over a celebratory dinner Mike toasts, "Once again the clever tandem has outwitted the miscreants. The world is safe again for at least a fortnight. Hear, hear!"

Grace nods and takes Mike's hand. "Sweetheart, I don't know how I could ever have lived without you. You deserve the best and you'll get it the moment we get home."

In the morning while Grace is outside with Cixi. *Where do you think they'll send us next?* Cixi asks. Grace looks at her furry friend. "Don't worry, we won't leave you behind." Mike calls Captain Samson at ONI to tell him that the report is on its way to him. "Captain, what do you want me to do now?

"Mike, this is probably our last official conversation. I'm being reassigned shortly. You'll be getting a new contact, Captain Lee Coyne. You'll be hearing from him as soon as he takes my place."

"Sir, that's not pleasant news for me. I've truly enjoyed our relationship and your support. I've learned a great deal from you. I hope your next assignment will be rewarding."

"Thank you. I'm still not certain what or where it'll be, likely somewhere in Europe, maybe NATO or SHAPE. I'm too old to go to sea. That being said, I must tell you I've seldom known an officer who has gotten into so many unusual situations as rapidly as you. I know you were hoping to go to China. Well, your wish has come true. In a few days you'll be receiving orders to the US Liaison Office in Beijing. As you know we don't have formal diplomatic relations with the People's Republic of China (PRC) as yet. Given President Nixon's visit and subsequent negotiations, it's highly likely we'll establish an embassy there by the end of the decade. You're to be assistant to the head of the political section. Grace will be hearing from the State Department shortly. She is being assigned as a political consultant, and you can thank me for that. The boss and I convinced State that it would be in the best interests of national security and that she would be a great asset there given her ethnicity and her background with her father. Good luck."

* * *

When Grace returns Mike opens with a downcast tone, "Honey, you'll never guess where I've been assigned next. I don't know if you'll like it, but as you know, when you're in the service you go where you're assigned."

"Tell me. How bad could it be? You're not leaving me behind and heading for some exotic port are you? You know, without me and Cixi to support you, you're of limited value to the navy," she teases.

"No, you're going along if you want to. I don't know if you'll like it though. It may bring back some bad memories."

"It doesn't matter. After escaping from the mainland to Taiwan and then watching Chiang operate there, it couldn't be worse. Wait a second, we're not going to Taiwan, are we?"

"No. But it might be almost as bad for you."

"Okay, Yankee dog. Where are you taking me?"

"How would you feel about the U.S. Liaison Office in Beijing?"

"What? Are you kidding? That's what we wanted. You're going to pay for keeping me guessing. You white guys think that's funny. You'll pay—you can count on it. Just keep looking over your shoulder. Do you suppose that has anything to do with the special delivery package that came while I was outside with Cixi? What do you think it is?"

"Who is it addressed to?"

"Me, but it's from State."

"Go ahead and open it."

"The letter says State is promoting me to Special Agent. They want me back as a political attaché at the USLO in Beijing. What the heck does a political attaché do?"

"I don't know. I'm not even sure what my job is. Captain Samson said we would be hearing from his successor shortly with instructions. My bet is these titles are masks for intelligence jobs, like the UN. In the meantime, we have about ten days to get to Beijing. There should be travel docs in your package. I expect to get mine in a few days. Until then, we have some free time. Let's go to The City and enjoy the Christmas decorations. We can have lunch or dinner with the Watsons."

They grab Cixi, train into San Francisco, and check into the Fairmont again. In the morning they walk Union Square enjoying the city's holiday ornamentations, the giant Christmas tree, and leisurely shopping. The air is crisp and the winter sun is brilliant against an absolutely crystal blue sky. The next day they take the Watsons to lunch at Tadich Grill. Opened in 1849, it's on California Street just east of Sansome. Clearly it's an institution reeking of old time charm and atmosphere. Since Jimmy's family has been in The City for over one hundred years, he's warmly greeted. Jimmy and Mike go for the Oysters Rockefeller—shucked oysters served in the shell, covered with Tadich's signature creamed spinach and four cheeses blend and baked to perfection with a crown tomato. Joanie orders a prawn cocktail and the Dungeness crab cakes. Grace goes for the lighter Crab Louis. A bottle of crisp sauvignon blanc fills everyone's glasses and is a warm toast to a bright future for all.

Joanie and Grace have a great time chattering away. At the end of the lunch it's tearful goodbyes knowing that it will be more than a year before they see each other again.

* * *

3 January 1976, Mike and Grace board a United 747 to Tokyo with a connection to Beijing. They're in business class on the upper deck, which has less than twenty seats. It's very quiet, well above and ahead of engine noise, and also offers great service. Wheels up just before 1300. Dinner service starts with a choice of beverages. Of course Mike would like Macallans but that isn't available. So he settles for a Stoli and tonic. Grace has a glass of wine, which she will barely sip. "You're really a cheap date".

"That's what you think sailor".

Shrimp cocktails are followed by dinner. They both opt for the salmon entree. The dessert offering includes a choice of sweets and/or cheeses and after dinner liqueurs. After a while they settle back and take an extended nap. Nothing to see but a dark blue ocean 30,000 feet below. Eleven hours after takeoff Tokyo's Narita Airport emerges from the mist. A short connection to Beijing and within an hour they drop through a dirty sky and a slight drizzle into the capital of the People's Republic of China. Having crossed the International Date Line, it's still Saturday, 3 January.

After the long trip they're happy to be met by a Mr. Chen from the USLO. China has over one billion residents most of whom seem to be at the Beijing airport, which isn't very large. Total cacophony. Chen talks quietly with one of the immigration officers. They move smoothly through immigration and customs until Cixi's cage arrives. Chen puts his hand in the man's coat pocket and Cixi passes.

Chen is an affable, round, five-six, middle-aged man who identifies himself as a general handy man at the Office. Chattering non-stop, he weaves them through the traffic tsunami. At least a million bicycles, carts and wagons of all descriptions, plus trucks and cars move erratically and noisily through the streets. Mike's relieved he's not negotiating this maelstrom.

They complete their trek through the vibrating maze and arrive at the diplomatic residents' compound on the outskirts of Beijing. Chen explains that Chinese citizens are not able to mingle freely with foreigners, especially diplomats.

The walled enclave houses many villas laid out in irregular patterns along tidy, well-manicured streets. The villas, built over a long period, show different styles. A small army of workers, men and women, overwhelm the streets with brooms, shovels, mowers, rakes and refuse carts. Chen pulls up in front of what will be their home. As they explore the interiors Cixi stalks cautiously, but imperiously, about the house thoroughly inspecting it. When she's completed her circuit she comes back to Grace and rubs against her leg, *It's no palace, but it's acceptable.* Chen says there are housekeepers to maintain the houses and watch children, if necessary.

He helps Mike with the luggage and offers to take them to dinner at a nearby restaurant. This is appreciated. They're tired, hungry and obviously have no idea of where to start. He tells them someone from the Office will come in the morning to give them a briefing on life here and take them to the USLO office in town.

In the middle of the night Mike sits up startled. Someone's shaking him. It's pitch dark out. Grace is pummeling him. "Michael, what's that sound?"

"What sound?"

"Can't you hear it?"

He listens. "Sounds like traffic to me."

"It's only four a.m."

"I guess things start early here."

"Hold onto me. I'm scared."

"This is your country. I'm the one who should be scared."

"Just shut up and hold me."

Cixi climbs on the bed and snuggles against Grace.

Five minutes later they're all back to sleep.

0700 they're awake but exhausted, staring at the ceiling. Their biological clocks are out of sync. "What time is it?" she asks.

"It's about seven here and mid-afternoon yesterday in California."

"Can I go back?"

"You can if you want, but I'll be very lonely here without you."

"Thanks for your concern and empathy."

"Honey, I've been thinking."

"I'll alert the media."

"No one likes a smart aleck, China girl. Maybe since we are now in your native land I should address you with your given name, Chan-juan. In fact, between us I could call you CJ. Would that be all right?"

"If it makes you feel good it's fine with me. Actually, in a way I like us having this private connection. You're pretty clever at times for a white man."

"Well then, *CJ, nǐ hǎo ma?*" (How are you?)

"Just fine, whitey."

At nine the phone rings. A cheery female voice asks, "Is this Commander Holmes?"

"Yes."

"Good morning, Commander. This is Donna Dorman from the Liaison Office. Is everything alright? Did you and Ms. Liu arrive safely and have a good rest?"

"Well, Donna. We're here. That's about all I can say for sure."

"I understand. It was a long trip wasn't it? If you don't mind I'd like to come and help you get settled. You're probably hungry and

I doubt there is any food in your villa. Maybe I can take you to breakfast and then grocery shopping. In case you're wondering, we don't wear uniforms here except for special occasions. How about ten? Would that give you enough time to be ready for your first trip into the Middle Kingdom? The ancient Chinese believed their empire occupied the middle of the earth, surrounded by barbarians. Some still think of Westerners that way. They call them *yang guizi*. That translates as foreign devils.

"So I've heard. I'm married to a Chinese lady. I'll speak with her majesty to confirm ten is suitable. We'll see you then. Thank you."

Grace prepares Mike. "A common breakfast in China is *congee*, a watery porridge. Another is deep fried devil. These are twisted strips of dough that have been fried. People in northern China typically eat steamed buns stuffed with meat or vegetables. They also have tea with breakfast. You'll have a hard time finding a box of Wheaties here, Yankee."

1000, Donna arrives. Cixi greets her with typical restrained dignity. "My goodness. What a gorgeous animal." Cixi stares at her, circles her, seems to nod at Grace, and retires to the easy chair she has claimed for her throne.

Donna takes them to a cafe where they have a choice of Chinese or American breakfast. While they eat she briefs them on local customs and answers questions. Next, they go to a grocery store that carries western style groceries.

"Your groceries will be delivered to your villa today," Donna explains. Since it's Sunday the office is closed. You have a day to relax and catch up with jet lag. I'll be back on Monday morning to take you to the office."

Later, they walk around the compound with Cixi. The cat draws a crowd of workers who prattle animatedly about this white empress. Cixi moves with calm dignity among her subjects. Mid-afternoon, as promised, the groceries arrive.

Monday Cixi seems content to relax on her throne when Donna arrives to drive them to the office. She turns them over to Cristina Ming, the office manager. She's five foot two, thirtyish, with her shiny black hair styled rather than pulled back in a simple bun. Ming is unusually well dressed for a Chinese working woman—no pajama outfit for her. It's clear that her suit is custom fitted. She greets them with open arms. "Welcome to China Ms. Liu. Have you been here before?" she asks in Chinese.

"I was born in Henan province."

"I beg your pardon. I had little personal knowledge of you or your husband, the Commander." She doesn't test Mike because he greeted her in English. He'll let her be surprised later. Cristina, in charge of the admin staff, is prim and seemingly very efficient. Her Chinese given name is Kew, which means beautiful or lovable, depending on the Chinese character used. "Let me show you your offices."

Cristina gives basic information on the LO layout, introduces staff members, and asks if they have any questions. She shows them their side-by-side offices and leaves with a sincere, "If you need anything at all, questions, help or services here or outside, just let me know."

The offices are 12 x 12 spaces with windows looking out onto a sea of signs and laundry hanging in the smoggy air from lines between buildings in the distance. "*The Great Wall it aint,*" Mike observes. They spend the rest of the day getting acquainted with the staff. The Americans are anxious for the latest California news. Some have heard about the Moffett Field murder case, and the story is told more than once. At the end of the day Mr. Chen gives them a ride to their villa.

"Someone will collect you at nine tomorrow, if that's satisfactory. We'll work out daily transport soon."

They find Cixi napping on her throne waiting for them. They drop down and just look at each other. They're not quite grounded yet. Cixi climbs on the sofa next to Grace. She looks Grace in the eyes, and purrs. *"All is well,"* she's saying, in Chinese of course. *"I'm home."*

"Sweetheart, are you okay?" Mike asks. Happy that we're here?"

"I'm fine. Still a bit tired, of course. Cixi and I are happy we're back in China, but it does bring a flood of mixed memories, mostly of my father and mother. It's going to take time to get back into the rhythm of the country and to people on the street speaking a language I was born into. All in all, I'm looking forward to getting back to my roots. When we were here in the 40's fighting the Japanese and the communists, it was very difficult. I was so young I don't remember much. We hated the Japanese, but not necessarily the communists. They were just a different political party that we couldn't reconcile with. In the States it would be like your Civil War."

"I can believe it was a difficult and confusing time. Now we know what Mao had in mind as he tried to unify this huge polyglot into a country. We have to give him credit for pulling it off, even if we don't like the result. Tomorrow we'll have a formal meeting with the director and senior staff, get our first briefing and learn why we're here. What I'm going to miss the most is my friend Mr. Macallan. I'll have to ration the two bottles I brought with me."

"Let's see what we can put together for our first dinner in the Middle Kingdom. Then I'll be ready for bed."

"Me too."

* * *

0900, Chen shows up smiling.

The day is filled with meetings, starting with Hugh Evans, the mission director, at 1000. Then they'll bounce among the various functional heads. At 0950 they walk up to Hugh's office. His secretary, Claire Morgan, is dressed very neatly and professionally in a black, fashionable, high quality suit. She smiles, welcoming them warmly. She's apparently Chinese-American and from the sound of her accent one would say she's from Virginia. She could be Grace's sister. Similar height, figure and smile. They bond instantly. Her Chinese language is excellent. Mike thinks, *Her Chinese is better than mine.* Westerners can't be totally fluent in Chinese or Japanese, just as they can't be in English. Slang and regional variations make languages difficult for foreigners everywhere. No matter how long you're in a foreign country you will never be as fluent as the natives. At 1000 Hugh's door opens and he comes out.

"Welcome to the Middle Kingdom", he says in Chinese.

Already a test of how well Mike does with it. Mike offers the traditional formal first time greeting, *"Nǐ hǎo, wǒ shi jiao Michael. Wǒ xìng Holmes. jiào Michael Holmes."* (Hello, My name is Michael, my family name is Holmes. I'm Michael Holmes.). Two can play this game.

Hugh gives Mike a smile and a slight bow, touché. "Come in." His office furniture is simple, yet modern. The large room is tastefully decorated with the usual photographs and flags of diplomatic offices. "We're so pleased to have the two of you join us. Michael, you've developed quite a dossier in the last few years. And Grace, your work at the UN has not gone unnoticed either. I've heard about your escapade with Ling in Hawaii. Clearly you're a formidable team, and I'm very happy to have you here."

This fellow is smooth. You have to be to succeed in a Foreign Service job at this level. "Mr. Evans, we're very pleased to be here. For Grace it is a special opportunity."

Grace smiles, "Mr. Evans, I'm truly looking forward to this assignment. You must realize how exciting it is for me to be back in China after more than twenty-five years."

He leans back in his chair and smiles broadly exposing a line of perfect white teeth. Evans is medium build, fiftyish, fit, with a full head of black hair. He's hung his coat on the hall tree to the right of his desk and his blue oxford dress shirt reveals a bit of muscle across the shoulders and arms. Mike's bet is he works out regularly. The smile is genuine, his manner welcoming and relaxing. "Please, both of you. It's just Hugh. We're informal among staff here. For the American staff it can be a stressful duty at times and we need to support each other. Before we get into the details, let me share with you the four "I"s on which we operate.

"The first is Integrity. There is absolutely no excuse for breaking this value. We're in a very sensitive situation and we need to rely on each other one hundred percent. A break in integrity brings immediate dismissal without any recourse. Second is Intelligence. It's simple. Just use your head. Think before you act. Next is Imagination. There are few boundaries to what we can and must do here. Look for better ways to serve our country and deal with the Chinese as well as other foreign service people. Finally, Intensity means give everything you've got to offer. Go beyond the rules in serving the people here, inside and outside the staff. That's my little lecture that everyone receives and that we try to constantly reinforce. My goal is to make this assignment the most effective, rewarding, and enjoyable time it can be for everyone on the staff."

Grace comments, "Those are great rules to live by generally."

"I'll spend the next hour or so giving you my version of China from a strategic level. The functional leaders you'll be with the rest of today look at it from their areas of responsibilities. To me China is the most fascinating country in the world. Even more interesting than Russia, which is saying a lot. Imagine trying to run a country of over one billion people. There are, I think, nearly 20 ethnicities, each with its own language and several dialects. To the best of my knowledge there are something like 290 living languages in China. Until the last couple years many groups have had little contact outside of their geographic area. Tucked into mountainous regions it's probably true that hundreds of thousands, or maybe millions, of people know nothing of the world outside their homeland, or maybe even their province. I have to give Mao tremendous credit for having pulled all this together—at least to the standpoint of making it governable. Though it helps to have complete political and military power to enforce his strategies.

From what we can see and hear Chairman Mao is quite ill. He's seldom seen in public. There has been a great struggle going on to succeed him. The maneuvering actually started almost a year ago. Mao is suffering from Parkinson's disease and along the way we think he may have also had a stroke. He had been a tall vigorous man in his youth, but lately he's been a recluse, and it's clear he won't be around for very long.

Premier Zhou Enlai has been the most influential leader along with Mao. Unfortunately, he too has been quite ill of late. He worked out Nixon's visit and played a major visible role in it while Mao actually was very limited, only meeting Nixon twice. Zhou introduced the idea of modernization to China, but Mao was never a fan. He's has never been out of the country and doesn't realize how far behind China is in industrialization. The Great Leap Forward and the Cultural Revolution generated a good deal of pain and animosity in the countryside, and economic conditions have deteriorated for many people.

"On the other side is Mao's wife, Jiang Qing, who leads the famous Gang of Four. She sees herself as the natural successor to her husband. That's never going to happen because she's used her position to hurt too many people. In fact, in March of 64' Mao kicked her out of his house claiming she was not an apt pupil of communism. Hua Guofeng seems to have Mao's ear and, but for Zhou, would be seen by many supporters as the next premier. Throughout the past ten years Deng Xiaoping has been bouncing up and down Mao's support ladder. Twice he's been demoted, banished, and then reinstated. All in all it's a great opera leading toward a new China, but still not very clear how it will play out."

"That's some story. So why are we here? What is our job?"

"America needs intelligence on China now more than ever because of what I just described. China is turning the corner and may soon become a great economic and military power. Your job is to gather as much useful intelligence as possible, and at the highest levels possible. Find people in key positions, cultivate them, and where possible, recruit them. It shouldn't be difficult to find the discontented. There have been and still are many factions who are not happy. I look at it as a giant roller derby, everyone going around and around, elbowing and butting each other for position. Since Zhou is ill, succession as well as near-term direction is up in the air. If Zhou survives Mao and opens China to western entities, there will be many opportunities to invest and prosper. If you can get into that stream you'll be very popular. The word gets around fast in this country. You'll find people coming at you to make friends and share information, in return for some favors. The key is we need high-level assets who are close to the seats of power and centers of information."

Mike looks at Grace and sees that she is thinking just like he is. Their long-term business model just got a boost.

"Thank you, Hugh," Grace says. "Your insights will be very helpful as we make our way through the new China."

Mike echoes her. "Hugh, this is exciting. We'll make the most of the opportunity."

"One more thing, folks. There is a tentative plan underway to have a multinational trade and technology conference either late this year or more likely early next year. It'll be in Singapore and last about six months. It won't be your standard set-up-booths-and-listen-to-speeches. I understand the concept will be more like a long-term world trade center with attendees coming and going looking seriously for import and export opportunities. Initially, the attending countries will range from Korea on the north to Australia on the south and probably India on the west. All in all, initially there should be about

14 or 15 countries participating. I expect that western countries like us, the Europeans, and South Americans will be invited also. That will add probably another ten to the list. Either way it's going to be a very big deal, especially coming as it will in the midst of the changes within China. You two are going to be there whether or not the US is an official attendee. That milieu will be the ultimate intell gold mine."

For the rest of the day they're briefed by the department heads. They seem to be an able group overall, with some sharper than others. Though it's a high stress place to work they appear to be handling it well. China is not exactly America's best friend. It's been almost four years since Kissinger and Nixon opened the door and progress toward normalcy is naturally slow. The Chinese are trying to find themselves as they navigate through shifting leadership and uncertain strategies. They're still very sensitive to western domination, given their early 1900s humiliation at the hands of the Europeans. There is a level of tension in the atmosphere. Everyone has to move with sensitivity in practically everything they do.

Hugh had suggested they take a few days and tour Beijing with Mr. Chen to acclimate and themselves as well as update their knowledge about everything from daily living to northern China geography.

While touring on Thursday January 8, there is suddenly great tension across the city and hurriedly prepared notices on newsstands and walls. Zhou Enlai has died!

They drive as quickly as possible through the crowded streets back to the office. Hugh's secretary runs up to them, "Did you hear about Premier Zhou? Mr. Evans wants to see you right away."

Hugh is on the telephone. He motions them to sit down. From the tone of the conversation and the discussion it's clear he is talking to someone in D.C.

After twenty minutes he hangs up and sits back, exhaling. "You heard I'm sure, about Zhou. That really throws a monkey wrench in the works. For the foreseeable future the political situation will be like a fire drill in an insane asylum. You've come at one of the most momentous times in the history of China, perhaps the world.

"Everything is question and speculation. The boys in D.C. are beside themselves. We're at the epicenter and they're looking for all the intelligence we can possibly provide. Even that won't satisfy them, I'm certain. No one knows who is going to come out on top of this mess.

Our notions of the old China are now totally obsolete. Great promise and great danger lurking everywhere. It'll take a lot of intell to understand what's happening behind the scenes, maybe not even then. I'll be spending most of my time with people from the other country's embassies. I bet Moscow is a beehive right now. With their long China border it wouldn't surprise me if they try some military probes to see what reactions they get. Use this confusion to make as much contact as possible. Everyone will want to talk. There won't be much valid data for a couple months but just get out there and meet as many people as you can across the whole spectrum."

Chapter 20

LET'S TALK

February 1976
Beijing

Taking Hugh's directions they start calling and making appointments with as many people as possible. Everyone wants to meet and talk with them, especially to get their views and perspective from the US side. Over the next sixty days they're out constantly at lunches, dinners, cocktail parties, wherever knowledgeable people are gathering. All news is speculation, but making contacts now will pay off. In mid-March Grace suggests it's time to contact Jiang Gao. "He must be terribly busy, but he'll be very interested to speak with us. We're a conduit to the US for him just like he is for us. We can ask Helen in the library to look him up."

"I agree. But we have to be careful in contacting him. I suggest we have Chen use a back channel. He's low profile and he knows his way around. He can ask Jiang to get in touch with us.

Ten days later Grace gets a call from Jiang. "I'm very happy to know you are here." We should plan to get together. Would you like to have dinner with me at one of my favorite restaurants?"

"Gao, it's very good to hear your voice. Of course. We'd love to see you. Give me a date, time, and place and we'll be there. One question, should we be concerned about surveillance?"

"Probably, but we'll be discreet. It isn't a problem now. The MSS is in high confusion, probably worse than most of us in Beijing. They probably know about you. But even if they do you're nowhere near the top of their agenda at this moment."

Wednesday evening, they meet Jiang at the Heavenly Garden, *Tian An Hau Yuan*. The sign outside says, Lost Heaven, which confuses taxi drivers. It's located in a small, quiet square amidst luxury retailers, trees, sidewalk cafes, flowers. Like they're trying to emulate Paris. The restaurant is large, but dim lighting evokes an ancient Asian atmosphere. It specializes in Yunnan Province cuisine, so if you're tired of Peking Duck, this is the place to go. When they arrive a few minutes late, due to a couple passes in the taxi, Jiang is there to greet them.

"What great pleasure it is to see you again, my friends."

"Gao, you're looking great," Grace replies.

Mike shakes his hand warmly and with a big smile. This young man might be a great help. Besides that, he's a nice, seemingly uncomplicated fellow. He appears to be more mature and self-assured now, more relaxed than in New York. Probably because he's on home ground. His smile is more genuine and his nervousness is almost totally gone. However, he still takes off his glasses and wipes them every few minutes. Old habits are hard to break.

"Gao, tell us what has happened since you returned to China. It's been almost two years hasn't it? Obviously, Mao's health and now Zhou's sudden death have upset the political arena."

"Yes, there has been a great deal of turmoil. You know that Jiang Qing is having problems. It's clear to me that it is only a matter of time until someone becomes our new premier—or at least our leader by whatever title."

"What do you expect will happen then?" Grace asks.

"I don't know who it will be, but I don't think it will be one of the old guard. I have a feeling that Deng Xiaoping might come back into favor. He's a clever politician. Mao likes him but not his views. Deng favors modernization, which Mao opposes. If he does regain power, after Mao is gone he'll push that with great vigor, but also with sensitivity.

"At the Bank we're already thinking about a financing program if modernization comes. It's going to take billions to reorganize agriculture and build out industry. He'll also spend billions upgrading national defense. I'm certain he'll establish science and technology centers to accelerate development. When he's ready, we may go to the IMF (International Monetary Fund) and the World Bank for some initial financial assistance. The first investment probably will be in agriculture. We have to feed our people better before we can expect them to meet the growth challenges ahead. That means land reform and improved crop yields, which will stimulate investments in farm equipment, better farming methods, upgraded fertilizers and pest control chemicals. We'll have to import most of that until our industrial capacity comes on line. Companies such as Tata in India, Komatsu in Japan and Deere and Caterpillar in the US will be prime equipment suppliers."

Mike asks, "When do you anticipate this will begin?"

"Not until Mao is gone.

"Is this general knowledge?"

"Senior executives at the Bank seem convinced that eventually Deng will rise again."

Grace asks, "Do you know people we should talk with to learn what is coming along?"

"I don't have any contacts in the defense area, but I can give you some names and positions in agriculture and industry that might be helpful."

"We would be most grateful. In return we can see to it that you are treated properly." Jiang realizes what's happening here. Inadvertently he began to give them the type of intelligence they're seeking.

He sits back as if he's been poked in the chest. He wipes his glasses with his eyes closed, returning to the conversation more deliberate. "Grace, is this what you were talking about in New York?"

"Yes, it is."

"I will have to give this some thought then, to put you in touch with people who might be sympathetic as well as knowledgeable. I'm not the only person who is upset or concerned with the directions things are going. One of our major concerns is graft. Once the money starts flowing, many people are going to want to siphon off some for their own purposes."

"I'm afraid we can't help you there. But if the contacts you give us are useful, we'll see that you're compensated accordingly."

"How would you do that? I cannot have money deposited in my account. The government will think I'm one of those thieves."

"Of course not. We could set up an account for you in Hong Kong under a fictitious name. It won't be the first such account. We can deposit gold coins to be held in a vault in your account's name."

"That's a good idea. I can do that. First let me think about the contacts I can give you. We can deal with the compensation level if they prove to be productive for you. Now let's eat. The Yunnan style food here is exquisite. I'm confident you will enjoy it."

A waiter appears and explains some of their dishes: *Qiguoji* (steam pot chicken) seems to be a favorite. There is spiced squab, ganba mushrooms, Xuanwei ham and sea cucumber "toads". They pass on the toads, opting for the chicken and mushrooms a side dish of ham with rubing, a mild white cheese.

After dinner Grace and Mike ride home in silence, but the vibrations are almost overwhelming. That was surprisingly easy. Gao is growing up and looking ahead to protect himself, come what may in the uncertain years ahead. When they're dropped off in front of their villa Grace suggests, "Let's go for a walk. I believe the walls of our house have ears."

They circle the neighborhood for half an hour. It helps settle dinner as well as stimulate active imaginations. After digesting a number of scenarios, they've had enough for one night. A cold wind is coming off the mountains. They head back to the villa and a warm bed.

"As they sip their breakfast tea Grace says, "Let's see if we can connect with Ling." Mike's already gone native and switched his morning coffee for tea. "Chen should make the first contact again. He knows his way around and won't arouse any suspicions. Let's bring him in and tell him about Ling."

On arriving at the office they call him only to learn he's on his way to pick up Claire. Apparently, twice a year she takes a long weekend retreat at a Confucian temple west of Beijing. Grace explains, "It's called the Temple of Eternal Light."

She says it in Chinese, which confuses Mike. Translations from Chinese can be tricky.

KIDNAPPED

March 1976
West of Beijing

1245, Grace's phone rings. "Grace, it's Hugh. Chen just called. Claire has been abducted at gunpoint from the temple grounds. I'm calling the Federal Police since she's got diplomatic status. Grab Mike and come to my office immediately."

In two minutes they're with Hugh. "Take whatever you need and get out to the temple pronto. I've instructed Captain Bennett to send two of his marine guards with you. I recommend you dress in fatigues because you don't know what you may run into. Mike, you may have to go into the mountains after her. Requisition small arms to carry with you. I don't care what the Feds might say. We have to do everything we can to get Claire back quickly and safely."

The Temple grounds are almost twenty-five miles west and then north another 10. Beijing is surrounded by Hebei Province, which marks the northern edge of the North China Plain. *Hebei* means north of the Yellow River. The Taihang and Yan mountains create a bowl along the western and northern perimeters of the province. As you rise out of the plains you approach rugged, lightly forested hills and valleys. There isn't much in the area except some small villages and farms. The van driver speeds as fast as the roads and traffic permit, and still it takes nearly three hours to reach the temple grounds. Federal Police are already there. Chen runs up, tears streaming down his cheeks. "I arrived just ten minutes after the men took Claire. If I had been here sooner I could have taken her away before they arrived."

Grace assures Chen that it isn't his fault. If he had been there earlier they might have taken him as well. Someone calls over to the police officer in charge. He comes with a very worried look on his face. This is the beginning of an international incident—he's in way over his head.

"I've gathered all the monks, guests, and workers into a meeting room to explain the situation." The place is packed and hot. They need to talk to people individually to learn what they've seen or heard. Grace, one of the Marines and one of the police officers take people one at a time into a resident villa and grill them. Mike does the same. After an hour they've a clear and rather consistent picture of what happened just before noon.

The kidnappers knew what they were doing. This wasn't a random act of kidnapping. They went directly to Claire, told her to put on a coat and walking shoes. Everyone else was held in the meeting room under armed guard. Then they left with her on a trail northward into the hills, warning the monks not to follow them.

With the Fed officer they work out a pursuit plan. He's notified his superiors of the situation and requests that they send aerial recon ten to fifteen miles up the trail while they approach from this end. Grace will stay as a coordinator and contact with Hugh. Mike will go with the marines, Zach and Ernst, along with the Feds. The marines have M1 carbines and pistols in shoulder holsters, better than carrying a pistol on the hip where it can get caught going through a forest. They're also packing two grenades each just in case. The kidnappers could be part of a much larger group. Mike has a carbine and the standard issue .45 caliber pistol, a lot of stopping power if they get into a fight.

The police had the foresight to bring flashlights and a dog that might be able to follow Claire's scent. It's already 1715 and will be dark shortly at latitude 39.88, two degrees farther north than San Francisco. In March the sun is low on the horizon by 1800. The valleys already in deep shadow. Only the mountain tops have a fading silver crown. The sky is thick with heavy dark clouds that threaten rain or even snow. Mike decides to start, regardless. "We can't give the bad guys another eight hours head start."

Grace gives him a quick hug and kiss, "Be careful." The dog and its handler lead, followed closely by Mike and the Fed officer. Zach and Ernst are on their heels. The kidnappers left nearly five hours ago. Traveling at a thirty or forty minute mile, they could be seven or eight miles up the trail already.

The trail's width varies from four feet to less than two, and it's not well traveled. They're constantly stumbling over rocks and into holes. It's muddy in spots, wet everywhere, icy and very dangerous because they can't see well. Periodically, there are invisible sharp drop-offs. The party plods along a continuously rising trail as it penetrates the rocky, forested mountains. There's a small stream along the left side about twenty feet below. After three hours, they're all flagging and it's quite dark. Mike calls a halt and tells everyone to find what shelter they can. They'll start again at first light. The temperature has dropped steadily. The good news is there is no wind.

The marines have brought rations. Ernst scrambles down to the stream for a couple helmets full of water. Heat tablets from the ration pack heat the water in metal canteen cups. The canteen cups fit into heaters. Dehydrated food and condiments come out of a tan cardboard box about 4 x 2 x 6 inches to make a small but hot, nourishing stew. Beyond that they have a couple candy bars from the pack and several rice balls from the monks. When they finish, Mike wraps himself in his poncho and crawls under a small tree. The cold air and moist ground begin to seep into his arthritic knees. He tries to keep flexing them, but eventually he falls asleep. Whenever he wakes up the joints are getting progressively stiffer and more painful. By morning his legs are nearly solid posts.

At the first glimmer of a frosty light cresting the mountain tops everyone is up, grabbing rice balls, ready to start. Except Mike, who can't walk, his arthritic knees nearly frozen solid. "Zach. I can't walk. Cut me a couple poles about six feet long. Then, cut notches in one end for a grip."

They pull him to his feet while they're slowly stretching and massaging the aching knees. The pain is worse than in Hong Kong. He condemns those bastards to an eternal fiery hell. When he stands or moves, his weight compresses the joints and stresses the tight ligaments. A signal goes screeching to his brain: *Get the hell off me.* He takes a step and topples. Zach and Ernst catch him. He can't flex the knees, no deep knee bends, but they have to get going. They shoulder his pack and he stumbles ahead, very slowly throwing each leg forward from the hip. His boots seem to hit every rock and rut on the trail. Each contact resends the signal. Nevertheless, somewhere ahead in this freezing hell Claire is in trouble.

Mike struggles to keep up. When it begins to snow, the rocky trail becomes extremely slippery, and there's no scent for the dog to follow. They move him and his handler to the rear and the lead is swapped every thirty minutes among Zach, Ernst and the Fed officer. Two hours along they are laboring. The fresh wet snow is making the trail even more treacherous. Everyone is staggering, sliding, tripping, and cursing. It's bloody cold. Mike's knees have loosened up a bit, but the pain signals are constant. Each step is like rubbing sand between the joints. He presses the group to keep moving as fast as possible. As they top a rise in the trail Mike calls a short break. He sends Zach and Ernst to scout ahead. Within fifteen minutes Ernst comes jogging back. "Commander, we found tire tracks just around the bend. They're pretty deep so the snow hasn't covered them yet."

Painfully, Mike follows him back over the rise and around the bend to a flat spot. When he reaches the tire tracks he looks ahead. A mile or so up the valley there's a faint light. This pumps everyone up and they take off with renewed energy. The air is dead still, but as they get closer we can hear sounds. There are definitely people there. They slow the pace, careful not to make noise. The dog is trained not to bark. He won't give away their presence. There's a buzzing in the air from a small recon plane flying over. Immediately the lights in the shack go out and there's silence. The plane makes another pass, then flies off. It's pretty certain it couldn't have seen anything. All it accomplished was making the people more cautious. The dim light in the building comes back on.

The Fed officer and Mike agree to each take a party of six and move ahead. The rest of the group will hold back for ten minutes and then move cautiously forward. They find one small, dilapidated cabin, just planks and a slant roof with no paint anywhere. Small cracks between some of the boards let a glimmer of light escape. It might be an old hunting hut. At 100 yards from the shack they stop and listen. It's about 0700 and dawn's light is finally oozing slowly down the hills into the valley. There's the smell of a fire and something cooking. The odor is obnoxious. The snow has stopped. The air is very still. Mike motions Zach and Ernst to follow him around to the right front while the Fed officer and two of his men go left to see what's on the back and other side of the building. Walkie-talkies help them coordinate movements. They see nothing other than this one scruffy building. Approaching thirty yards there's a loud noise from the shack. They hit the ground and Mike's right knee bangs into a rock. He trades a scream for a low curse. There's talking inside. They hear a woman's voice shouting, but it's not Claire. The woman sounds angry, seems to be giving orders. The men are replying, they can't catch the words yet.

* * *

While Mike and Grace were organizing and leading the rescue team Claire was abducted and being badly treated. Later, she described what had been happening.

"We were in a yoga class when three men burst into the room carrying rifles and pistols. They looked around then went to the monk leading the class. Shoving a rifle barrel in his face they ask, "Where is the American woman?" They couldn't tell because everyone in the room is Chinese. The monk pointed to me. One of the men grabbed me, and shouted, "Yankee bitch, get you coat and shoes on.""

"They dragged me outside. One of the men cut the rope hanging from a temple bell. He made a noose to put around my neck. He dragged me along as he jogged up a trail into the hills. I was terrified.

"The men set a fast pace, jerking the rope if I slowed down. The trail was uneven, rock-strewn, rutted, slippery. Within an hour I was stumbling and falling, out of breath and coughing. The rope cut into my neck. When I fell again they stopped for a few minutes until I got my wind back. Then they yanked me up, kicked me, and started again. This went on all afternoon. If I asked a question they just jerked the rope harder.

"As it started to get dark we came to a small truck parked where the trail flattened and widened into a rutted lane just wide enough to carry the truck. There was a driver in the truck. One of the men got into the passenger seat and pulled me in on top of him. He laughed and said something to the driver as he groped my breasts through my coat. By the time I saw a rough shack, it was nearly dark and the temperature had dropped to freezing. The man threw me out onto the ground, got out, picked me up, and dragged me into the shack. The other men followed. "Just one filthy room with some rough benches around the walls. There was a small fire, but the room was very cold. When I collapsed onto the floor I was kicked in the back and rolled over. I looked up at a thickly built man with an ugly face and long matted black hair. Someone grabbed me from behind and stood me in front of him. Except it wasn't a man. It was a woman about five feet four very heavy, solid. The left side of her face was paralyzed in a perpetual sneer. Her blind left eye stared straight at me, never blinking.

"In Chinese she said, 'Welcome Yankee bitch. Welcome to you homeland, you traitor,' and slapped my face. Something hard in her hand scratched my cheek. I reached up and felt a trickle of blood. 'Put you hand down,' she shouted and slapped me so hard I fell back into the man behind me. He propped me up to face the evil leer in the corner of her mouth and her right eye. The left eye never moved.

"'We have questions to ask you and you better answer them. We fifty kilometers from Beijing, hidden in mountains. Here no one can find you. If you want to live, you answer my questions. If you don't, we make you very uncomfortable before we kill you and throw you body to the vultures.'

She turned and said something about eating. The man shoved me into a corner away from the fireplace. I wouldn't let myself cry although I've never been so terrified in my life.

"The group filled bowls from something at the fireplace, and some type of stew. The smell made me retch and they laughed. One of them said, 'Not hungry?' and kicked the bowl out of my hand. After eating they sat around the fireplace and talked in low tones. I couldn't make out anything they said. In an hour or so they put mattresses on some of the benches.

"The woman lurched over to me and said, 'You better get some sleep. Tomorrow you be very busy answering my questions, or else.' She dropped a filthy blanket on me and walked away dragging her left foot. Despite being frightened beyond imagination I fell asleep.

"A little after dawn, the group began to stir. One of the men built up the fire, but little of the warmth reached me across the room. I told them I desperately needed to urinate. On orders from the woman one of the men pulled me up off the floor and took me outside. I didn't see an outhouse. He motioned me to walk over to some bushes and do it there while he watched.

"Back in the shack another man gave me a piece of some stale bun. 'You like our food now, bitch?' the woman yelled across the room. The men laughed. I kept chewing on the moldy crust. The woman got up and motioned me to come to the middle of the room and stand facing her. 'You assistant to head of American Liaison Office, are you not?'

"I shook my head, 'I'm just a secretary.'

"She slapped me and yelled in my face, 'Don't lie to me. We have comrade working in you office and comrade say you are director's assistant. As assistant you must see all important papers that go through director's office, No? '

"'I only see the administrative papers. I'm not cleared for classified material,' I answered."

"She slapped me so hard I fell backwards into a man behind me. 'You lie. You see all important papers or you cannot work with him. Try again. You see everything important that come to his desk don't you?'

"'No, only the admin papers.' I pulled back as she swung at me again, but the man was so close behind me that her hand hit my nose. A trickle of blood slid down my lip."

"'You don't seem to understand, traitor. I know you see all important matters. So I give you one more chance. You know about all important matters, don't you? You know names of American spies working out of you office, don't you?'

"'I told you I'm not cleared for secret documents. "

"'You must think I stupid, you turncoat. Since you don't want to cooperate I have to help you. Take off you clothes. '

"I hesitated, dumbfounded. *She must be a psychopath,* I thought.

"'You hear me. Take off you clothes. '

"'It's too cold here. I'll freeze.'

"'You won't freeze because I going to keep you warm. Last time, take off you clothes.'

"I refused. She nodded to the man behind me and he and another man pulled off my coat and ripped off my clothes. I was naked in front of those men.

"'You very pretty. My men would like you. You like them?'

"I couldn't breathe. I was so frightened I couldn't answer.

"'No? See if you like them?' She nodded to the man behind me and he reached around and grabbed my breasts.

"'No!' I shouted and tried to pull away from him, he held me tightly against his chest and shoved his hips into me.

"'Now, let me repeat request for the last time. I be specific. It may help you memory. Give me names of Chinese traitors who working for you as spies.'

"I told her I didn't know.

"She paused for a moment staring at me with that blind left eye. 'I not a bad person. I have feelings too. Perhaps you like cigarette while you try to remember names.'

"'I don't smoke.'

"'I do. I think I share my cigarette with you. You might like it when you try it.' She lit a strong smelling cigarette and blew the smoke in my face. She held it in front of my breasts and said, 'You certain you don't want one?' I couldn't believe her threat. 'Oh go ahead.' She pushed the tip into my left breast. I screamed and fell back, but the man wouldn't let me move away. 'I guess that means you don't like pain. Well, I have much more for you if you memory not get better quickly.'

"'I don't even know if we have people spying for us.'

"Her leer hardened. 'Of course you do. That why you have office here, to spy on us.' She pushed the cigarette into my right breast and held it there.

"I can't back away because the man is holding me. I screamed again and then fainted."

* * *

A second scream is certainly Claire. Mike fires his pistol once into the air. Silence inside the shack. one head looks out a window.

"You are surrounded," he shouts in Chinese. Come out with your hands up."

No sound. No reply except, "Michael. It's Claire." A slap and a curse.

"You can't get away. You're surrounded by the Federal Police."

The door opens a crack and a woman's voice shouts, "Go away or I kill her."

"We're not leaving. And you must release her now."

Another scream from Claire and a body crashes onto the floor.

"Once more, I tell you, leave now or bitch die."

"And I tell you, we're not leaving. If you kill her I'll strangle you with my bare hands, then burn you and the shack to the ground. There will be no part of you left to bury. And your soul will live forever in pain."

The door opens wider. Claire's framed in the opening, naked. Someone is holding her by the hair from behind. The woman yells, "Go away. If you no go, I kill traitorous bitch now."

"We're not leaving. You will surrender immediately." To Zach and Ernst Mike whispers, "If you get a clear shot, take it. This woman is insane. She really could kill Claire." He instructs the Fed leaders by the two way radio to quietly surround the shack from his side but hold fire.

The woman leans over Claire's shoulder and swears at me. "You go or I kill now." She pulls Claire aside by her hair and stands in the doorway. Instantly, two shots reverberate against the hills and her head disintegrates. Claire falls back out of sight. Other shouts from inside, "Don't shoot. We come out." In a few seconds a single file of four men step over the woman's body and stumble through the doorway with their hands up. The Feds grab the men.

"Claire, are you OK?" Mike rushes the building with Zach and Ernst close behind. Claire lies naked on the ground sobbing. Ernst tosses Mike her coat and a blanket. He wraps her and holds her until she can stop. The Fed leader comes in.

"Get two helicopters up here ASAP to take Claire to the hospital in Beijing. My men will go along as guards. The other one will take me back to the temple."

Chen can drive Grace and Mike to Beijing. Before they leave the temple he needs to talk to the head monk. It could be they tipped off the madwoman about Claire's presence.

The Fed leader searches the shack. "The helicopters should be here within fifteen minutes. They can land in the meadow to pick up the lady and the marines and then you. The woman leading this is named Cho Bai, a terrorist who believes all foreigners are evil. We've been looking for her in connection with the bombing last year at a wedding reception for the German consul's daughter. Several people were killed and many injured. The authorities will be happy to know she's dead. We'll interrogate the four men, then collect anything that might help us know more about her plans or other people she may have had."

Mike suggests they throw a couple grenades into the shack so he can keep his promise to burn her. But the officer dissuades him saying it would cause him problems with his superiors. Mike relents only because he has done his job well, and Mike knows what it means to have a negative report on your record.

Choppers arrive and fly them out of this frozen hell. The head monk professes no knowledge of Cho Bai. Grace had been talking with him at length all day. Her conclusion is that he is telling the truth.

INSIDE JOB

March 1976
Beijing

Zach and Ernst return to the office from the hospital. The police have put a guard on Claire's room. Mike tells Captain Bennett to post another one of his marines at her room as well. At this point he doesn't trust anyone with her welfare. Mike tells Zach and Ernst, "I'm going to put a letter of commendation in both your files for your work on this mission. You performed at the highest level of the Marine Corps tradition."

They salute, thank him, and leave with smiles.

Mike has conveyed the basic story to Hugh by radio. Back at the Office Grace and Mike shower and change into street clothes. Then, they check in with Hugh to learn what he's heard about Claire.

"She's under sedation. The poor girl had a terrible time up there. Zach and Ernst told me about it. The doctors want her to have complete rest for a couple days before we start bothering her with questions. When she can handle the flight we'll evac her to Japan to the hospital at Camp Zama. From there I expect they'll send her home to Richmond for treatment at a government trauma recovery center."

"When do you think I can see her?" Grace asks.

"I don't know, but I'm in daily touch with the doctor and will let you know when she's ready for visitors. Why don't you two go home? You've had a tough couple days."

They take Hugh's offer and spend the weekend recuperating and talking over what happened. Grace believes Claire was chosen because she would be easy to pick up at the temple. They thought they could break her easier than one of the professional staff. "We need to learn about Cho Bai. When we go back to the office let's get Research to do an in-depth on her history."

Monday Hugh tells them Claire is recovering, but slowly. She'd like to see Grace. "Is there anything I can take her?"

"She has enough flowers from the staff to start an arboretum. She just wants to talk about what happened."

While Grace visits Claire Mike goes to Research. In a couple hours they come up with a newspaper archive about an accident Cho was involved in five years ago. She had a twin sister. Both were accomplished musicians on traditional Chinese instruments. They formed a duet with Cho playing the *guzheng*, a 21 string instrument similar to the Japanese *koto*. Her sister played the *xiao*, a flute. They were on their way to a performance in a car with their parents and their friend when a limousine ran a stop sign. The impact killed Cho'sparents and sister, and gravely injured Cho. The girlfriend received only minor injuries. The limousine was from the German Embassy. The driver had diplomatic immunity and could not be prosecuted.

Cho's family was financially comfortable so she was able to retain the servants and a health care person to support her recovery.

After the accident Cho dropped out of sight and was not heard from again until about a year ago. There was information that implicated her in the bombing at the German wedding reception. She'd been in hiding since then, but had distributed several papers railing against foreigners. The police had not been able to trace the source, but her name on them implicated her. The research group is continuing to dig for more data on her. They didn't know who the girlfriend was that survived the accident.

Grace came back from the hospital with a worried look. "How badly was she hurt?" Mike asks.

"Claire's injuries were more psychological and emotional than physical. It may take a very long time for her to recover from the trauma. Claire did say Cho claimed she had someone on the inside at the office who told her where Claire would be. But she had no clue who that might be. It could be any one of a number of people, for it was common knowledge where Claire was going."

"So, there's a skunk in the woods and we have to find it. Did she say he or she?

"No, just a comrade. I think we should start with Chen. He seems to be everywhere and know everything. I don't believe he's the stool pigeon, but he might have some ideas."

"Good idea. Let's get him in here and pick his brain."

* * *

"Mr. Chen, we need to find out who tipped Cho Bai about Claire being at the temple. We know that Cho hated foreigners. But, why did she go after Claire? Cho told Claire that there is someone on our staff that fingered Claire. We need to uncover the traitor. The only lead we have, and it may be false, is that when Cho was injured in her auto accident there was another girl in the car who was not hurt. She was identified by the newspaper simply as a friend. Can you find out from the newspaper if anyone remembers the story and who the girl might be?"

When Chen agrees and leaves, Mike turns to Grace. "CJ, I'm going to talk to Hugh about putting hidden cameras in the office so we can look for any suspicious behavior."

Over the weekend the cameras are set in place. Every morning they monitor the tapes but don't see anyone doing anything out of the ordinary. It doesn't take Chen long to report he has found someone at one of the newspapers who covered the accident and remembers the friend—Ming Kew. That's the office manager, Cristina.

Grace and Mike discuss a plan to expose Cristina. They need to provoke her into some incriminating action. "CJ, we know that Cristina has always wanted Claire's position but couldn't have it because security regulations require US citizenship to hold that job. Maybe we can convince Hugh to put her in the position temporarily until State sends a replacement. He can keep classified material out of her view."

"Good idea Yankee. Once she's in that position we can set up opportunities for her to do something that she shouldn't. If and when she does we'll have her. Let's go see Hugh."

He agrees to the plan and the next day he calls Cristina into his office to make her the offer. "Cristina, I wonder if you could do me a favor? It's going to take the State Department at least a couple months to find and send a replacement for Claire. You've asked me about the job before and I told you that regulations require a US citizen with a Top Secret clearance to hold that job."

"Yes, I understand, but I think an exception can be made for me. I can do that job very well. Being native Chinese I know things that I can share with you that Claire could not know. It would help you do your job and be more successful."

"Well, that's possibly true. I can't break the regulations, but in this case maybe I can bend the rules a bit. That's what I wanted to discuss with you. I believe that I could put you in the position as my executive assistant until State sends a permanent replacement. That's about all I can do, but I think you would like the work. It would give you a break from office management details for a few months. And you would see things at a higher level that ought to be interesting for you. Would you be willing to take the job under those conditions?"

Cristina looks directly at Hugh for a few seconds and then nods her head. They discuss details on the handover of her job to her assistant. As soon as she can make the change she'll take Hugh's offer.

The changeover goes smoothly. Cristina is happy to have the job even temporarily. Now, they have to watch her actions closely without letting her know she is under surveillance.

Each morning Grace or Mike review the previous 24 hours' tape. Nothing is apparent for the next couple of weeks. Then, one Monday morning Grace is looking at the tape while Mike is studying local news. "Michael, could you come here for a moment?" she says rather casually. "I want you to see something."

When he sits down in her office, she turns the tape recorder on and simply motions him to watch. The tape is time marked 3 April 1976. In a few minutes he sees Cristina get up from her desk with a piece of paper in her hand and walk into the vault room where classified documents are kept. Grace flips to another tape of the vault. Cristina is looking at the paper and obviously reading from it as she dials the combination on one of the secure cabinets. In a few seconds she pulls the drawer open. Over the next hour she methodically goes through the files, drawer by drawer. Periodically, she pulls out one or more files and goes to the copier. After making copies she puts the file back in order carefully, closes the drawer and spins the dial.

Grace flips back to the camera in the main room. Cristina pulls a large envelope out of her desk and puts the papers into it. She walks over to the desk of one of the young clerks and puts the envelope in her bottom drawer. Then, she returns to her desk. She straightens out her papers and leaves the office. The time stamp is 0146 Sunday morning, the fourth. The office is not guarded as if it were a consulate or embassy. No one will know that she used her key to access the office in off hours.

When Cristina goes to lunch Grace and Mike walk casually to Hugh's door and knock. "Got a minute Hugh?" Grace asks.

"Certainly, what do you need?"

They go in and close the door. This is not uncommon as they often have private conversations with him. But this time is not a common case. They lay out findings for him and he is simultaneously relieved to know that we've solved the mystery, while upset that it's her. When trust is violated, it's very distressing even though it was anticipated.

"Hugh, as soon as she returns from lunch we should bring her into the conference room along with Captain Bennett and confront her," Grace says.

At 1315, Cristina returns and Grace asks her to join them in the conference room. She asks if she should bring a pad to take notes and Grace nods so as not to make her suspicious. When Cristina steps into the room she's startled to see Captain Bennett. Looking around at the four of us she realizes this is not going to be good for her. She sits upright on the edge of her chair.

Hugh opens by saying, "Cristina, I'm very disappointed in what I learned today. Can you tell me what you were doing in the office around midnight last Saturday?"

A deep blush covers her face and she immediately starts to wiggle in her chair. "What do you mean?"

"I mean that we know you were in the office Saturday night and you opened the classified files in the vault."

"Well, yes, I did come in to catch up on some work. But that's all."

"Midnight, Cristina?"

"I was home and I couldn't sleep so I decided to come to work and finish some things I had pending. I want you to know how efficient and committed I am to this job and to the Office."

"What were you doing in the vault and where did you get the combination to the files?"

"I found the combination on a piece of paper in Claire's desk. I thought it was all right to go into the files."

"Cristina, you know I told you explicitly you were not to handle classified material."

"I guess I just forgot. I'm sorry. I was concentrating on my job. It won't happen again, I promise."

"Why did you make copies of classified documents?"

"I didn't."

Mike steps in. His face turns red and hardens. He moves six inches in her direction. His black eyes bore into her. "Cristina, I'm tired of your lies. You did go where you were not authorized to go. You did make copies of classified material without the proper clearance. We have a camera tape showing you doing that. Then, you put the papers you copied into an envelope and put the file in Meili's bottom drawer. Mike offers, "Cristina, if you'll give us others in Cho Bai's organization we might release you without any charges."

She sits back as though she's been punched. She's stunned, looking at her hands folded in her lap, wondering what she can do now. Mike's paralyzing stare never leaves her for a second. No one speaks. Finally, realizing there was no way out she blurts,

"Yes, I did it and I would do it again. You foreigners come to China and try to impose your ways on us. For centuries you come in and cut up China to suit yourselves. You treat our people as peasants. You beat us and cheat us and expect that we will take your abuse. Well, that time is over. China is growing stronger every day. Soon, China will rule all Asia and then, one day, the world. Everyone will bow under China's might. Cho Bai was my dear friend and look what you did to her. You killed her family and crippled her and we could not do anything to avenge her loss. Well, Claire paid a small amount of pain, but not as much as we would have given her if you had not arrived so soon. Now, you cannot hurt me because I am diplomat also. I curse you and I leave you." With that she stands quickly and makes a move toward the door. Captain Bennett blocks her way.

Mike, Grace and Hugh leave her in the conference room with one of the marine guards. They're concerned that she might try to commit suicide. Grace and Captain Bennett go to Meili's desk. They open her drawer and remove the envelope. Grace asks Meili, "Do you know what's in this envelope?"

"No, I didn't even know it was here."

Cristina believed no one would suspect the young clerk if anything went missing. Eventually, Cristina could take envelopes out of the office when she thought she had everything she wanted.

Hugh calls the federal police to take Cristina and hold her until he can determine if she had committed other crimes as yet undiscovered. Then, he turns the case over to his deputy to follow up.

Chapter 22

LING DELIVERS

May 1976
Beijing

"Well, Sherlock, I think we did a pretty good job with Claire's case."

"Yes, madam. It appears we have clearly become a powerful force for righteousness. I expect evildoers everywhere are cowering in their dens in fearful anticipation of being exposed by our brilliance. In another matter, I must share my deep personal feelings regarding you and assure you of my undying love and devotion."

"Sweetheart, you are so silly and I love it. I love you more than your little heart can imagine. Please take care of yourself. You are truly exceptional."

* * *

Chen has managed to find Ling on the staff of *Guojia Anquan Bu*, the Ministry of State Security, the intelligence branch of the PLO (People's Liberation Army). Its headquarters is a large complex in Xiyuan in the west side of Beijing near the Summer Palace. He lives in an apartment in the complex. The longer Mike's in China the more respect he has for the ingenuity of these people.

Chen explains. "It take great discretion and patience to find Mr. Ling. I must move with great caution so people not notice me. Someone always know what you need to know. It is simply matter of finding that person who can answer your question. After I learn where Ling live I spend several days watching for him to leave complex. Finally two days ago he come out and I follow him to shopping area. I approach him as if to ask directions, in case he being followed. One must assume that man with Ling's record would be under surveillance.

"I was correct. Ling is still under suspicion because of what happened in Hawaii. His case has become even more sensitive since you and Ms. Liu arrived. Of course MSS know you are here and your contact with Ling in Hawaii. Both Ling and you are being watched. Ling tell me it is extremely dangerous, nearly impossible, for you to meet him. Yet, he aware of his obligation to you. In his present condition he could tell MSS of your arrangement with him, but he believe that is unwise. They might banish him to a remote office, if they find out. His hope is to find some way he can help you and benefit from it. But, that must be through third person, a back channel. That could be me, if you and Chan-juan agree."

"Does Ling have a recommendation?"

"He say he knows one or more people in the military who might be willing to work with you. Once he know what you want he can select and test a man. Then he will put him in touch with me. If you communicate through me we can learn if that person is interested in what you have to say. If all goes well then you can meet that man to do business directly. Is that acceptable to you?"

Mike looks at Grace, "The plan sounds reasonable and is as safe as it can be for now. How will you communicate with Ling?"

"We will arrange drop in shopping area. Once each week I will go there and either meet him, drop message or pick up message. I can go tomorrow if you agree with plan."

"Go ahead with your scheme. Well done, Mr. Chen. I think Ling knows in general what we want."

Grace smiles at Mike, "It looks like we're on our way. Isn't Mr. Chen clever?"

"A great resource. If we have our business one day, he'll be a good man to know."

Two days later Chen reports he met Ling who agrees and will talk to a man in the navy who he thinks might be interested. "Ling says man is at your level. He works in technical side of naval weapon development. Ling says man's career not going well. He is egotist and has angered some senior officers. He probably not going to be promoted and maybe even removed to less sensitive position shortly. He needs to talk to man while he still in position to provide current intelligence. Now, we must wait for Ling."

Nothing happens for nearly a month. Chen finds one message that says it will take time to develop the man's interest. Mike is impatient, *What good will it do if the man is transferred soon?* Grace reminds Mike that Westerners are not as patient as Asians. In their position all they can do is wait to hear.

As diplomats they're free to travel within the greater city limits, but to go into the countryside they need a pass from the state security office. Since there is a break Chen offers his young cousin as a guide. She's a graduate student in Chinese history and knows not only the city but the background of this rather intriguing place. Her name is Li Na.

Na is chubby and smiles constantly, through somewhat misaligned teeth. With a bit of orthodontics she would be a pretty girl. Just starting a graduate program in history at Peking University, Na's dressed in typical student garb, loose dark blue dress and black tights to which she has added a colorful scarf. A gray, light-weight, knee length coat and knit cap complete her ensemble.

She tells them Beijing's records go back three thousand years to the same period that the earliest Egyptians appeared. China has a history of dynasties coming and going, often violently. In 1253 the Mongols invaded China and by 1300, under Kublai Khan the Forbidden City of Beijing was built. In 1890, under the aegis of the

Empress Dowager Cixi, the Boxer Rebellion besieged the home base of the foreign legation. This brought in an international military force that routed the Boxers. Cixi and the Emperor escaped but the Qing dynasty never recovered. Sun Yat Sen pushed for reform and became president of the new republic. Sun died in 1925 and the next decades were marked by struggles between Chiang Kai-shek, his successor, and the communists under Mao Zedong. By 1949 the communists had forced the Nationalists to take refuge in Taiwan.

There is much to see in and around the city. Na starts them at The Temple of Heaven, a triple-gabled, blue-roofed Hall of Prayer for Good Harvests that is a wonder of Ming architecture. It's cool inside and they're reluctant to leave. The Summer Palace, where the Imperial family would escape the heat of the central city, overlooks beautiful Kunming Lake. The top of a pavilion offers an amazing view down over the city and the plains below. Na tells them the next site, Jingshan Park, is built on a hill made from earth excavated to create the moat around the Forbidden City.

The old city is marked by narrow alleys where the people go about their daily lives as they've done for centuries. The thousands of small shops and restaurants remind Mike of cells in a beehive with the bees buzzing in and out of them. *What a place to hide or drop a message,* Mike thinks.

Although Grace knows the history of China, she'd never visited Beijing when she was growing up in Henan province. At the end of the tour, Grace thanks Na. "It was a great lesson for me to see some of the history of my people that I didn't know. Now, I'm even more proud of being Chinese." As she reminds Mike, "My people were writing poetry, designing silken gowns and inventing gun powder while yours were wearing scratchy wool and fighting in the forests of northern Europe."

A week later Chen shows up at their office. "Mr. Ling is moving very cautiously because he knows he is being watched. We must be patient. This is very dangerous game for everyone. May I suggest we make it a habit to carry a weapon?"

While they wait for Ling they keep in touch with Jiang meeting at a quiet restaurant where they can make sure they're not being followed. Grace is inconspicuous. Mike is not.

Gao tells them over lunch, "I'm very involved in planning the first phase of a major financing program that will support the industrial modernization program. It will cost many billions and last far into the future. The bank believes China must modernize no matter who is the leader. It's imperative to be able to compete with the U.S., Japan, and Europe's economic powers such as Germany. Within a couple months we will have some information that you'll find interesting." He adds with a gleam in his eye, "While we wait for that, I am quietly compiling data on the hidden personal investments of China's leadership. That could cause a scandal that would destabilize the political hierarchy. They'll be sorry for what they've done to Jiang Qing."

But things begin to heat up during the summer (pardon the pun). Mao restores Deng to a leadership position, his last major act. On September 9 Mao dies and the race is on. Hua Guofeng is the acknowledged successor to Mao and most likely will be the next premier. It will be a battle between Hua Guofeng and Deng. Inside this tornado Mike and Grace chase down every rumor and speculation.

September 9 Chen asks for a short meeting. "Mr. Ling has identified and qualified a naval officer who is interested in what you have to say. You will have to decide where and how you can meet him in private."

"CJ, we need to set up a safe house somewhere in town. Any suggestions?"

"We're under surveillance at least part of the time, if not continuously. I'm thinking Chen can make contact with a woman who runs an escort service. There are several that serve both foreign and local patrons. By their nature they are discreet. I believe we can make a deal to have access to one of her apartments as needed. Since normally both Chinese and foreign men frequent it, it should be easy for us to set up meetings with the naval officer there. Just don't you get any ideas about sampling the local talent. The deal will be for the room only, Yankee."

"Gee, you don't let me have any fun mom."

"I take that as, *"Yes, ma'am!"* I'll make the arrangements through Chen. As soon as it's secured, Chen can set up a meeting there."

The man agrees to meet Mike and Grace and on 1 October at 2100. They make sure to lose their tail and be in the apartment when the he arrives. The room is painted red and accented with erotic art. A bed, sofa, small table and lamp, two easy chairs, a side board with a tea service and liquor, and a tall armoire complete the furnishings. The bathroom includes a shower large enough to two people. On the wall is a rubber hose. In checking for surveillance equipment, Mike finds some interesting apparatus stored in the armoire. "Grace, look at this. Could be exciting."

She walks over and looks intently at the masks, scarves, cheap cotton ropes and a velvet whip. She scrunches up her nose, but can't resist lingering. "Don't get any ideas big boy."

Grace makes tea, but after thirty minutes their man hasn't arrived and Mike is concerned that something has gone wrong. Grace says, "Be patient Yankee. Remember what I told you about doing business in Asia."

Twenty minutes later Mike's about to give up when there's a knock on the door. Grace goes to open it with Mike out of sight behind the door, and his hand on his Prather pistol.

Through the peephole Grace sees a well-built man of about forty. "Yes, what do you want?"

"Good evening, is Miss Yee in?"

Yee is a code name. It's common, but not like Smith is in the U.S. Grace opens the door and beckons him inside. He's startled when the door is closed and he sees Mike behind it. Grace assures him that all is well and Mike puts his gun back in his leg holster. "Please sir, have a seat." Grace motions him to the sofa. They take the chairs.

"Sir, would you like some tea?"

He hesitates for a second or two, looking around the room and at Mike. He accepts.

Once settled with tea Mike starts, "Sir, you know who we are and generally why we're here, but let me give you some details about this venture."

He nods and seems to relax a bit.

"Mr. Chen has given you a broad outline of our purpose. Our goal is to obtain useful, high-level intelligence regarding China's military strategy and development plans. Mr. Chen said that you would be agreeable to furnish information along those lines. Am I correct?"

"Perhaps."

"Good. Can you give us some background data on yourself, your position in the navy and the work you are involved in?"

"Yes, but first I must be assured of the safety of this arrangement. I am loyal to China, although I have some concerns for my career and future opportunities."

"Of course. I'm also a naval officer and understand your position. We want to assure you we will take every precaution to protect you. As you can see, we have made some effort to secure a safe meeting place."

"Sir," Grace interjects, "I am Chinese by birth. My home was in Henan Province. My father was a general on Chiang's staff. I, too, have concerns about the future of China in the geopolitical sphere. Our goal is to do what we can to contribute to a balance of power between the U.S. and China so that neither side feels it can or must destroy the other. Our goal is truly world peace, which we assume all thinking people share."

The man takes a sip from his tea cup and sits back, less tense and seemingly reassured. "Thank you. Yes, I too want a peaceful world for my children to grow into."

"About your family. How many children do you have?"

For fifteen minutes he relaxes talking about his family with Grace. Mike would have gone directly to point of their business. Grace is wiser. She knows how to be patient, to get a man to reveal things of importance without realizing he's doing it. What a partner.

Eventually, Mike brings the conversation around to the business at hand. "Now that we know each other I believe we can speak directly, Commander Wei." That's the name Chen had given them. "What are you working on and what is your position?"

"I work at the naval technology center. My unit is weapons development. Personally, I'm involved in design and testing of a new, ultra-high energy, plasma cannon to be powered by a large electrical battery on board a ship, or from shore. This will increase the shell's speed and range. Instead of propelling a conventional gun powder shell, it will expel a shell-like container of neon gas that is converted into plasma upon firing. The energy onto the the plasma is created when electricity is injected into the gas shell. This creates a magnetic field that ionizes the gas within the shell resulting in an extremely high temperature container. The container, is fired at very high speed using our new cannon technology. As it strikes the target it explodes, dissipating the plasma on the target, and incinerating it. Think of it simply as a huge burst of energy, or in laymen's terms, an extremely high electrical shock. "

"How will it do that?"

"When the plasma shell strikes the target the escaping energy is so great that it will blow away and/or melt the hull or superstructure of the enemy vessel or of a building. The propellant's path will be aimed by a mathematically predetermined curve at the time of firing. Just as you can calculate and adjust the trajectory of a cannon shell we can set the speed and distance of the plasma shell by virtue of the amount of energy we put behind it. That is basic artillery geometry—mass times force. It's the same as the explosion of gun powder in a cannon. But our cannon has many times more force than the current ship cannons. I'm being simplistic, but this is the concept. Eventually, we may be able to reduce the energy source to fit in a submarine, or perhaps even an aircraft. Imagine a fighter plane firing plasma missiles. They could immobilize an aircraft carrier with just a few hits."

"That's incredible. It advances the applications of the laws of physics."

"Of course it seems impossible now, but so did controlling the splitting of the atom until it was accomplished. Tesla developed the first plasma ball in 1890, but his technology wasn't powerful enough to take it out of the laboratory. This weapon will have other new, high energy physics features as yet unseen in current weapon systems. Those capabilities are what will make it powerful beyond belief."

"How far along is the development? Is there a test scheduled yet?"

"Very soon. The theoretical design and blue prints are complete. We've built a working model that is yet to be fired. That will happen with a couple months, or sooner."

"This is at the naval technology center where you work?"

"Yes."

"And you're involved in the design of this weapon?"

"I was until recently."

"What happened?"

"I've pointed out repeatedly that there are minor flaws in the control system that could cause it to fail. But my superior, who is not a physicist, wants to get the system to the test stage as quickly as possible. He has removed me from direct activity in weapon development. I'm now the chief administrative officer handling all the documentation. It makes me a librarian rather than a physicist."

"I'm sorry to hear that," Grace says. "But can you still access copies of the specifications and blueprints of the mechanism?"

"Yes, that is my primary responsibility. I can make copies of the system, but it's a big job. There is a great deal of documentation involved, as you might imagine. Also the blueprints are large, each nearly one meter square."

"If you can deliver a full technical description we would be willing to pay for that. If after evaluating it we want copies of the blueprints we would pay for them also. Can you bring us the technical specifications as the first step?"

"It will take some time for me to bring the specifications out piece by piece. It's quite a large document, and I have to work very carefully to get it past security."

"Commander, if you can do that, we can do business. How long do you think it might take?"

"I believe I can have the full specifications together in a couple of weeks, barring any changes in the security system."

"Excellent. When you have them, please contact Mr. Chen to set up a time for us to meet here and transfer the papers. We'll examine them and offer you payment at that time."

"Very well. I will contact Mr. Chen when I have them."

After Wei leaves Grace asks, "Is this weapon truly possible?"

"Honestly I don't know. It's very far ahead of all current and planned weapons systems that I know. If it does what he says it can, it will be like the introduction of gunpowder was in 900 AD. It will change warfare forever. The more you think about the technology behind it, the more you can imagine how it will change life in the world as it's adapted to every day applications. Things as common as today's plastics evolved from WWII applications."

* * *

Wei contacts Chen and sets up a meeting for 20 October. Again he's early an hour late. He looks frazzled when he arrives. "Sorry I'm late. I wanted to make sure that I wasn't being followed."

"Do you have reason to think you might be followed?" Grace asks.

"No, but I've never done something like this before. It makes me very nervous."

"I understand, Commander. But if your routine at work hasn't changed, there is no reason to believe that you're under surveillance."

"Thank you for your assurance, Ms. Liu."

Mike also assures him. "I'm certain no one suspects you of anything out of the ordinary. Were you able to make copies of the technical specifications?"

"Yes, that is why I'm nervous. I have them here in my briefcase."

Wei opens the black leather case and pulls out a document, almost two inches thick, unbound. He doesn't seem to know who to hand it to. Grace reaches for it. She puts it on her lap and flips through it quickly. She hands it to Mike.

"Michael, I think you can understand most of this. I'll help you with the technical terms."

It's a pretty standard format for technical specs but in Chinese vertical format. Text and diagrams cover probably two hundred pages. "This must have taken you some time to copy. It's very impressive. We'll take this back and study it. If it is what it looks like, tell me how much you want for it?"

"Sir, I'm not sure. As I said, this is the first time for me. It's top secret data. I will have to rely on you to set a fair price. Will you need anything else about this weapon system?"

"If it is what you described, then we'll want to see some blueprints for the actual machinery. Do you think you can bring that out?"

"That will be more difficult. The schematics are on large pages. It takes time, making copies when no one is around."

"Yes, we understand. Let us study what you've brought us. Mr. Chen will relay our opinion and degree of satisfaction. If we want you to bring the blueprints we'll send Chen with money for this document and a request for the prints. Is that workable for you?"

He hesitates for a moment, head down, thinking about the offer. "Very well. I will wait to hear from Mr. Chen."

"Good. In any event, we'll pay you for what you've brought. How do you want it paid, in yuan or gold or something else?"

"I think yuan would be sufficient for now. If we make a larger, long-term arrangement we can discuss the form of compensation. If there's nothing else, I must leave. It will take me an hour or more to reach home and I don't want my wife to worry. Thank you."

"Xiè xie nǐ Commander," (Thank you) Grace says as she takes him to the door. Grace and Mike spend three days reading and trying to understand the potential impact of this weapon. "This technology is above my pay grade, but it's something extraordinary. I don't know if it'll work, but that's not our decision. There is clearly enough here to warrant passing it on."

"Why do you think he is willing to engage in such a dangerous game? Is he greedy, angry with someone, egotistical or what?"

"I don't know, but he reiterated what Ling said about his career not going well. It could be a combination of greed, anger, or even revenge." He's upset by what's happening in his career and the stupidity of his boss. And he's going for the gold to secure his future and prove that someone appreciates his work."

"I think you're right on. How much do you think we should involve Hugh?"

"We have to show it to him, but I know he won't have any idea of the magnitude. I think we should only tell him the background. We don't have to mention the blueprints. We'll have him send it by courier ASAP to Commander Coyne at ONI and we'll send an encrypted message letting him know that a top secret package regarding a new weapon system is coming. We'll give him a brief background on the agent and ask him to have it evaluated immediately by the tech people. If they're interested, he can let us know about going for the blueprints. Also, we need to know what they're willing to pay for the specs and for the blue prints."

20 November they hear from Captain Coyne. His message is brief. "Proceed. Offer 25k for step one and 50k more for step two."

They send Chen back with the first payment and instructions to deliver step two ASAP. They withhold the step two price until they hear how Wei feels about the 25k.

It takes Chen ten days to connect with Wei who, it turns out, was traveling to a test site in the Gobi Desert, similar to Los Alamos. Wei agrees to the 25k and to proceed with step two, but insists he wants 100k for that. He knows the value of the blueprints—fifty-five pages delivered in segments, several at a time. Wei is proceeding with the utmost caution. If he's caught he'll be convicted of spying and probably executed. That's after being tortured to find out who he's working with.

It's a couple weeks before Wei is ready to meet again. On 6 December they wait at the safehouse, late again. He's very nervous. His life hangs on the successful acquisition and passage of this extremely sensitive information.

Wei sits down as though he has just run a marathon. He passes over a heavy valise with trembling hands. No wonder he's sweating—twenty blueprint sheets folded in quarters weighing nearly twenty pounds.

Mike unfolds one sheet. It's a clear print of some piece of machinery. All notes are in Chinese of course. The boys in D.C. are going to have a fun time translating all this. Continuing through the package he unfolds most of the prints one at a time, passing them to Grace. She looks at each one for several seconds then stacks them on the table.

"Commander, you've done a great job. We thank you. Our people will be most intrigued by what you have delivered. How long do you think it will take you to deliver the total system?"

"That is most difficult to predict. The critical issue is how often I am alone with the print tray. It could be days between delivery of more. My concern is that I expect to be transferred to the test site within the next month to six weeks. We're preparing to test the cannon. I'll work as fast as I can, but I can't guarantee delivery of the total system."

"We hope you can accelerate the process," Grace tells him. "We understand and appreciate the sensitivity of your position. You've done very well so far. We have another 50k for you when you finish the project."

"That is a problem. This weapon system is clearly the leading edge of technology, Commander Holmes. You said so yourself when I told you about it. I think it should be worth twice what you are offering. You see the prints are authentic and in clearly readable condition."

Mike looks blank, but his mind is active. *He's absolutely correct, but I can't cave in right away. If I show weakness he may continue to raise his price. I don't think he's experienced enough a negotiator to try to extort an outrageously high price from us. Nevertheless, it looks like some bargaining is about to start.*

Grace breaks the silence. "Commander, you are correct regarding the advanced nature of this system. However, you said it had not been tested, that all you have is a model. I mean no disrespect, but we don't know this isn't a hoax. It could be something that's just a fairy tale designed to extort money from us. How do we know that this is actually a true representation of a valid system? It might even be some machine you've tested previously and discovered it doesn't work."

They're confronting the validity of his data. Wei is startled that Grace should bring up such a possibility. She's gambling that if he's a fraud, it will come out now. If he isn't, he has to do something to save face. For a long minute he sits looking down, and then at each of them.

"Ms. Liu, I am shocked. You have my word of honor as one of your countrymen and as an officer in the Chinese navy that everything I have told you is one hundred percent true and accurate to the best of my ability to communicate it."

Mike steps in. "I don't mean to insult you, Commander, but keep in mind that you are asking us to give you a significant amount of money for something that has not yet been proven workable. We have a responsibility to our government to deliver what we have promised."

"I understand. If I expedite delivery of this total system will you agree to a price of USD 75,000?"

"Commander," Mike interjects, "we intend to send this material immediately by courier to our superiors in Washington D.C. If they believe that it is a reasonable representation of a valid system, we will pay the seventy-five thousand. Provided you can deliver the total system within the next thirty days."

Wei sits contemplating the totality of the situation. He lifts his eyes first to Grace, then to Mike. With the look of a man who is asking for trust he agrees, to the terms.

Grace reaches out to him with a gesture of reassurance. "Thank you, Commander. You can be absolutely certain we will keep our end of the bargain."

* * *

Over the next five weeks they have two more meetings with Wei. In the first he brings another twenty-two blue prints and in the second nineteen more. Then, comes the surprise. "I'm being sent to the test site this week. I don't have any more access to the blueprint file. There are approximately fifteen more diagrams still at the center."

"Commander, what are we to do now? This is incomplete. It's not what you promised."

"Is there any other way we can get the prints?" Grace asks.

"No. There is no one there I can trust with this. You must understand that."

Mike asks rather pointedly, "There must be some way to complete this. So far you have given us about eighty percent of the prints, but they're not of much use without the remaining twenty."

"I don't know what to tell you. Spying and stealing is not my business. I wish I had never agreed to this."

"Commander, we understand and appreciate your concern," Grace interjects, "But is there some way you can get us into the building at night so we can access the prints ourselves?"

Mike looks at Grace like she's totally crazy. She returns the look signaling patience to hear what Wei will say. Patient or not, they can't just waltz into a secure weapons center and dance out with the prints.

Chapter 23

BREAK-IN

December 1976
Beijing

Wei thinks for a long minute, "The center does not have 24-hour on-site security. The military can't imagine that anyone would try to get into their complex. There is only a key and button combination lock, and watchmen who come by the building hourly. I have an extra key. I can draw the layout of the center so you can go to the blueprint files and copy the remaining prints."

Grace looks at Mike as if to say, "See, I knew there would be a way."

He's thinking. *This is a very high risk. If we're caught, we'll be in the same position as Ling was in Hawaii. I doubt the Chinese would be as easy on us as we were on Ling.* All he can see are dingy jail cells and torture. If they're very lucky, a prisoner exchange might be worked out, but that could take years. On the other hand, what else can they do? They're so close to a major coup they can't quit now. "CJ, I'll do it."

"No, you won't. We'll do it together. We can move much faster if there are two of us going through files and making copies."

"I don't like exposing you to the danger. If we're caught the result will be most unpleasant."

"I know that. But it's my job and this is the only way it will work."

Mike turns back to Wei. "Okay, we'll go in. You have to draw us a detailed map of the building access, give us the key and combinations to all locks, a path to the print files, and where in the files we can find the prints we need."

Grace says to him pointedly. "You understand the danger, Commander. The access code, the time schedule to avoid the watchmen, and the location and detailed layout of the print files must be perfect,"

"I understand."

It takes over an hour for Wei to draw the building plan. They rehearse precisely how it will happen. Chen will drop them at the building and wait at a safe distance to pick them up. Timing and speed to complete the work need to be flawless or the two intrepids will spend what little life is left for them in a terrible position.

Since this is probably the last time they will see Commander Wei, Mike wants to know more about the device and what Wei sees as its flaws.

"The most important problem is lack of heat and energy controls. You have to understand the nature of plasma in order to imagine the energy in this weapon. Plasma temperature is commonly measured in Kelvins or electron volts. It is, informally, a measure of the thermal kinetic energy per particle. Very high temperatures are usually needed to sustain ionization, which is a defining feature of plasma. This system will build up massive amounts of energy, thus heat, prior to propelling its plasma energy pulse. When the plasma ball strikes the target it releases its energy onto the target, superheating it instantly and thereby causing failure of the target's structure. Whether metal, concrete, or other material. I'm absolutely certain the propulsion system needs better valves and switches to manage the heat buildup. As it is presently configured It could self-destruct. If it does, the explosion will be almost beyond descrition in its intensity."

"Will you be in charge of the tests in the Gobi?" Grace asks.

"No, but I will be involved. I don't like it. In my opinion the physics are not well understood. As it is currently designed it might get out of control and obliterate the people assigned to fire it."

"Do you think then that it would be better if this device was never completed?"

Wei sits silently. Mike thinks that for the first time he sees the true danger of this system. When he speaks they can hardly hear him, *"Huo shi"* (perhaps yes). The concept and the theory underlying it are brilliant. In time and with testing it could be the next great weapon the atomic era has introduced. But at this point this system is not well understood. In the wrong hands it could hurt many people, military and civilian. It's almost as powerful as a small atomic blast. The worst part is the people in charge of its development don't comprehend that, or don't seem to care."

"Commander, we're going to pay you the full 75k even though we have to finish the job. From here on you have a large responsibility to everyone," Grace counsels. "It might be better if you saw to it that the proper safeguards were not put in place before the test. Think about it as you prepare for the test. May God and Confucius help you see the right thing to do."

* * *

Saturday 1 January 0200, the time Wei said would be safest to enter the building. It's a very cold and damp night. A freezing wind sliding down off the mountains threatens to scour all life from the frozen plains. There is a chance of snow in the air, and heavy dark clouds coming out of the northwest. This is the type of night you wish you didn't have to go into. They're thinking. *Why aren't we sitting in front of a nice fire with Cixi and a glass of port to warm our cockles?*

Mike looks at Grace. She gives him the "Courage, Yankee" grimace. Chen is driving. They're dressed in heavy black jackets, woolen black shirts, and thermal black pants, black gloves and sneakers—government issued night combat uniforms. Not chic, but serviceable. As they approach the naval weapon development center Chen drives slowly so they can sense the environment. Where are the watchmen? Are there bright street lights in the area? Where is the entrance to the building? How far is it from the street? What escape routes do they have, if any?

They pass by once more. Grace and Mike step out and shut the door quietly. It's bone-chilling cold. Chen leaves quietly. They don't see anyone, but can hear faint voices at a distance. It could be the watchmen. In eighty yards they're at the door. Mike holds the tube while Grace puts the key in the lock and hits the four digit combination 6-2-8-0. They hear the bolt slide free. In a second they're inside and the door is closed. It's welcome warmth. First step: successful.

They've memorized Wei's floor plan. Up the stairs on the right to the second floor, turn left immediately, using a small pencil light proceed seventy paces until reaching a solid door on the left. It has no lock. Inside they can turn on their flashlights. This is the file room.

Wei said the file tray they want is the fourth from the left in the second row. The copy machine is at the end of the room. It's going to consume a lot of time running over and back some thirty feet to make copies. Mike looks for the file tray and Grace checks to see if the copy machine is turned on. It is in a rest mode, good. They find the right tray, but the file is locked. Wei forgot to tell them that. They can't force the lock and expose the theft. It's a dead end if they can't get past the lock.

Fortunately, Mike has the bump key and lock picks. Will it work on Chinese locks? While Grace holds the light steady Mike inserts the key, pulls it out a sixteenth of an inch, twists and nothing happens.

He's sweating inside his heavy suit. He tries it again. Jiggles it. Nothing. They've come all this way and a two bit file lock is blocking the successful completion of one of the greatest intelligence coups ever. He tries once more, and still it won't open.

"Let me try. You need to speak Chinese to it," Grace teases. He can't hear if she is swearing or praying. It sounds like "*Qǐng kāimén*" (open please) as she inserts the key. A little jiggle and voila! Open. He gives her a quick hug and they pull the tray out. The blueprints are numbered and too big to photograph with their cameras. They look for number 56 and up. Mike thumbs through the stack and together they pull out the first fifty-five and place them atop the file. They take eight or nine at a time and together walk them to the table next to the copier, careful not to bend the pages. Gloves keep them from leaving fingerprints.

The first sheet goes onto the glass plate of the copier. They hold their breath and press the "Copy" button. Just like it is supposed to work. In about 15 seconds the first print is copied. They look it over carefully to test readability. It's clear. They repeat the process on the next sheet. Color copies are slow because the image is large and these copy in blue. After the fifth copy the machine seems to labor. Maybe it's overheated. They don't want to lose time, but they have to stop and wait for it to recycle itself. In all it takes nearly half an hour to copy all sixteen prints. They had planned to be out before now. But they can only work as fast as the copier will cycle.

When they have the sixteen they take the originals off the top of the cabinet and carefully reinsert then in order. In the end the stack looks as neat as it did when they opened the tray. Close the file, push the lock back. Roll the sheets, paper is thick. rolling takes time, bind them together, slide them into their tube container. The carrier weighs nearly ten pounds. Plan called for them to be out of here before the watchmen came around at 0300. It's already 0249. Check everything carefully. Slowly exit the file room. Quietly close the door.

Reaching the stairs they hear voices nearby outside. Sounds like two men talking just outside the door. One of them tests the handle to confirm that it is still locked. What will they do if the men come in? Mike's carrying his 9mm Browning HP, but if he has to shoot them to escape that will create big problems. All the good the gun might do is stop them from shooting Mike and Grace. Now just to wait.

In a couple minutes they see a little flash of light. The men have stopped for a cigarette. They're stomping around in the alcove just to the right of the door trying to stay warm. Mike and Grace slide down the wall to the floor just above the stairs to wait. It's 0308. Damn that slow machine.

0320 it sounds like the men are moving off. Grace looks out the window and sees Chen's car driving slowly past. He must be getting worried, but the watchmen don't seem to make anything of it. They wait another ten minutes until the men are checking another building. Then they slip out the door. Grace takes the tube while Mike closes the door. He loses his grip on the icy handle and the door slams shut. After a few cautious steps they begin to run toward the street. There is a shout that sounds like "*Tingzhi*" (stop). The guards must have heard the door slam. Grace is still twenty yards from the street and Mike's aching knees are barely keeping up. They hear gun fire and a bullet whizzing past. In a pitch dark night at one hundred yards, plus there isn't much chance they'll be hit. Mike turns, pulls out his gun and fires off a couple rounds in the guards' general direction. By the time they shoot again Grace is almost at Chen's car. Then, Mike hears a thud. Grace yells, "I'm hit." She falls. Mike pulls her back to her feet, picking up the roll of blue prints and throwing both into the back seat. He jumps in, hopefully not on top of her. Chen pulls a U-turn that slams the door shut and accelerates quickly. In about a mile he pulls into a dark alley and stops. Sirens behind them.

Grace moans, "It's my back. Right side, below my ribs."

Mike has his flashlight out. He unzips her parka and pulls up her shirt. "You've got a large bruise and a small hole. The bullet must have nicked the tube carrier. It didn't penetrate her back very far. When he tells her that she gasps, "Thank you," and passes out from the shock.

The tube carrier is on the floor. He sees there is a grazing bullet hole on the edge of the lower half. The thickness of the cardboard and a dozen sheets of heavy paper deflected the force of the bullet.

0415, they're back at the LO. Mike has a chance to look more closely at Grace. There's a clear puncture wound in her back. Gently he rolls her over. No exit wound and almost no blood. Still, Grace's lower back is aching. Mike calls Hugh. "Do we have a discreet doctor we can get here to look at Grace, right away?" They do and he'll have him there ASAP.

Mike tapes a gauze pad from the office's first aid kit over Grace's wound and covers her with a blanket on the couch in Hugh's office. Her breathing and pulse are normal. Looks like she's resting, not in shock.

He lays the prints out on Hugh's table. They look good despite the bullet path that scratched a few of the sheets. Grace wakes up and asks about the prints. "The prints are fine sweetheart. Good job. You get a Purple Heart for this."

"I'll settle for a diamond ring," she murmurs and goes back to sleep.

The doctor finds a lump where the bullet is resting. It entered laterally rather than straight in. Just under the tissue, didn't touch the kidney. "No internal bleeding. I'll give her a painkiller for the wound and a relaxant to get over the shock." Once the local anesthetic takes effect, he probes and finds the slug just an inch into her back below her rib cage. He cauterizes the wound, and puts a couple stitches in to close the hole. Close call. Too close.

Chen drives them home. 0700, Mike has helped Grace undress and get gently into bed. They're still so charged up, they can't sleep.

Mike takes out the Macallan's Elchies decanter and pours a relaxing shot. He gives Grace a bit of brandy, but she barely sips it. Cixi is given three drops of Bailey's in some warm milk. Cixi climbs into bed next to Grace. Half laughing and half shaking they slowly unwind and finally drift off just as the dawn sky begins to lighten.

Chapter 24

JIANG'S VENDETTA

January 1977
Beijing

Sixteen January, Grace has recovered from her wound although she's not ready for volley ball. The blue prints have been sent by courier to ONI. Chen can't find Wei to pay him. Apparently, he's been sent to the test site.

Grace calls Jiang Gao and makes a dinner date for the three of them. Since they're under surveillance, they drive around the city for twenty minutes before making a quick turn into a dingy alley behind a neighborhood Japanese restaurant. A smiling Gao's there when they arrive.

"I've been very busy. Deng seems to be gaining power, so we want to be prepared for a long term, multi-billion dollar, funding program."

"What do you think will be his first priority?" Mike asks.

"Actually, he'll probably move on a couple of fronts simultaneously. Agriculture and military programs are number one and two. We've got to reverse the effects of the Great Leap Forward. Land reform and resettlement are necessary to put food production back in the hands of the local farmers. Experience showed very painfully that they are more efficient than the collective farming system. If we support them with better methods, equipment, seeds, and fertilizers we should greatly increase their yields.

"On the other side, Deng will most likely move as fast as he can to build the strength of the navy and air force especially. The era of massive infantry units is past. China must protect its coastal waters, particularly the South China Sea, where there are disputed territories. Then we have to modernize our naval strike force."

Grace glances at Mike. How well they know that.

"Eventually, we'll need to build one or more aircraft carriers. All this calls for the investment of many billions of dollars over the next couple decades."

Grace adds, "It looks like you have a very busy career ahead of you. How do you feel about China's leadership now?"

"I can see that Jiang Qing could not have led the country into the modern era that Deng foresees. On the other hand, it's increasingly clear the leaders are getting rich from the development of new China. I'm collecting evidence on where and how they're enriching themselves. I don't know what I'll do with it yet. Perhaps you have some ideas."

"That depends on what you'd like to achieve." Grace suggests.

"I want China's leadership to be honest and trustworthy—above reproach, as you say in America."

Mike points out, "If that's your goal, then any data you have regarding misuse of funds can be either made public or put into Deng's hands to deal with. If he aspires to be the great man leading new China, he must fight internal corruption. Otherwise it will eat the heart out of his new tiger. The history of undeveloped and developing countries is consistently marked by corruption from the top of government down to the local levels. Still, we have to admit there are only a few countries can prove politicians don't get rich feeding at the public trough."

"I'm aware of that. I saw evidence at the UN. There were people using that assignment to better themselves financially, at a cost to their country."

Grace asks, "Specifically, what are you finding here?"

Jiang leans forward with intensity. "It's ironic that in a socialist system where equality is the presumed ethic, people at the top are enriching themselves through the labor of the proletariat. It's an abomination of the espoused doctrine of socialism. What I'm discovering is that our leaders at the highest level have their hands in the till, as you say in America. I mean they are skimming money from state-run industries. I can name officials in almost every segment from agriculture and mining to technology and heavy industry."

"Are you saying that China's ruling party is taking money out of national commerce?"

Jiang leans in again, even more excited, "Absolutely, and I can prove it. The funds of those industries flow through the central bank. I have names and amounts."

"Would you trust us with some examples that we could use in back channels to serve your purpose of fighting government corruption?" Grace asks.

Jiang stops talking for a few seconds to consider the question. He picks up his sake cup and drains it. She refills it for him. He takes off his glasses and wipes then. A few more seconds of silence. "Yes, absolutely yes. I trust you and Commander Holmes to use this to help me change the leaders and/or their behavior."

"It's a great honor and a profound trust you're giving us. Organize your data and let's set another meeting to go over it together. We have a safehouse where we can meet in private without fear of being seen doing business."

"I suggest we meet in about ten days, at your safehouse."

"Here's the address. Memorize it, then give me the paper back. What time is best for you?"

"Can we meet at 9 p.m.? Most people will be at dinner, so there's less chance of discovery."

* * *

30 January, Mike and Grace drive to the safehouse and park in the back lot.

2000, Jiang arrives with a large black briefcase. After a few minutes to warm up with the hot tea Grace has prepared, he opens the case and pulls out a large sheaf of papers— twenty or thirty pages.

"These are the most senior federal officials. This is a representative sample. There are more, but this will give you an idea. I'll continue until I reach the provincial level. There the funding is local and more difficult for me to trace. You can imagine the magnitude and effect this can have on China's leadership. It's a financial atomic bomb. My problem is, if I expose these powerful people, I'll surely be killed."

Grace and Mike move closer on the sofa and lay the sheaf on their laps so they can view the pages together. The top sheet shows a name immediately recognizable; one or the top five politicians in China. Grace gasps. It's a person she's known of for many years, a distant relative. The page lists a number of commercial enterprises with notes detailing the connection or position the subject occupies and amounts paid to him on specific dates. Assuming the data are true and accurate, this is an indictment—a prima facie case of bribery and graft.

Mike passes the sheet to Grace and looks at the next page, another of the top five. This is incredible. The data could be used several ways to extort, blackmail, slander or otherwise ruin the person's life.

"What do you think, CJ?"

"Devastating. Gao, if you have this on many more officials you could destabilize the government overnight. We'll have to think carefully about the best way to handle this."

"Look through these and let me know what you think is the most productive way to use them".

"You realize you've given us a most sensitive task. You have our word it will never be identified with you, and will be used in the most positive manner for the good of both our countries."

Gao leaves and they pull out a few more sheets. The story is the same, corruption at the highest levels.

There's a knock on the door. Gao must have forgotten something.

Mike looks through the peep hole. Not Gao. Two very determined men staring at the door.

Louder knock. "Open the door, police."

Grace calls out, *"Zhǐ xū yī fēnzhōng"* (Just a minute please.) She opens the armoire and pulls out the mask of a cat. Mike signals her to open the top buttons on her dress. Now they're pounding, "Open the door, police!"

Very quietly Mike turns the key, stands behind the door and pulls out his pistol. Grace backs away from the door to the bed. One hand on her hip and the other at her neck she stands provocatively. "Come in, its open," she calls in a husky voice.

Two husky men barge in with guns raised. They stop abruptly when they see Grace in the cat mask and her hands lingering over the buttons on her dress. "They didn't tell me there would be *two* handsome men."

Mike slams the door. In one quick move he fires into the leg of each man. They go down with screams, falling on top of each other. Grace pulls the cover off the bed and throws it over them. They struggle to untangle it. Mike tips the armoire on top of them. He motions to Grace to head for the door. She grabs their coats, while he scoops up the papers and briefcase. Snatching a wolf mask off the floor he dons it and bolts through the door. Grace closes it behind them and locks it.

Hearing shots and noise, a few people look out their doors. They see two masked people dashing for the back stairs. Once outside they tear off the masks and run to their car.

Driving directly to their villa Mike suggests they have a drink and don't even talk about the material. It's almost certain the place is bugged. In the morning, in the security of their office they read through the entire stack. More than a dozen individuals are cited.

"CJ, we need to show these to Hugh. This has severe political implications."

Hugh sees international repercussions. If this were leaked it would affect Deng's leadership, setting back the modernization of China. If Deng had it he would have ammunition to purge enemies from office, and hold the rest under a Sword of Damocles. Their careers, actually their lives, would be in the palm of his hand.

If outsiders saw it, the US and other great powers would reassess how they're going to work with Deng. They would hold the sword over him as well.

After spending the morning discussing this Hugh says somewhat sarcastically, "You two never bore me, but I don't know what I would do if I had another team like you.

"Given the sensitivity of this I'm going to courier it directly to the Secretary of State in a top secret SCI pouch. No one other than him will have access. We need to protect Jiang. Only the three of us can know who generated this. I'll have to let my boss know that something of this sensitivity is being sent to the Secretary. Then it's up to him to involve whom he chooses.

"This is a spectacular coup for you two. The only problem is that due to its extreme sensitivity no one beyond the president's National Security Council will ever know what you've accomplished. That adds another tiny wrinkle. There may be a sword hanging over us as well. This material is so dangerous someone in DC might decide we should take a permanent vacation.

"Given the plans to China's new secret weapon that you've "borrowed" and now this explosive evidence you've uncovered that could bring down the government of China, what are you planning for your next act?"

Chapter 25

GOODBYE BALI

February 1977
Beijing

"Hugh, when we arrived last January you told us we would be going to Singapore sometime next year for an international trade and technology fair. You haven't mentioned it since. What's happening?" Mike asks?

"That thing got so big and unwieldy it's been indefinitely postponed, if not cancelled."

"So what do we do now? We can continue to work on Ling for other recruitment leads. We could also take a couple weeks of leave and go somewhere warm. We've not had any time off in the past year."

"That's probably a good idea. We're into Chinese New Year so not much is going to happen for the next month. Why don't you book a week or two in some place like Bali? If you seek more activity Singapore has everything you could want. You could even do a week in each place."

Mike looks at Grace, "What do you think CJ?"

"Seems like a great idea to me. I've always wanted to go to Singapore and stay at the Raffles Hotel. Sounds so romantic—palm trees, the scent of frangipani, rickshaws, ceiling fans and louvered teak shutters in the darkened Long bar, Somerset Maugham telling tales of the South China Sea. I'll call a travel agent this afternoon."

"I don't think they have rickshaws anymore and Maugham is long gone, but the rest of it sounds great. Let's get our golf clubs out of the closet and go. Chen will take care of Cixi. We can obtain visas here."

In a few days they've booked Singapore Airlines to Singapore for a week, and as Hugh suggested, Bali for another week. Mike has never seen Grace so happy to get away from the cold barren plains of north China. They're set to leave on February 9th. They'll catch an early morning flight and in seven hours be in Singapore lounging at Raffles Long Bar with a couple Singapore Slings in their hands.

The following Wednesday Hugh calls, "Can I see you two for a minute?"

When they enter his office he isn't smiling, but he isn't frowning either. He has a very strange look on his face; sort of like wonderment. No matter what, it's clear that sunshine and palm trees isn't going to happen.

"Do you want the good news or the bad news first?"

"Bad" says Grace with a frown on her pretty face.

"You're not going to Singapore or Bali, at least not any time soon."

"I could have guessed that," she replies dropping heavily onto the sofa. "The good news better be really good to offset that."

"See what you think of this. I've just received messages from ONI. You're to be in Washington the week of the February 22nd. You'll attend a series of briefings regarding your two latest adventures. Briefing is doubtless a misnomer. The military is very, very interested in the weapon data. They're actually suspicious of it. The politicos are salivating over the Chinese leadership financial data. They too aren't true believers as yet. You're going to have a couple weeks of intense discussions with the boys of the Potomac. Be sure you have your act together before you have to take them on. In lieu of a ticker tape parade you're probably going to face an inquisition.

"Both of your orders are on the way along with classified travel docs. It looks like you are hot cargo. You will report to the Beijing airport on the day designated in your orders. All arrangements from there on have been set. I expect you'll be routed directly to D.C. Your personal effects will be shipped to storage in D.C.

"You'll be in D.C. for an unspecified time discussing, rather defending, your data. Then, get this kicker. Assuming you still have jobs, after D.C. you'll proceed to London. There is a major conference on intelligence and investigative practices, of all things. You've been scheduled to speak on *Teamwork in Intelligence*. I didn't know there was such a thing. "Nevertheless, when that's finished you won't be coming back here. Your new duty station will be London where you'll be attachés at the U.S. Embassy."

He pauses, "Tell me this, I've been in this game for twenty years and I've never seen anything like you two. How do you do it?"

EPILOGUE

Deng Xiaoping was restored by Mao in the spring of 1976. When Mao died on 9 September 1976, Deng openly supported Hua Guofeng as Mao's successor. A rival group called the Gang of Four was led by Jiang Qing, estranged wife of Mao. On 6 October they were arrested and imprisoned awaiting trial. Gradually, Deng out maneuvered Hua and emerged as the real power. He doesn't have Hua's title, but he's clearly a more able politician and leader. Once in charge he begins to implement his modernization agenda across four fronts; agriculture, industry, national defense, and science and technology.

Mike and Grace are called to Washington to face America's powerful military and political leaders regarding the intell they provided on China's new naval weapon and the widespread corruption within China's top politicians. They'll be battling the skepticism, and sometimes hostility, that arises when people are faced with information that runs counter to their assumptions and beliefs.

This is the lead-in to the next book in the *Mike and Grace* series.

www.ingramcontent.com/pod-product-compliance
Lightning Source LLC
Chambersburg PA
CBHW070440120726
47910CB00003B/867